LifeShift

A Sci-Fi Adventure

Michael Kott

For the Bremen High School Class of 1957

A Note from the Author

While this is a work of fiction and uses characters of Greek and other mythologies, it also incorporates known world mysteries. Many Native Americans, when asked where they originally came from, pointed to the Pleiades. Recently a theory has been put forth that Mars once had a large ocean of water, much like the one described by Alex.

Care was taken to describe locations as they appeared in 1960, not as they are today. For instance, when I drove the route from Needles to Barstow in California in the late 1950's, early 1960's, it was pretty much all desert. I'm sure that now, with Interstate 40 replacing old Route 66, it is quite different.

If you have visited Sequoia National Park and seen the General Sherman tree you know there is now a fence around it. There wasn't in 1959-60, so Merope could have danced around it then, and not broken any park rules. The fence was added years later after it was suspected that people walking close to the tree were compacting the soil, encouraging water run-off and causing damage.

CHAPTER 1

THE INCIDENT

Illinois – May 1957

Click.

What was that? The sound appeared to come from down the tracks I had just walked. I ignored it as I needed to get this train checked in.

Click.

There it was again! Definitely slightly louder, so it was closer. My chest tightened as I considered the faint, but familiar, sound. I turned and shone my flashlight down the tracks, but the hazy light was unable to penetrate more than a few feet into the inky blackness.

My anxiety increased, but I managed to take some deep breaths and silence my nerves. Finally, I turned from the darkness, plodded over to the middle of the next freight car, and pointed my light up onto the left side of the weather-beaten boxcar. The railroad owner's faded initials, DL&W, and underneath, the serial number 55067 in serif lettering, were reflected back to me.

I directed the light to the stack of waybills in my other hand. The tracking document showed the car belonged to the Delaware, Lackawanna and Western Railroad, and the serial number matched. I checked it off and moved over to the door, grabbed the thin metal seal, and pulled to confirm it was intact and had not been tampered with.

I peered again into the night, but beyond a few yards, all was opaque. I had trouble concentrating on the job; darkness seemed to close in on me in a way I had not experienced. My eyes continued to stray to the open tracks, hoping they would discover the source of my apprehension—and prove it wasn't what I feared.

A sudden, gentle breeze brought me the acrid smell of cinders, a product of burnt coal. The odor filled my nostrils; I loved that unique smell of the railroad yard. Looking up, I took in a sea of stars, one positive benefit of working the dark, suburban Chicago night. Relaxing somewhat, I began to trudge to the next car.

CLICK. And again! Was it a little louder this time, like something slowly coming toward me? I twisted around, my light momentarily illuminating huge script letters—*Route of Phoebe Snow*—on the right side of the freight car. At the sight of the familiar DL&W slogan, I pushed my fear away and pointed my light down the tracks. I was isolated, a half-mile from the yard office, and still had half of the seventy-five cars to inspect. As I walked down a set of empty tracks, out of the glow provided by the yard tower lights, I realized I was trapped between two parallel lines of freight cars.

The switch engine crew was humping—that's railroad jargon for sorting cars—back at the head of the yard. The conductor had assured me earlier that no cars would be sent rolling down this track, but what if he had forgotten I was down here?

CLICK! Much louder, much closer. The noise sounded like what I hoped it was not, a fully loaded freight car pressing the rail down into the ties as it slowly rolled along. The sound came from back toward the yard office, but was it on this track—the one I was standing on? Or another one? Impossible to tell at night, but an eerie feeling told me to get off the empty track. The word *danger* popped in and out of my mind like a semaphore, and I retraced my steps, past an open hopper car filled with coal, and stared back into the night.

My hearing seemed unnaturally acute—as if all sounds had been turned up and made clearer. I could hear the singing of cicadas and the low moan of the switch engine as it wound up to let another string of cars loose. The slamming of couplers echoed as slow-rolling cars crashed together somewhere in the yard's maze of tracks. A dog barked in the distance, probably in reaction to the noise of the freight yard.

Suddenly, my skin tingled as if a low voltage electrical charge were running through me. Up and down the tracks, to my right and left, were long strings of freight cars.

Run, a voice whispered.

But I had nowhere to go.

CLICK!

Suddenly, there it was, seeming to float out of the night. I was so surprised that, despite my premonitions, I momentarily froze in its path. At the last second, something screamed into my brain, and I bolted from the tracks and dove under the hopper car. Safe, I turned and shined the light up on the boxcar as it slid by, noting its distinctive glacier green paint scheme and the serial number 27368. The huge mountain goat herald of the Great Northern Railway seemed to stare down at me as the forty-foot-long car slowly rolled past.

Now I could clearly hear the squeak of the axles, the creaking of the rails being depressed, the moan of the wooden ties crushed into the earth, and the friction of the metal wheels screeching on steel rail. I didn't need a waybill to tell me it was fully loaded with tons of grain. I'd have been a puddle of mashed goo if I hadn't heard it coming in time.

After it rolled past, anger filled me and I slammed the stack of waybills to the ground. How could they forget I was down here?

I cursed that lazy jerk, Gary Goshen, who had the yard clerk stint before me. He should have checked this train in before I showed up for the evening shift. But Gary liked leaving things for me, the 'kid,' to do while he screwed off. It could have been finished while it was still light out, rather than having me do it now, late at night. He resented they had even given this job to me, a teenager still in high school. I was just temporary help, filling in while the regular guys went on vacation, but Gary was full time. While he thought the job demanded some kind of skill, it was basically just making sure no car was missing or tampered with. Who couldn't do that?

But I'd be past all this soon enough. In two weeks, after graduation, this job as a replacement yard clerk ought to be enough to help me get one full time at this or another rail yard.

The sound of slamming couplers from somewhere in the yard brought me back to my predicament. Unsure if there was another car silently on its way, I decided it was better to be safe than sorry. Even though it meant walking all the way back to the yard office, checking with the switch engine crew, and then walking back here to continue where I left off.

As I trudged down the tracks, I kept the flashlight trained ahead and my ears open. When I neared the office area and the safety of the yard lights, I saw the switchman, Moe Haskins.

"Hey, Moe, what the hell are you guys doing? You humped a car down Track Eight where I was checking in the five-eighteen train."

"Hey kid, I didn't switch any car down eight."

I nodded, and wondered how long it would take before they stopped calling me kid.

"A GN grain car? 27368? It almost pulverized me!"

Moe stared at his sheet, then looked at me incredulously. "That was supposed to go down Track Six, kid. Hell, I don't even remember us switching it. What the—?" He stared at the sheet, then looked back up at me. "I'm awful sorry, kid. Thank God you're all right."

What could I do? I didn't want to get known as a troublemaker and lose my chance at a full time job, so I simply shrugged it off. At least, that's what I tried to do. I was shaking as I trudged back down the line of cars that still had to be checked in. I walked with one shoulder almost touching the various rolling stock on the neighboring tracks, and I stayed off the number eight with its ribbons of steel— just in case.

After I finished checking in the entire train, I walked back to the yard office to get ready to go home. Moe was sitting at my desk when I walked in. He apologized profusely to me again and wondered aloud how the car got onto Track Eight.

"We're going to retrieve that car and get it back on the right track," he finally said. "You want to come along, kid?"

I was finished for the night, but it would be forty minutes before my dad came to pick me up, so I nodded. The new diesel switch engine, with a weather-beaten red caboose attached, was idling noisily right outside the office. Moe and I got on the caboose and he waved his lamp at the engineer. With a lurch, the diesel slowly began to cross over tracks and switches.

The old wooden caboose swayed from side to side as we gradually shifted over to Track Eight. I stared out the window as the sides of freight cars slid by. We slowly click-clacked over the steel rails as we made our way in search of the misplaced car. After a few moments, a blast of the engine's horn told us we had found it.

"Come on, Alex. Let's take us a look," Moe said, and stepped off the still-moving car.

That was the first time he had called me by name. I stepped off the caboose and walked past the idling switcher to the freight car. It had rolled about a hundred feet past the last car of the train I'd checked in earlier.

As we walked over, I kept my distance. My anxiety had strangely returned. Moe checked something by the coupler and then indicated to the switch engine to couple on to the car. Once they were joined, we got back on the caboose and the diesel pushed us back toward the office.

As we bounced along, I glanced at Moe and saw that his face appeared oddly indifferent.

Suddenly, he looked over at me and started speaking in a strange, almost feminine, voice. "More than one unknown force was at work here tonight..."

"What, Moe?"

"That little bitch interfered," a different feminine voice said angrily. It sounded like it came from my left, but there was no one there. "She helped him cheat. She's responsible..."

"Me? I cheated?" I asked. "Who helped me do what? When?" Who was Moe talking to?

"Death... She helped you cheat death tonight." The words, directed at me, came from Moe, but in that strange feminine voice.

"I knew he was one of them. It has started..." the voice from my left mumbled.

"That little bitch said they'll be coming together. She said it's time to start the quest," Moe replied in the same eerie tone.

"Who's a little bitch? What quest?" I asked Moe. I had started to get scared again, but he didn't appear to hear me.

Then, a third feminine voice spoke. "I told you he was protected. He has a mission. However, by attempting to terminate him, you've caused a dangerous ripple in the events of this entire planetary sector. You must not interfere with what has been set in motion." The voice seemed to materialize from above us.

Moe's face contorted as the feminine voice to my left said, "Not to worry, we'll fight her and the others." Then it—or she—was gone.

"What mission?" I directed my questions to the unseen voice overhead. "What kind of ripple? What did I do?"

Moe turned and looked at me. But of course, it wasn't Moe anymore. Was it ever?

"You shouldn't be here, Alex Monroe," he continued in that feminine voice. "This night, Alex Monroe should have ceased to exist in the life books of Earth and been scheduled to be reborn elsewhere...away from here and off this planet. Our work should have been done if not for...that little blue wench..."

Then Moe closed his eyes and lapsed into silence as we rattled down the tracks.

When we reached the office, I jumped off the caboose and ran inside. I didn't see Moe the rest of that night.

* * *

As usual, dad picked me up at midnight and we drove home in silence. I didn't want to talk about what had happened. I wasn't sure myself.

That same night, I had the most amazing dream.

I was in someone else's body, sharing it as he continued to have control. I could look out and see what he saw, feel what he felt. He walked along a pathway bathed in a greenish glow. When he reached the end of the trail, he was standing on the edge of a towering cliff. Far down below was a churning sea. All around lay stunning white, red and black rock formations, but I was mesmerized by the crashing waves on the shore far below. Terror gripped me. The water, I realized, must be a thousand feet down, and that ocean I was looking at, that orange-colored ocean, could not be anywhere on Earth.

I felt perfectly awake, and could make out minute details of things around us. The buzzing of peculiar insects in the strange, red grass off to our right, the multi-colored flowers growing along the path, the breathing of the body I was in. A cool breeze, blowing in off the churning sea, caressed his skin.

From behind us, above the thunderous sound of the waves, I heard a voice call out, "Sylvane!" The body I was in turned, looking back up the path, and through his eyes I saw a girl running toward us. She was beautiful. Hair as black as the coal loaded in a hopper car flowed behind her as she ran. As she got closer, I could see she was small, barely five feet tall, and dressed in a strange, jacket-like attire that seemed semi-transparent. I could make out that she wore something under it, but it also was unfamiliar. All of her clothing ended about mid-thigh, and she wore no shoes. She leapt up on him, wrapping her bare legs around his waist and throwing her arms around his neck, and stared into his eyes. I could feel the heels of her bare feet pushing against his backside.

"Did you miss me, Sylvane?" she asked, as she planted kisses on his face.

Apparently, his name was Sylvane. "Veronique, what are you doing here?" he asked.

I could not resist staring at her eyes. They were absolutely compelling.

"Your father will not like that you came at this time," Sylvane continued.

"My father never likes what I do," she pouted. "He treats me like I'm still seven years old. You and he are unaware that I've recently reached the age where I know who I really am." Her eyes penetrated his like a searchlight.

"What do you mean, 'who you really are?' And why are you staring so intently at me?" his lips asked.

"I see someone from the far future reflected in your eyes, Sylvane," she laughed, and her fingers gripped Sylvane's shoulders hard. Then she pressed her fingers to his temple, and I felt him freeze as I surged forward.

Her cherry red lips came towards me, and her amber colored eyes bore into mine. I seemed to be swimming in between worlds. As I spiraled away, I heard her voice saying, "I don't know who the Hades he is, Decima. Why is he in there? Why the hell was I called back? I don't need this shit."

The next second, I was lying in a darkened room. In the dim moonlight, I could only make out shapes of objects around me.

I tried to see if Veronique, the black-haired girl, was nearby. Her words echoed in my mind; I smelled her scent on me—all around me. And those eyes—

Where the hell am I? I looked out the window and saw a huge moon hanging low in the sky. Something banged in the wind. I heard the chirping of crickets. The sound of a car driving by.

Suddenly, a dog barked outside and then whined. That sounded familiar.

"Blackie! Shut up!" someone hollered.

That exclamation came from the next room. Finally, my mind returned to normal. The griper was my dad. Blackie was our dog.

"Goddamn raccoons!" I heard my dad mutter as he got out of bed. My normal life came crashing back. I was Alex. I lived in southwest suburban Chicago, went to high school and worked for the railroad.

Then, last night's events from the railyard and Moe's strange multi-voiced mutterings swarmed in my head. Those female voices— were they connected to my dream somehow? Then, I fell back asleep.

"Alex, are you going to school today or are you just going to sit there?" The words, from outside my room, startled me. I glanced out the window and saw the sun had risen, chasing the moon back to bed.

I didn't answer immediately.

"Are you sick?" My mom's head peeked in and awaited my answer.

"I'm fine. I'll be out in a minute."

She stared at me for several more seconds before she left. I swung my feet out of bed and prepared to start my day, putting the dream behind me.

I hoped.

Chapter 2

Irene

That morning, I hurried through breakfast. I was still distracted by the dream, and wanted some time alone. Though I was certainly in no hurry to get to school, either.

High school had not been one of my best times. While most of the senior guys had cars, I still rode the bus. But the biggest problem was girls. I shouldn't accept all the blame here, either, because my parents were partly responsible.

* * *

It had not been my bright idea for us to move out into the sticks after I completed eleventh grade in Chicago. Even now, after almost a full year in the suburbs, my heart still ached for Brenda Koenig, the one I left behind at Lindblom High School. When we met that first day of high school, I had thought she was my soulmate. We had even been born on the same day. She was as shy as she was pretty, and we leaned on each other those early days, coping with the strangeness that was high school.

Because Brenda was so cute, with her golden brown hair and blue-green eyes, it didn't take her long to take high school by storm. But she never forgot me: the picked-on guy who remained quiet and shy. My interests didn't match the ordinary, or popular, so I was an easy target for those who liked to cover their own faults by belittling others. We stayed close those three years, and then I had to leave.

We lived on a street barely a half-mile long. To the north was forest preserve, to the west a huge farm and rolling prairie. The closest town was a few miles away, and most of my time was taken up with chores on our new pseudo-farm. At my new high school, I became a bigger social outcast than in the city. I had no Brenda, and these kids had grown up with each other. I was an intruder.

Girls—I loved them, but I could not understand them. At school, our two most popular cheerleaders, Susan Stage and Patty Zerbean, would glide by my locker every morning. They were close to the same size, and were like salt and pepper: Susan with light blonde hair while Patty's was sort of blue-black. Susan would occasionally glance my way, her usual condescending smile perched on her pouty lips, while Patty seemed to dismiss my very presence.

At one time or another, I had a secret crush on both. Susan had the most luscious lips, and Patty was a marvel of female form. I guess it was a form of absence makes the heart grow fonder, except in this case it was contempt breeds love.

* * *

After arriving at school that morning, I hurried to my locker, still distracted by the incident out at the railyard and the unusual dream. As Susan slithered by, she paused when she saw me, then gave me a sympathetic smile. I was clueless as to what it meant. Quickly on her heels followed Patty, who actually furrowed her brow after squinting over in my direction.

Finally, almost directly behind them came Irene Westover, who looked at me questioningly, her eyebrows raised as if in alarm.

* * *

Irene, who had transferred in the year before I did, was an enigma to the entire school. Popular with most of the girls, she avoided boys, including me, like they had the plague. In fact, we'd never had a one-on-one conversation. I knew she was very intelligent because I had overheard a number of students call her the curve breaker.

Irene and I even had a class together that final semester. What I thought unusual was, despite being one of the prettiest girls in school, she had never dated anyone.

* * *

That morning, I shoved those thoughts into the back of my mind in time to watch Irene as she glided past.

As she turned the corner, taking one final glance in my direction, I heard her say, "Great, you're finally here! Meet me in the cafeteria at lunch."

I hurried after her to my American History class, but when I stepped into the hall I saw no one in the corridor where she had spoken. Just Irene, smiling and holding the classroom door open for me. While we had never spoken, we had fiercely competed for the best grades in our class. At times her grasp on history was so great, it was as if she'd lived it herself.

* * *

A few weeks earlier, we had been required to write a term paper for my American History class on any subject we felt appropriate. American History was one of my favorite classes, primarily because Irene was in it, so I decided to write the paper on the subject of UFOs.

The title was "UFOs – Extraterrestrial Visitors or Secret Nazi Aircraft?"

* * *

When I was around eight years old, I had practiced reading by thumbing through my dad's newspaper. One day, in 1947, I read this story about a man in the state of Washington who had been piloting his small plane and claimed he saw a group of 'shimmering craft' flying in formation over a mountain range. He described them as boomerang-shaped and said they flew 'like a stone skipping over water.' That incident was credited with starting what later became known as the flying saucer craze.

Most people laughed about it, but for some reason, I took it very seriously. After seeing that story, I scoured the papers every day for more articles and kept them all. At times I had to really search for them. Most were buried in the paper and written like it was a big joke. I could imagine the writer snickering as he wrote. However, I couldn't shake the feeling UFOs were something real and important.

Later that same year came this huge story out of Roswell, New Mexico. Papers from all over screamed out the headline: *Flying Disk Crashes in New Mexico.* Wreckage, consisting of strange materials covered with unknown symbols, had been reportedly recovered by the Army Air Force. Among other things, eyewitnesses said the material was indestructible but very lightweight. If you bent it, it would always return to its original shape.

The next day the AAF claimed it was all a mistake. Forget what we said yesterday, they seemed to imply: today we're saying it was merely a weather balloon. Years later, eyewitnesses to the recovery would point back to the original story and claim it was an alien craft with alien bodies, and the military had threatened them in order to keep the secret. Regardless, back in 1947 I was very unhappy to be only eight years old and incapable of going to Roswell to see for myself.

By the time I got into high school, I had amassed quite a collection of articles on UFOs, which was what I preferred to call them. In the newspaper articles they were always called *flying saucers.*

Just after starting my last year in high school, I came across an article written by a research group in New Mexico investigating UFOs. By this time, ten years after the Roswell incident, the Air Force had been made a separate service from the Army and was supposed to be conducting a probe of the so-called flying saucers. Everything I read, however, outside of the Air Force study hinted at a cover-up. I wrote to the research group and they allowed me to join, even though I was in high school. From then on, I started getting a newsletter from them once a month. It covered the latest sightings, the current thinking about UFOs, and an in-depth analysis of unusual incidents. Even though I personally never saw one, I was a believer.

When I started working at the railyard, I met Mark Wallen, one of the GTW railroad police, who was also interested in UFOs. He turned my quest in another direction. Mark had been an intelligence officer in the Army Air Force, and right after the war ended in 1945, he had assisted in following up on stories that Nazi Germany had been secretly building very advanced aircraft. The aircraft designs supposedly included one that was disk-shaped, and another that resembled a flying wing.

Witnesses to UFO sightings all over the world frequently described them as either disk or boomerang (flying wing) shaped. Was it a coincidence? I thought not.

One night, about two weeks before the incident with the boxcar, Mark had stepped into the yard office for a cup of coffee. We talked about the things he'd seen in Germany in 1945, while I waited for my ride.

He said the boomerang description of the objects in the story from Washington closely matched what he'd seen after the war over six thousand miles away.

"I don't understand how they could even think of such advanced aircraft," I told him.

"It was really strange," he said. "Everything pointed to the entire German advanced aircraft program being somehow connected to a group of female psychics. From what we learned, the Germans not only designed and built several different versions, but they had actually flown a disk-shaped craft."

Probably because I grinned at that, he shook his head and continued. "I know it sounds crazy, but we were told the lead psychic got the plans to build the craft from inhabitants of a planet orbiting the star Aldebaran. The women in this group were all described to me as long-haired, beautiful women who claimed they were picking up the transmissions from this planet."

"Did you find these women?"

"No. I don't know for sure if they even existed. The German SS, their secret police, destroyed all of the records of the group before my men could get them. I was told a number of different stories about the fate of the group. Some said there were five mystics and that they had actually escaped the country prior to Germany's surrender. Others thought they were executed or they died in the Allied bombardments. No physical trace of them has ever been found."

"That's bizarre," I said.

Mark nodded and said, "Several people claiming knowledge of them even said they left in a spaceship to another planet."

That got me laughing, until Mark gripped my shoulder with one strong hand.

"You know, Alex, at first I laughed too when I was told the story." Mark looked at me seriously. "I know it sounds crazy, but what I can't get out of my mind is, if it was all such a big joke, why did the SS go to so much trouble to cover up their whereabouts? And, if they didn't design these strange craft, who did?"

CHAPTER 3
CIRCE

I took my seat in class and looked over two rows to where Irene sat. Seemingly preoccupied, she appeared to glance in my direction, then gave the front classroom door a quick peek, and finally gazed out the window.

While I was spying on her antics, Mr. Marlowe finished attendance and then held up a handful of paper. "I've been teaching history for fifteen years," he said, "and I thought I was beyond being impressed with a term paper, but one of you did just that."

Then came the moment from which my life would never fully recover. The classroom door opened and a new girl walked in. However, she was not just any girl. I watched as she tossed back her curly, coal black hair and glanced around the room. When she looked briefly at me, her exotic amber eyes momentarily flashed to a deep emerald green, and a slight smile appeared. She then turned her head and locked eyes with Irene. I was sure then that she was the person in the hall.

"Are you the new student?" Mr. Marlowe asked.

The new girl broke eye contact with Irene, glanced back over in my direction momentarily, and finally, turned her attention to Mr. Marlowe.

"Have you seen me before?" she asked as she handed Mr. Marlowe her admittance slip.

"No, I've not had that pleasure," Mr. Marlowe, ever the gentleman, cheerfully answered her.

"Then I must be the new student," she said with a straight face. There were several snickers from up front in the classroom. However, my first thought was, what a little smart ass.

Mr. Marlowe frowned momentarily at her humor attempt, but quickly recovered and said, "Class, this is Circe Nicks. Please make her feel welcome. Circe, why don't you take the empty seat here up front?

Instead, she pointed at me and said, "How about I sit there, in that empty seat behind Alex?"

"Okay. Do you know Alex?" Mr. Marlowe asked.

"Does Jupiter know Io?" she snapped.

"Pardon?" asked Mr. Marlowe.

"Sorry. Yes," Circe replied. "Alex and I go back a long, long way, right back to the beginning of time." Then, ignoring the open-mouthed stares of the other guys, Circe sauntered slowly down the aisle with her eyes focused on me.

When she drew alongside me, her eyes glowed like a setting sun and she smiled at me before sitting down. From this close, I could see her dark, curly hair was tipped with silver, and my breath stopped.

Circe was Veronique, the girl in last night's dream.

"As I was saying, class, one of your papers was absolutely unique." Mr. Marlowe's voice brought me back to the classroom. "I want to congratulate Alex on writing the most interesting term paper I've seen in fifteen years of teaching."

Huh? I was stunned.

"He took a subject, flying saucers..."

UFOs, I mentally urged, *call them UFOs.* Around the class there were giggles from some of the girls and guffaws from the guys. I glanced over at Irene, whose stony glance was directed first at Mr. Marlowe, then at Circe. When her jade eyes came to me, they sparkled, and I could swear turned violet for an instant, but held no trace of being upset that I had beat her out. At least she didn't laugh at me.

"While you all chuckle at Alex and his A-plus paper," Mr. Marlowe continued, "let me tell you it was hard not to laugh myself when he suggested the subject of his paper to me. However, after reading it, I must say I'm impressed. Not only with the job he did, but with the subject of UFOs and the possibilities they are connected to work done in Nazi Germany in the twenties and thirties. It makes you stop and think."

Mr. Marlowe then walked over and handed me my paper. He liked to walk around class when returning assignments and make comments on the work you'd done. I'd always thought that was pretty neat. "Great job, Alex," he said softly. "I hope you don't mind, but I made a couple of copies of your paper. I sent them to some colleagues at the University of Illinois."

Feeling a little embarrassed from all the attention, I just nodded.

He then turned to Circe behind me and said, "The term paper is seventy-five percent of your grade, Miss Nicks, so you'll need to make it up."

"Can I do it on the Odyssey?" she asked. "I can report to you the true story of how I lured Odysseus to me, and supposedly turned his men into little oinkers. By the way, my name is Circe, not Miss Nicks. I abhor last names. I only gave the school one because it was required." She glanced at me and set a hand on my shoulder, a ring on one of her fingers catching my eye. The band was silver and in the center was set a black stone, like a black diamond, that seemed to emit silver flashes.

"Very enlightening, Miss...uh—" Mr. Marlowe said.

"If you don't like that, I can do it on the Greek Goddesses," she interrupted. "I'm equally well versed in either..."

"I appreciate your interest in Greek mythology, but this is *American* History, Miss...uh...Circe. I have some suggested titles if you'd like to look them over."

"Mythology?" she protested. "I was speaking of the truth behind the supposed stories from ancient Greece. Did you suggest UFOs to Alex? And how are UFOs American History when they've come from other worlds?"

"Uh, no, he came up with that subject himself," Mr. Marlowe explained. "I hardly think UFOs are from other worlds, Circe. It's an American phenomenon."

"I can name you twenty worlds that have sent planet hoppers here," Circe said. "And it's not just an American experience, it's a worldwide event. Always has been."

"Nonsense." Mr. Marlowe shook his head. "I see you are a jokester, Circe. Refreshing, but please think about a fitting subject, and get back to me by tomorrow. I'll need a subject title by then and you must complete it before school ends. That gives you less than two weeks. Is that acceptable?"

"Sure," she replied. "I'll see if Alex has another A-plus subject up his sleeve."

Mr. Marlowe frowned at her implication, then continued walking around the class to return the papers. Unable to control my urge, I turned around in my seat. With her shoulder-length curly black hair and striking eyes, Circe was hard to look away from. She was slim, but well proportioned. Easily the most beautiful creature I had ever seen.

"Like what you see?" she asked. She licked her impossibly red lips with her tongue, then left the tip of it sticking out. I had never experienced a conversation with a girl so obnoxious or forward. Actually, no girl had ever talked to me in a sexually aggressive manner. It was hard enough being the new guy, and being relegated to the bus for transportation had left me out of participating in after-school sports and activities. I wanted to get up and run.

Seemingly sensing my unspoken wish, Circe reached out and gripped my forearm. "Oh no," she said. "You're not running away from me. After all, you're responsible for me being here. And besides, I might need your help. You heard him. While I look into your little fracas last night, I've got to follow the rules of this school." She seemed to sense what I was thinking, but she talked like she was some kind of detective.

"What are you talking about?" I asked. "I'm the reason you're here? What fracas?"

"I am a kind of a detective, but later with all that stuff. This guy wants me to write a paper, and I can't draw attention to myself. You got any ideas?"

She relaxed her grip on my arm, and her fingers made little circles on my skin. I urged myself to relax, but her touch was stimulating me in ways I had never experienced before.

I tried to ignore her fingers and focus on her question. "I just wrote about UFOs because I'm interested in them. I don't know much about anything else." Her touch was driving me to distraction. "You asked him about the Odyssey and Greek goddesses. Are you into all that Greek mythology stuff?"

"Mythology? Watch what you say about my history." She looked at me with a furrowed brow, like I should know better. "And just why wouldn't I be? I am one."

"One what?"

"Greek goddess. Pay attention."

I decided this girl may be beautiful, but she was also a flake. Even if that was true, how could she know she was connected to the ancient Greeks?

"You'll see," she said, as if in answer to my unspoken thought. "What period do you have lunch?" she added.

"Uhh, fifth."

"Sit with me. We can talk about why I'm here and your paper, and maybe you can help me with mine. Mr. Marlowe seems nice, so I don't really want to mess with his memory."

"Are you sure you want to sit with me?" I asked her, choosing to ignore the comment that she could somehow affect Mr. Marlowe's memory for now. I was still digesting the goddess bit. Though if our school play ever needed a goddess, she could sure fit the lead role.

"We Fates have lots of roles we play," Circe said, as if I had spoken that last thought aloud. "For each life, your fate is cast at the time you're born. This one will surely be interesting for you. However, someone is trying to change it, and that's why I'm now involved. But only for a little while, though, so don't you—" she planted a small finger on my nose "—fall in love with me."

This time, I was speechless, though questions were flying through my mind. But I knew one thing for sure—she was obnoxious and at times bordered rude, but I was already in love with her.

"Be patient, Alex. Gradually, you'll learn the answers you seek. Don't forget: fifth period, look for me."

With that she smiled over at Irene, who had been watching the two of us with her hand propped under her chin and a smile on her face. Again I imagined a flash of violet from her eyes. Circe waved to Irene with a waggle of fingers, and I turned around, as I knew I had been dismissed.

When class was over, Irene walked by, collected Circe and gave me a tight little smile. When I looked back, both had already gone.

The rest of the day went mostly as usual, though my moment of glory did get me additional attention from my classmates. Some joked around that I had come from outer space, and others repeated thoughts that I was odd. But a few were impressed that I, Alex Monroe, had dented the normally serious façade of Mr. Marlowe.

When fifth period rolled around, I went to the cafeteria not really expecting to find Circe. I figured by then she had met some of the more popular guys in class and found out she had almost made a fatal social blunder by latching on to me.

The cafeteria was built with these huge glass windows through which you could see inside from way back in the hallway. As I approached, I could see Circe was already inside, standing in a far corner and talking with Irene. Then, as I reached for the door, I saw Circe and Irene quickly embrace and kiss before both slipped out the opposite exit. Didn't anyone else see that? Two girls—kissing? On the lips? Students just funneled around them like they weren't even there.

So much for Circe meeting me. Leave it to Irene to clue her in about who she should and shouldn't hang out with.

Not wanting to eat lunch alone yet again, I scanned for one of my few friends who sometimes ate at that time. As I stood just inside the door, someone nudged me from behind.

"So, do we have like a regular table?" Circe asked, wrapping an arm around my waist. "So I know where to meet you each day?"

I was speechless. I realized I had never seriously expected her to meet me, especially after she left with Irene. But here she was.

"How about that table by the window?" she asked, with a squeeze to my side. I nodded, and she proceeded to practically drag me to the table.

We settled in, and she looked up at me with a smile. "You bring your lunch?" she asked.

"Yeah, but you can buy lunch, too." I had a million questions I wanted to ask her, but she intimidated me.

"Would you share your lunch with me?" she asked, lowering her voice to a whisper. "Decima told me to rush straight here, so I didn't bring much money."

That sounded strange, but I was getting used to her weird statements by now. "All I've got is this sandwich." I held half of it up with disdain. "My dad likes this lunchmeat concoction with pickles and—"

"That will be fine," she interrupted. Whisking the half-sandwich out of my hand, she took a bite. "Decima is head of the Parcae. She rushed me here from California," she said as she chewed. I noticed she was also speaking again as if she were answering my questions aloud.

"No one, but you and my sister, can see the real me outside of our class unless I let them. That's why Sis and I can get as intimate as we wish. We're Fates, we always kiss each other on the lips. Only you saw that kiss. And just so you know, we're both bisexual. Stop thinking dirty thoughts about her...and me. You know nothing about us."

She peeked under the bread, and I waited for a look of disgust to cross her face. "It's called pickle-pimento loaf," I said. "I hate it, but my dad loves it. Who are the Parcae? Why did they send you here? Is Irene actually your sister?"

Circe looked back at me with a smile, then took another bite. "They sent me here because of your incident last night. We still have no idea who the Hades you are, but you must be one of us."

"They sent you here because of me? Who is us?"

"This sandwich is good," she said, ignoring my questions. "I like it. May I?" She indicated my milk carton.

"Sure," I said, amazed.

She reached over, picked up the carton and took a sip. "I was hungrier than I thought. Would you share your sandwich with me each day?"

I nodded. Was this a new way of robbing me of my lunch?

"Thank you," she said, as her eyes scanned the lunchroom.

"Why me?" I asked again. "What are you talking about, that I am one of you?"

"Why you?" She got serious fast. "'Cause you messed up the rhythm of this world last night and it's my job to find out what happened. And, of course, fix it if I can. Decima tells me that life plans made thousands of years ago have apparently come to pass. You are to lead a long-rumored great quest. In short, you're one of us. Don't ask me what the quest is, though, because that has been entrusted to the minds of certain Eternals, most of who are at this school. Your interaction with them will ring that out."

I remembered something else I had been wondering. "Are you really Veronique? The girl from my dream last night?"

She answered me with a slight nod of her head. "Yes. I got involved after I found you hiding inside Sylvane. But let's just hold all that for now. I'll get together with you later and explain in more detail."

I nodded, but I don't think my brain was completely engaged.

"I've had enough of school for today," she said. "I'm going to go, but I'll find you later."

"You can't just leave whenever you want to," I said. "You'll get detention."

She looked over at me for several long seconds, then her face blossomed into a grin. "Oh, for the love of Zeus, you're hilarious. My sister's right. You're such a...goody-two-shoes. *You* can't leave, Alex. I can do whatever the Hades I want. After all, I'm a goddess."

CHAPTER 4
DREAMS LOST

As I walked to work later that afternoon, I still couldn't shake the nagging feelings from the night before. I had been tempted to dismiss the episode—the voices, Moe's weird behavior— as a hallucination. Then that girl, the actual girl in my dream fantasy, had shown up at my school. And, she not only knew about the dream, she seemed to know all about me. All day, my mind had bounced between the events of Monday night and the beautiful face of Circe.

However, I decided now to keep my mind on my work, as I didn't want to get caught up in the same situation as the previous night. One brush with death was one brush too many.

* * *

As luck would have it, I had an even longer train to check in. The switch engine had been scheduled to take a cut of cars over to the Chicago Heights Yard, so I grabbed onto the ladder of the boxcar situated directly behind the engine for a free ride. That, I figured, would save some steps. And after what had happened the previous night, I was making a special effort to stay away from Moe that day. As the switch engine picked up speed, my mind drifted back to Circe, school, and my paper...

* * *

"Alex! You want off here?" Harry, the locomotive fireman, yelled.

His question broke me out of my daydream and I quickly realized we were already at the end of the yard.

In my haste to get off, I failed to position my body as I had been taught, so when I let go of the ladder to step off the slowly moving train, I took a tumble on the unyielding ballast—the stone they spread around the rails to keep weeds from growing.

"Alex, when you gonna learn?" I heard Harry's voice snicker, then the rest of the short train rolled on by. As it exited the yard, the low moan of the diesel horn reverberated through my body as if in mockery. I got up, pulled some of the sharp cinders out of my hands, and wiped the blood on my pants. Just some scrapes and cuts; my pride had been the biggest casualty.

As I walked back down the long string of freight cars, checking them in that night, I was grateful there was a full moon and several empty tracks behind me. I'm not sure why I still felt anxious. With the switch engine gone, there was no car humping, and therefore no chance of a repeat of what had happened the previous night. It took me about thirty minutes to get to the last car, a flat car on which had been loaded a large object covered by a dark tarp. The waybill said the cargo was a huge electrical generator. On the dented and battered side of the ancient flat car it sat on, I could barely make out the faded initials, IHB, and under them the numbers 11564. The serial number and the railroad: Indiana Harbor Belt.

Even though I had been moving in the direction of the office, I was still a quarter-mile from the yard lights. A final check of the chains on the flat car's consignment and I was satisfied it was secure. Before I started back, I leaned up against the car and wiped some fresh blood from my hands. That was when my mind flashed back to that day in school, then the dream of the previous night—

It struck me like a great white shark hitting its prey. I was suddenly transported back to the alternate reality world.

If that's what it was.

* * *

It was dark and I was back inside Sylvane. He was sitting on a rock outcrop of that same cliff from the previous dream. For a moment, the only sound was that of the waves punishing the shore far below us.

Even in that dream state, I almost jumped when a hand was laid on his shoulder and, from behind, Veronique whispered in his ear. "Let's go down to the beach."

He turned and I glanced from her small pink fingers (one wearing the same ring she wore as Circe) to the sky behind her. My mind then went numb, and it took a few seconds to reset my mental circuit breaker and process what I had seen.

I had counted three moons! The highest was a deep blue color and was positioned up and to the far left. The middle one was slightly lower and appeared to be blue and orange. The lowest one was settled to the far right and glowed with a yellowish green color.

As I stared at the orbs in that strange sky, through Sylvane's eyes, Veronique reached over and turned his face to hers. "The beach," she softly whispered. "We agreed, Sylvie. We do it tonight, under the moons. Remember, you consented to put your shyness aside and keep me company while my father is fishing. We're doing it, and you're not backing out. In fact, since you were late and tomorrow's my birthday, I want you to carry me there." She punctuated that by first poking his chest then putting her arms around his neck.

I was conscious of lifting her up off her feet, and she responded by tucking her small body in close to Sylvane's chest and wrapping her legs around his hips. I could actually feel her soft, bare skin crush against his. Those solid amber eyes never left his (ours?). What if I could—?

At my mental urging, Sylvane held onto her with one hand wrapped around her back as he reached up and stroked her silky hair, then gripped a lock and pulled it close. She smiled, then her hand came around and brushed the hair away.

"Stop that, Alex. What is it you need? Some sort of proof that Circe and I are one and the same? How about this..."

Eyes like gold held me trancelike as her lips closed on...mine.

* * *

Suddenly, my mind was catapulted back to the railyard, where my fingers gripped the chains that held the generator on the flat car.

As I stood there, immersed in the sounds and smells of the railyard, I became conscious that the sweet scent of Veronique/Circe still hung in the air. The taste of her delicious lips was still on mine, as well, and I could feel her tongue swirling in my mouth as those strange moons floated overhead.

I must have leaned on the low deck of the flat car another ten minutes as my body, both mentally and physically, returned to normal. When I prepared to walk back, I became conscious my shirt was soaked with perspiration. My heart pounded in my chest and I realized— I was afraid. I gradually became aware of crickets chirping and other noises of the night. Had it been that quiet or had I just not heard them before?

I thought maybe I should talk to someone about this. But who?

"What are you doing? Are you being sick? My kiss never made anybody sick before." When I looked over, I saw that Circe had silently come up behind me.

"What are you doing here?" I stupidly asked. "You're not supposed to be here on railroad property."

"You are a nincompoop. A beautiful girl appears in the night and all you can say is, you're trespassing?"

"I...I...what are you doing here?"

"Finishing what we started on Trivane. You kind of disappeared fast, and I don't know if I satisfied your doubts." With that she seized me by the shoulders and kissed me into another dimension. At least, that best describes the most wonderful feeling I'd ever felt. "Okay, I've got to go before, according to you, I get arrested or something."

"One question?" I said hurriedly.

She nodded.

"Where the hell is Trivane?"

"Someplace you and I once lived together," she said, then turned and walked away, fading into the night as quickly as she had appeared.

* * *

"Alex, how are you tonight?" Mark asked as I walked back into the yard office.

I looked over to him sitting at my desk, nursing a cup of coffee. "Okay, I guess. No, actually, things are getting a little crazy, Mark. I think I'm losing it."

"Tell me about it," he calmly replied.

I told him about the freight car, the dream-like experience the previous night, Circe coming to my classroom and finally, the dream-like vision that evening. I didn't mention Circe's actual in-person appearance moments ago in the railyard.

He listened without comment until I finished.

"You're probably just overtired working this job and going full-time to school," he said. "I'm sure this girl resembles the one you dreamt about, but she can't be one and the same. Your mind is just playing tricks on you. Relax, Alex. I'll walk down and check out that freight car. Later, I'll stop back here." He walked out and, through the window, I watched him trudge down the tracks.

After that last experience in the yard, I was glad to be back alone in the office shack. I sorted the last train's waybills and tried to force the visions out of my head. Instead, I focused on the need to somehow establish a relationship with a more down-to-earth girl. I had realized that, if I could not get up the courage to ask out a real girl when I was surrounded by them in high school, what would happen to me after I graduated? Other than those in the strange visions, I surely wasn't going to meet one working in the freight yard.

Why couldn't I have met someone like Brenda at my current school? I had not talked to her in a year, but I vowed to call her the next day and see if she would be willing to help me out.

Later that evening, having completed all my paperwork, I looked up to see the clock inching toward eleven. The switch crew had returned and was now busy humping the cars from the 1015 New York Central freight. I remained alone in the yard office.

As the memory of Circe's sudden appearance and the vision of that weird world returned and threatened to overload my senses, I finally bolted out of the chair and walked outside. The whine of the diesel switcher, muted slamming of couplers on humped cars that had reached their destination, distant sound of barking dogs, car and truck traffic from the bridge over the yard, and the scent of burnt coal and diesel fumes battered my nose and ears. The night sounds and smells of the yard once again quickly enveloped me.

Flashlight in hand, I surveyed the switcher work briefly, then decided to walk alongside Track Six. I knew none of the 1015 cars would be routed down this track; however, I walked outside the rails just to be safe. To be super-safe, I occasionally glanced back up the track toward the yard office. After I had walked a distance outside the range of the yard lights, the sounds became fainter and I saw the object of my search up ahead. My flashlight flared along the side of the glacier green boxcar of the night before.

The car sat coupled to two other special grain-loaded boxcars, all scheduled to be taken in the morning to a large bakery in Chicago. I flashed the light up on the side of the boxcar and saw stenciled:

WHEN EMPTY RETURN TO
GREAT NORTHERN RAILROAD
FARGO, NORTH DAKOTA

On instinct, I decided to reach up and touch the steel side. All noise around me ceased as if I had been suddenly plunged into a vacuum. Even now I can recall the strange cold that surged through me. When I took my hand away, I again heard sounds. Standing there shocked and alone, I refused to accept what had just happened. I wanted to see if it would repeat, but my hand refused to move. Knowing it was just twenty minutes to midnight, I ran like a frightened deer back down the tracks, and was grateful when I reentered the cone of light from the yard towers.

Once back inside the office, I gripped the desk, hoping my hands would stop shaking. I was sure something strange was happening to me, and I just wanted it to go away. Was I going crazy? My frantic brain flipped through images of recent events, and Circe's face popped into my mind. An immediate calm came over me.

I stared outside as a brightly colored red, white and blue Bangor and Aroostook Railroad boxcar was pushed past the office by the diesel switcher and suddenly released. A yard spotlight illuminated the words STATE OF MAINE emblazoned in huge letters across the car as it careened down one of the yard tracks. The wail of the diesel switcher told me they were about to wrap up work for our evening shift.

When I left work that night, I recalled that I had not seen Mark when I went to check on the freight car, and he had not stopped back at the office as he'd promised.

* * *

I wanted to talk to my dad about this, but having to come at midnight to pick me up did not put him in the best of moods. He usually said nothing and didn't appreciate being asked questions. Back then I thought he drove on radar.

On that drive home, something from the latest dream came back to me. When I had thought about Veronique's skin and hair, the fingers belonging to Sylvane had responded. That night, the overriding question was, Just who was Sylvane? And was he aware of me when I was inside of him?

CHAPTER 5
MISS HELDEBRIDE

At my locker the next day, I looked up just as Susan and Patty came along. As usual, Patty ignored me, but Susan, a few seconds behind her, stopped. Her usual condescending smile was not perched on her cheerleader lips. Instead, she wore a sort of coy look, and she was aiming it at...me. She walked toward me and didn't stop until she had practically forced me to back up into my locker.

"Alex," Susan said in a low voice. It was a thrill to hear her actually say my name. "What are you doing on Saturday?"

Mesmerized by her attention and sweet smell, I simply stood quietly. My eyes feasted on her deep blue ones, then strayed to her meticulous short blonde hair that I had always admired. Both Susan and Patty wore their hair in a close-to-the-head style reminiscent, I thought, of the 1920s. A band of very curly hair formed their bangs, while additional locks of curls encircled their heads like a tiara. It was as if they had copied each other. Susan, however, always wore bright colors, while Patty mostly wore clothes that were shades of blue.

"Hmm. You don't talk much, do you?" Susan whispered as her lips formed a pout and she pushed up against me, forcing me further into my locker.

I nodded, still bereft of voice.

"Alex? That's your name isn't it?" She said that a little louder, for the benefit of those around, I guessed. After all, she had an image to uphold; she never spoke to someone like me. I understood though. Her full pink lips went from the cute pout to a pucker, then they slipped into a subdued smile. I thought I saw the color of her eyes momentarily turn towards an even deeper ocean blue as she waited for my answer to her simple question.

I nodded to her as she looked up at me.

"Answer me, Alex," she urged softly. "Speak. You're hanging me out to ridicule here."

"Uh…" I was confused and tongue-tied.

"I said, what are you doing on Saturday?" she repeated a little louder.

I couldn't conceive that after having virtually ignored me for the past year, that morning she had pressed her gorgeous body up against mine and asked me for… a date? Me? A week previously I'd have thought that impossible, but that morning, I began to believe that since Circe had shown up, my world and fortunes seemed to have changed. Was that visitor from my dream responsible for the turnaround?

"Alex?" Susan insisted. Her brow furrowed and a small pointed finger poked me in the stomach. Obviously, she was not used to waiting for answers. "It's not anything like a date," she whispered. "I just need to deliver a message to you, so please just say yes." "I don't have a car." I said. "I…"

"Who said anything about a car? I have one," she said. "My parents bought me an Austin Healy 100-6 for graduation. It's just my size, don't you think? We're not going for a ride, though. I just need to deliver a message."

I nodded while thinking she was probably being manipulated by Circe.

"Alex," she shook me. "Stop thinking about her. No one's in my head. Besides, Circe, you, and I are on the same side. Just listen. If you're still here, I'll come find you and, if it's a ride you want, we'll take my little bug for a spin. You live out in the sticks, though, don't you? In the woods or something?" I didn't know what to say. "Will you just say yes for the benefit of these shmoes looking on?"

"Well, sure, yes, but I live by the woods, not in them," I managed to croak out. Her very presence was distracting me. "What do you mean, if I'm still here?"

"That's okay, I'll find you wherever you are," she murmured, then her voice dropped to a whisper. "Sorry, I didn't mean to worry you. What I meant was, they want to get you on the way to your destiny, so you may be gone by then."

* * *

With all that had happened in the past few days, I decided to simply nod at Susan's mention of destiny—and was she reading my mind too? I looked around and saw that a small crowd had gathered. I was uncomfortable with the attention that Susan had suddenly lavished on me, and I was glad that Irene didn't walk by.

Susan's voice continued in a whisper. "Don't forget. If you're still around, meet me Saturday morning in that little parking area off Central Avenue at nine." She punctuated that by using one of her fingers to tap my nose. "Don't be late."

With that, she turned suddenly and her golden curls brushed against my chin. As she disappeared down the hallway, I wondered what life had dealt me this time.

* * *

The next day in Miss Heldebride's English class, while we were reviewing our final test—on which I had somehow, despite my complete lack of preparation, gotten a B—Don, who sat in front of me, turned and handed me a note.

"Pass this back to Patty," he whispered.

Patty was in my English class, but never talked to me. I took the note, but before I could pass it, Miss Heldebride called my name. Thinking she had seen our exchange, I stood up and clumsily slipped the note in my back pocket.

"Alex," she said, "I can't believe you only got a B on this test. How long did you study for it?"

Relieved she had apparently not seen the note pass, I nervously shifted my feet. "I didn't, ma'am."

"You didn't?"

"No, ma'am. I concentrated on studying for my hard classes."

There was sprinkled laughter from around the room.

"Well, Alex, I can see where you put my class. You know, with a tiny bit of effort that B could have been an A."

"Yes, ma'am," I nodded. She shook her head in dismay and opened her class book while I sat back down. She always asked people questions like that in class.

"Alex?"

I again stood up at the sound of Miss Heldebride's voice, bumping my desk in the process. Snickers abounded at my reaction. "Yes, ma'am?" I replied.

"I want to see you after class."

"Yes, ma'am." I again sat down and wondered what Miss Heldebride wanted of me. I completely forgot about the note.

At the end of the period bell, as the rest of the class raced out, I stopped by her desk.

While she studied me, her fingers patted her sleek bun of blonde hair. She usually wore it up at class, but I had seen her with it down during one of the football games. She had the longest hair I had ever seen on a woman; it went all the way to her thighs.

"Miss Heldebride," I started. She made me so nervous. "I'm sorry about not studying for your test."

"I didn't ask you to stop after class to talk about that, Alex. I realize you've been...preoccupied. However, you should try to be more like Miss Zerbean. She seems to do very well on tests."

Everyone thought Patty was Miss Heldebride's pet student. However, that morning she said Patty's name like it was distasteful.

"What I wanted to know," she replied, interrupting my thoughts, "is where you are going after graduation?"

"Going? You mean like...college?"

She nodded. "Of course I mean college." A slight smile appeared on her face. I was sure she could sense my nervousness. "Where?"

"I can't afford to go to college, ma'am."

"Jocelyn," she replied as she stood up. "Call me Jocelyn. After all, do I look that much older than you?"

I nervously shook my head and wondered where she was going with that. Teachers weren't supposed to act and talk like they were students.

"You're practically out of school," she finished.

She then walked to the side of the desk where I stood. Miss Heldebride was tall, at least five-foot-ten, and the gossip was she had only last year graduated from college. With an eye on me, she hopped up and sat on her desk.

As we were the only two left in the room, I was nervous in her presence. Miss Heldebride was probably the most beautiful older woman I had ever seen. Grown woman, that is. Even though it was probably true that she was not more than five years older than me, I never compared women like her to girls my age.

* * *

I was also tense around her because I knew she was not one to be trifled with, especially by boys. I had heard some of her first male students thought they were being cool by whistling at her and asking her out. They quickly found themselves in Mr. Bricker's class. If you were to rank our English teachers by knowledge of their subject and teaching ability, Miss Heldebride was the best and Mr. Bricker the worst. Our principal, Mrs. Mason, was fully into women's rights, so she supported Miss Heldebride in everything she did.

* * *

"We were talking about college, Alex," she said. "You do know there are agencies that can help you, don't you?"

I didn't know what to say to her regarding college. I couldn't afford to go, probably even with help. And if I did go, I had no idea what I would study. I hadn't really thought much past high school, yet. However, I didn't want to get on her bad side by saying the wrong thing. While I stammered in front of her, she reached back to get her purse. She snared it out of a drawer on the opposite side of the desk, pulled out a card, wrote something on the back of it and handed it to me.

"Relax, Alex. Boys think I'm a bitch, don't they?"

"I would never call you that. I think you're beautiful," I said. Immediately my thoughts turned to, *What the heck? Where did those words come from?* I actually told her she was beautiful? A teacher?

"Well, aren't you the sweetest thing? It's okay that you think I'm beautiful. I can be a bitch, though, but I don't bite my good students."

That really unnerved me. I was shy around girls already, but having a grown woman—a teacher!—speak to me like this was almost unbearable.

"I'm sorry if I embarrassed you, Alex. Listen, however, this is important. I gave you my card because I have a friend in the financial aid office of Antelope Valley College." Her voice dropped to a whisper. "You know where that is? In California?"

I nodded because I was afraid of her, not because I knew.

"I wrote her name and a number on the back. My home number is on the front, but it's only good until graduation. Don't tell anyone. I'm planning to move back to California too, but let that be our little secret. Call me if I can help you..." Her fingertips rested on my hand after she handed me the card. "... anytime, day or...night."

It was a touch like I'd never felt. Different from Circe or Susan, but equally stimulating. I wondered what was happening with the females at our school. Or was it me?

"In fact, you can call me about anything..." she continued, then smiled. "Your future however, is west, Alex. Go west. We must get you to California where I can get you a scholarship. You can discover things there."

Could she really get me a scholarship? But why was the west so important? Was I missing something? Did I need a guidebook for speaking to women?

For a moment, her blue eyes were locked on mine.

"I have lunch," I said, uneasy not only with the situation, but also in her presence.

"As do I," she laughed, hopping off her desk.

"Have a good day, Alex," she said.

* * *

After school, I found the note for Patty in my pocket. It read, "Have you got a guy for *Cheerleaders Seduce a Geek Day?*"

So that was why Susan approached me the previous morning. It had to be a cheerleader prank. I even pictured her probable conversation with the other cheerleaders: "Girls, I got Alex, the biggest geek of all." The vision of them all laughing stuck in my head.

On Friday morning I looked for Susan, intending to tell her I was onto her little game, but I could not find her.

I wondered how women could change so quickly. A few days previously Circe had shown up, then Susan did her thing, and then Miss Heldebride appeared to...what? Discover me?

Once in my American History class, I glanced over to where Irene was busily writing something. She had obviously not been affected by whatever was in the air causing the incidents of the last couple of days. Irene's eyes came up and she stared from me to Circe's empty seat. When Mr. Marlowe came in the front door of the classroom, I heard the back door open at the same time.

Seconds later, soft fingers fluttered across the back of my neck and I heard Circe's voice whisper, "Did you bring my sandwich today?"

Luckily, I had, just in case.

* * *

When I arrived at lunchtime, I found Circe was already sitting at our table. She glanced up as I approached and gushed, "Thank goodness you're here. I'm starved."

I pushed my brown bag lunch over to her and asked, "You're really in my dreams, aren't you? Crazy things have been happening to me. You said you'd explain all of this."

"Yeah, sorry about that, but look at it this way. You can't deny you enjoy the changes. Women you've long fantasized about seem to be coming on to you. Now, when you're not supposed to even be here."

"I'm not supposed to be here? What the heck does that mean? I live here." But my mind was racing. How did she know about what had happened with Susan and Miss Heldebride?

Circe seemed to ignore my verbal questions and continued to focus on what I was thinking—and her own agenda. "You know, Susan Stage and that teacher, even your principal, are not who you think they are. All I can say is it appears that a journey, planned eons ago, has been set in motion. You are an important part of that upcoming trek. In fact, you might be the most important part. Apparently Susan and your teacher are involved." "What are you talking about? I'm not going on any trip. I'm in high school."

"For a few more days. The fate council will fix everything, and when they do, you'll be taking leave of this area."

"Leave? I can't just leave."

"Later with that. Face facts, Alex. You're not who you think you are. Somewhere back in time you were selected for a mission and were deep-sixed into obscurity. I don't know the mission yet, but I will get the facts soon."

"What?" I asked. "Deep-sixed into obscurity? What the hell does that mean?"

"Shush, you big mouth. I can't explain it all here," she hissed. "If someone overhears, it's more work for the memory erasers. I'll meet with you on the beach on Trivane one night this weekend and try to elucidate. For now, keep silent about this all."

"Trivane?"

"Trivane is where you and I meet in your dreams...and more."

"Wait. What kind of quest?" I stared at her with a shocked look. I wasn't Alex Monroe? Who was I?

Circe smiled at my expression, then ate my entire lunch.

* * *

43

Confused and quite out of it, after school I walked out of the north side of the building, as I had every day for the past year, to wait for my bus.

"Hi, Alex, sign my yearbook?"

I looked up and froze. It was Irene. I was speechless.

"Are you okay?" she asked.

I nodded, but was still unable to speak. In fact, I think I actually trembled a little in her presence.

"Here," she said. "I'll sign yours while you're doing mine." She talked to me like we were old friends. I assumed that Circe had set this up.

I stood trance-like as she reached up and pulled the yearbook out from under my arm. That caused my chemistry book to dislodge too, and it fell, hitting the curb on edge and cartwheeling past Irene's feet.

"Oh, I'm sorry." Her motion, as she turned and bent down to pick it up, sent her gorgeous reddish hair cascading down around her head. A sudden burst of wind whipped her blouse up a couple of inches off her back and exposed the top of black panties. Trying not to look, I came to my senses and opened her yearbook, just as she turned and handed me the chemistry book. For a moment, her emerald eyes held mine. Again, they seemed to tempt me with tiny flashes of violet. "You okay?" she asked.

I nodded and, still very nervous, took the book from her. After I re-tucked it under my arm, she reached over and lightly gripped my wrist. Her touch was nothing short of magical.

"You ought to be careful working around trains," she said as she traced the scratches and scabs from the puncture wounds of the previous night on my hand. She released my arm and turned her attention to my yearbook.

While she wrote, my mind raced. I had struggled to think of something intelligent to say and something clever to write, but came up blank in both cases. Finally, I feebly scribbled,

To Irene, One of the nicest girls I've ever known! Alex Monroe

I couldn't think of a single interesting thing to say. I was a total idiot.

"Finished?" she asked, those gorgeous green eyes focused on me. They were a steady green this time, no sparkles of lavender.

I nodded and handed her the yearbook as she returned mine.

"You didn't need to put your last name, Alex. I know who you are." She looked at me with a smile.

She hadn't even looked at what I wrote. How could she know how I signed my name?

"Oh, there's my bus," she announced. "Bye, thanks." Her eyes held mine for a moment and then, as she turned, I saw that beautiful hair gleaming red, then exotic brown and gold as it was caught in the late afternoon rays of the sun. She hopped up on the step of the bus, turned and fastened eyes the color of indigo on me, then disappeared inside.

Stunned, I simply stood there. I had been caught completely by surprise by her seeking me out and asking me to sign her yearbook. She had actually talked to me. Me. And what did I say? Nothing. Not one damn thing. I'm sure she thought I had a speech impediment, or worse yet, I was the dumbest guy in the Class of 1957. When I opened the book, on the first page I saw what she had written:

Dearest Alex,

You wrote a great paper on UFOs. Maybe someday in the future, when you're a famous writer, I can say I knew him when...he was living on Earth. Hope you fare well with the Fate Council's choices. You are apparently leading some quest, and it doesn't appear that I've been selected to go with you. Drat! However, Decima tells me that you will not be disappointed.

In the future - Call me anytime! Let's live a life together!

KE6-7645 (For a few more days)

Love, Irene

Under it was a strange, short message.

Be careful as you prepare for this mission. You're facing forces you're ill-prepared to deal with. For now, trust no one but Circe, and don't tell anyone about this warning. A special word of caution: There is more to Susan and Patty than you can possibly imagine. However, be especially careful of Jocelyn Heldebride.

Right after I read it, the words faded in the sunlight. When I boarded my bus and sat down, I looked again, and the strange short message was gone. Had it ever been there? Did I imagine it?

I shook the short message out of my head and wondered about her other words. What did she mean about me living on planet Earth? Where else would I be? And there was that name again, Decima. Who was Decima?

As I looked at Irene's signature and the word *Love*, I started to fantasize about a relationship with her. Could she have really liked me all that time? No—she was just being nice. I mean, everyone signs a note with love, don't they?

When I got off my bus, I got another shock. The scratches and scabs were gone from my hands. They were completely healed.

* * *

That evening, when I reported to work, I discovered my railroad future had taken a step backwards. The midnight-to-morning shift guy had decided, after fifteen years on the night shift, it was time he worked days. Since railroads ran on seniority, it bumped me to nights— permanently. To make matters worse, someone else in a less meaningless job, but with more seniority, decided he wanted the night clerk's job. That meant my whole future as a railroader went up in smoke. I ended up quitting the railroad that same night. At least there would be no more watching for humped cars late at night.

Yeah, sometimes life throws you a curve. I had swung at it and missed.

* * *

That night, I mentally played back the after-school conversation with Irene. I found it curious she had known the reason for the scratches on my hands. Since we had never talked, how could she even know I worked for the railroad? Of course, I couldn't explain how they had healed so fast, either. And maybe that was a bigger mystery ...

With my mind occupied by thoughts of Irene and how to approach her on Monday, I forgot Circe's promise she would clarify

47

things for me in a dream experience. It was Sunday night when that happened.

CHAPTER 6
DREAM ON

When I entered the dream state, I found myself in Sylvane, lying on the beach with Veronique. We were probably ten yards from where the swirling remnants of small incoming waves ended before flowing back into the orange ocean. However, at nighttime, the water, like it did on Earth, looked dark and ominous. Sylvane, with me inside, had his head propped up with one hand and stared out at eddies of retreating water.

Veronique balled her hand into a fist and rapped Sylvane on the head. "You in there, Alex?" she asked. Sylvane looked up, but I suddenly felt in control of his body. "I promised you an explanation, remember?" she added.

I thought of it, and Sylvane's head nodded. Somehow she had enabled me to take complete control of his body. "What about Sylvane? Won't he wonder about this?" I asked.

"He won't remember a thing tomorrow. He just fell asleep on the beach."

"Okay, how about we start with something easy," I said. "Just who the heck are you? For that matter, how am I involved in this? What's happening to me?"

"Calm down, I never said you could ask me questions. Your part is to keep quiet and listen. Understood?"

"Yes, master," I mumbled.

"Good, you're subservient. I have a thing for the obsequious. It's what drew me to Sylvane. Oops, that's you too." She paused while she snickered at her little observation, and her eyes perused mine. "As an Eternal, I have the ability to go back to former lives and, by avoiding that boxcar, you've somehow temporarily gained a similar power, only you don't want to accept it, preferring to think you're dreaming. Whatever. I was really not supposed to know you in your life as Alex, but you've apparently invoked some Eternal plan. I'm not sure if not getting crushed the other night was what did it. However, I do know it is part of a quest that has been rumored of for thousands of years. And you appear to be the central figure in this search."

"Huh?" I interrupted. "What are you—?"

"We don't have a lot of time, Alex. You need to let me explain some things or I'll have to end this and the wrong people will get involved and you'll never know the truth of what happened. So shut the Hades up."

I stopped asking questions.

Veronique, her face sporting a playful look after I stopped questioning her, stuck her toes in the path of a lumbering purple crab that simply scurried around them.

"I thought time was of the essence," I probed.

"After all your ignorant questions, don't you dare attempt to hurry me," she glared. "You may also be an Eternal, but for now, I'm the Eternal in charge here and I'll take my sweet ass time."

"I'm sorry, I..."

She laughed loudly. "You're such a geek; it's my nature to play little games with all creatures, including crabs and even you. Right now I'm not sure there's much mental difference between the two of you." She enjoyed another chuckle at my expense, then continued. "I was just letting the suspense build for you. Besides, it's fun for me to see you so uptight and nervous. After all, you may be my superior one day."

Then she turned serious and planted amber eyes on me. "In your present lifetime, I exist as Circe," she said. "In this previous lifetime, I was Veronique and you were Sylvane. We were living here on the planet Trivane, and at this point in our lives, we had a little fling. That's all it was, a coming of age involvement for me with some submissive guy on the beach. Who knew that someday the guy would turn out to be you? Anyhow, it didn't last once I got my memories restored. So, let's just say you were lucky to meet me. And, incidentally, me you.

"However, forget that; let's talk about what's important. If you were merely Alex Monroe, your dying should have slipped by relatively unnoticed in the big scheme of things for planet Earth. By not following that life script, you've unleashed forces even I don't quite understand. Yet evidently, according to the Parcae, it's initiated some long ago plan that involves you. So, there is more to this than meets the eye."

*"**You** don't understand what's happening?" I wailed. "Some plan? Just who the heck are the Parcae? And you? Are you Veronique or Circe or...someone else?"*

"Oh, you figured that out all by your little self. I'm impressed. I'm Lachesis, that's my Eternal name. So, actually, I'm all three. Here on Trivane I was Veronique. In our present lifetime on Earth, I am Circe. Like every Eternal, I'm born each time with a name common to the planet I'm on, but as an Eternal I also have a permanent name. Lachesis."

"Is that supposed to impress me?" I asked. "I never heard of you. What do you mean, you're an Eternal? And why did you call me one too?"

She let out an audible sigh, looked out over the water and seemed to speak to the stars. "Son of a Hera. What the Hades do they teach in Earth schools these days? And, why do I have to cater to all the unaware misfits?"

"Look," I started. "I've no idea what an Eternal or whatever is. All of this has to be some kind of put on anyway. How are you getting this stuff into my head? Who are you really?"

"I've just told you. My name is Lachesis. More than thirty-four thousand years ago, I was born for the first time on this shithole planet you call Earth, in the land known as Greece. At the time, I had two sisters, Atropos and Clotho. My mother was Nyx and my father was Zeus."

"Thirty-four thousand years ago? Don't make me laugh. Civilization only goes back maybe ten thousand years. Besides, how can you be thirty-four thousand years old?"

"I hate to be the one to break your bubble, but life on your Earth actually goes back over ten million years. Life on Trivane went back one hundred million years before its unfortunate collision with Methazar. In fact, most life on Earth was originally transferred here from there. Well, by way of Aldebaran and other planets. And, I'm not thirty-four thousand years old in this lifetime. That was just the first time I was born on Earth. I suppose you don't believe in reincarnation either."

"You expect me to believe that people have been living on Earth for ten million years?"

"I don't give a flying jazoole what you believe; nor do I have time to give you Earth History 101 lessons. Just accept my word for what it is: fact."

"Wait a minute." Circe's talk on her first day in my class about Greek Gods came back to mind. "Your father was Zeus? Like in Zeus, the Greek God?"

"Wow, comes the dawn. Yep, that's my daddy," she nodded.

"That's crazy," I said. "Greek Gods are mythology. Made up. Fiction."

"You keep believing that, Alex. But how do you explain me? Here and at your school?"

"Smoke and mirrors," I replied. "You're like some kind of magician. Or a hologram."

All the while I talked, she just slowly shook her head and smiled. "Want me to pinch you?"

"You said you had two sisters, Atropos and...Clotho?" I asked. "Are they as old as you? Wait, who are you, really? And what about Irene?"

"In the days of ancient Greece, the three of us girls were known as the Moirae, the Fates. Your mythology says we were supposedly responsible for where and when people were born, and how long they lived. Blah, blah, blah. So much bullshit. In actuality, we are only responsible for ourselves. Well, that's not entirely true. We do have something to do with the whole process. But you needn't trouble yourself with that. Atropos, who you know as Irene, is my older sister. Clotho is the youngest and yes, we've all three been around, bouncing from life to life, world to world, for millions and millions of years. So have you, the creature you now know as Alex. Earth humans normally don't recall their past lives. That's why we suspect you, like I, are not an Earth human, but an Eternal. You've either been masked from your true identity or you're just not old enough to recall who you were or are. I suspect it's both."

She stopped momentarily to wiggle her toes at another crab.

"But back to the present," she continued. "When you dodged death's edict that night, you caused my consciousness to be yanked back to this previous life on Trivane, apparently your last one with one of us. Seems like I always get summoned to clean up disasters. Atropos says it's because I sleep around so much. Maybe she's got something there...else why would I know you, some meek little toad on Trivane?

"Anyway, I assume that as soon as they figure out what went wrong with you, or what your quest is, they'll fix it, and then I'll be on my way, back to my fun life as Circe, the dancer in...well, that's none of your beeswax."

"I don't understand any of this. If what you're saying has a speck of truth, then what happens to me now?"

"Not my concern. I'm only to contain you until they research and decide. It usually only takes a couple of days."

"What do you mean, contain me? And who are they?"

"Parcae. Didn't we already cover that? They want to try and keep you from spreading the mess around by telling people some outlandish story that we'll have to clean minds over later. Right now I'm just supposed to be observing you. I got a reading from you when I saw you in the classroom and passed it on..."

"Reading?"

"You'll recall I sat by you, and when I touched you, I scanned your memory of the incident and sent it back to the powers that be. You have a scan block in your memories—it's strange. They only reflect your current life –not the past ones. Anyway, when you showed up in school the day after you were supposed to die, you gave someone quite a shock. She immediately sent Decima a What-the-Hades-I-have-no-idea-what-he's-still-doing-here mentalgram, and Decima sent immediately for me. I got there in five minutes."

"What do mean, I gave someone a shock? And they sent a message?"

"Yes—why is that hard to understand? But I don't know who the someone was, though obviously she was watching you."

"How is Irene involved?"

"Irene is a better analyzer than me, so Decima had her search back in your memories, and she found the details of the incident and how you avoided that boxcar. Irene believes you were somehow warned. She mentioned the block too, but she also got partly into your last life."

"Warned?" I asked. "Wait a minute. When did Irene search my memories?"

"She met you after school Friday, before she caught her bus."

I pictured her touching my hand, pretending to be concerned about my cuts and scratches. Wait, did she cure my scratches, too?

"She found your sense of hearing had been heightened—you knew something was up, didn't you? That was your warning. And yes, she did fix your little boo-boos.'

"Yes, I was not myself that night. I still don't understand what you're doing in my life on Earth, or how you're reading my mind."

"I told you, I'm one of the Fates. Part of my role in the process of reincarnation is to investigate anomalies. And all Eternals can read minds."

"Anomalies?"

"Yes, abnormal happenings, you know? Failure to die when you were supposed to is not considered congruent. You're a glitch. Investigation of such irregularities is up to the last born of us that has reached the age of enlightenment."

"You are definitely losing me. Can you explain—?"

"Oh for Zeus's sake! Stop interrupting me and I'll get there."

Fully chastised, I nodded.

"Each new lifetime, my sisters and I are free to choose anywhere we wish to be born. Our lifetime is unusually long, but we never age past your human age of twenty-five. When we get to that age, we move every ten years or so. That way, people don't get suspicious about how we stay young. Irene likes to attend high school and tease boys, so she moved to your little town and..."

"Wait. Are you saying she's really twenty-five years old?"

"Actually, in this lifetime we're not just starting out. Irene is in fact fifty-seven. I'm fifty-seven also, but I'm younger than her. I don't normally like doing high school. Boring. Teasing boys? Boring. Where's the sense in that, if they don't even know they're being tormented? But it has been fun these last few days. With you. You're kind of cute as Alex."

"How can you be fifty-seven? You're like...seventeen, for Pete's sake."

"I told you we stop aging around twenty-five."

"Where did you come from, then? Where are you living?"

"Let's just say somewhere in California. I was waiting for my sister Clotho to arrive. We made plans... Now she's probably already there, but doesn't have her memories yet."

"What's this age of enlightenment you mentioned?"

"On our seventeenth birthday, we recall who we are as Eternals and follow through on the plans we set in place the previous lifetime. Clotho got involved in some crap in Germany and died, so she had to be reborn in 1939. Hey, that's the year you were born! Anyway, she should be just recovering her memories. I need this debacle to be solved so I can go back home and have my sisters join me."

"To you it may be some debacle, but to me it's my life."

"Don't be offended, you'll be born again. Besides, I'm sure you're pleased with all the attention I've gotten for you. You don't seem to have many girlfriends, so I thought I'd liven things up. You see, there are a few Eternals at your school, and some agreed to help."

"There are more Eternals at my school?" I repeated, astounded.

"Yes. Your English teacher, Jocelyn Heldebride, is Eris, the Goddess of Strife, according to your... mythology. She got that nickname because she used to sneak around in the dark with Hera back in the old days and cause all kinds of trouble. Strife, you get it? My Mom back then, Nyx, loved the color black. Eris loves blue-black; she calls it midnight blue. You like her? Play your cards right and you'll get to see more of her. Much more."

"Jocelyn Heldebride is a goddess?"

"She's an Eternal and should be out of your league. But, Eris has a preference for meek boys who don't know who they are as an Eternal. However, forget her. We need to find out what is so special about you and your quest that someone took the trouble..."

She seemed to consider that. "Look, it's almost dawn on Earth, so you need to get back. This type of thing, you avoiding death, has happened in *the past, and normally within five days it's discovered and remedied. However, only Decima, my sister and I, plus whoever saved you, knew for the first couple of days, so it might take longer. For now, just go along with me as sort of your girlfriend in school. In a few minutes you'll wake up in your bed at home, and—"*

"So this was another dream?" I interrupted. "I'm dismissed?"

"If you really think this is some fantasy, Alex, then analyze this when you awaken," she said, and pressed her lips to mine.

Hard.

* * *

When I awoke and rolled over in bed, I saw that my alarm clock was set to go off in two minutes. After turning it off, I realized my lips felt kind of sore. *No, that couldn't be*, I thought. I quickly jumped out of bed and went into the bathroom. In the mirror, I could see a bit of Circe's red lipstick still smeared on my mouth. I touched my top lip, and then stared at the hint of red pigment on my fingertip.

That morning, I finally told my parents about quitting my job. Right after, I quickly left the house. However, I knew they were very disappointed. My dad felt I should have at least tried the railroad job offered me when all the musical chairs stopped. But I was worried it would be some desk job, which would not suit me. Sitting inside all day would have driven me mad. But, since I had quit my job, my immediate future was up in the air. Everyone else had summer jobs lined up or was preparing for college, and now, a mere week before graduation, I had nothing. But then again, according to Circe, I was to lead some quest. Me? Ha!

We lived near the forest, so on my way to catch my bus I usually walked through the woods in an effort to ready my mind before classes. On that morning's stroll, I had originally hoped to try and formulate some plan for what I'd do when school ended and I graduated. But while I walked, I couldn't help thinking of the dreams again. What nagged at me now was: Circe had intimated they would set things right. Did that mean I would, in reality, die? Would they somehow force me to leave? That kind of thinking didn't help.

"We all die, at some time. But it is not permanent for all of us." The voice seemed to come from a sudden breeze that rustled the leaves in the forest. "But it is not in your future that you should die here on Earth."

"Who are you?" I stupidly asked aloud. Had I even heard that? Or had the voice just appeared in my head? I was seriously starting to doubt all my senses.

"You heard me," the voice said. "You don't know me...yet. I'm a friend of Circe and...you. You must listen to all she tells you. She speaks the truth."

The breeze stopped as suddenly as it started, and I knew the voice was gone. Just then, the bus approached and I tried to put all of it out of my mind. But after I got on the bus and sat down, another reality sunk in. I had no driver's license and, after quitting the railroad, had no prospects for a steady job. In berating me that morning, my dad had said the country was in a mild recession and jobs were not growing on trees. Why had I been so impulsive the previous night?

Watching the trees roll by outside the window, I again tried to rerun the events that led up to my railroad job resignation, but the memories weren't there. All I could recall was the succession of job switches and my saying, "I quit."

Had I even thought it out? Had someone put those words in my mouth?

* * *

"Are you okay?" Circe whispered in my ear for the third time since class started. She talked out loud, and it made me nervous. What if Mr. Marlowe heard us?

"No one can hear us. You're speaking with a goddess. Give me some credit."

Reluctantly, I agreed. No one seemed to notice us talking. I also noticed, since she had arrived on the scene, my life had changed drastically. I had had a job. I had been happy. Now, look where I was. I thought again that without a steady job, I couldn't buy a car and I had no future to look forward to.

"Alex, before I came on the scene you were a noxious vegetable," she whispered in my ear. "You were never really happy, so get over your brooding. All the girls you desired in this school are Eternals, and I've gotten their attention for you, so you owe me. You should be happy I got you out of that lame job, too. We'll talk at lunch. I have kind of a surprise for you."

I shook my head in silent frustration. Anyway, I *was* once happy. But that was when I was with Brenda.

"Oh yes," Circe whispered in my ear. "My sister told me about your Brenda fixation when she zipped through your memories the other day. Irene and I had a good laugh, 'cause I'm sure that girl would have dumped you years ago. Cheerleader, right? They usually grow up to be quite mean little girls," Circe whispered.

"You don't know her," I said, loud enough for heads to turn.

"Just think your answers, Alex. I can read your mind. That way your mouth won't get you in trouble. Anyway, I know your friend Brenda's type."

What's your lunch surprise? You'll ask me to write your term paper? I thought the words in my mind and hoped to get her off the subject of Brenda.

"No, I've got something for my term paper in mind already. Hey! Want to cut school and do something fun tomorrow? We'll put a little adventure into this sad life of yours. What's left of it, anyway."

Yeah, me cut school. Fat chance of that.

"You're starting to annoy me," she whispered.

What? How?

"You're so infuriating. Start doing things for Alex," she said, with a tap on my shoulder that I knew was a dismissal.

One thing she said was true. If, as she claimed, Miss Heldebride, Susan Stage, Patty and Irene were Eternals, they were addictive. I was in love with all four. Make that five. Circe had also been correct when she said I was in love with her.

Oops, make that six if we're counting normal Earth girls. Brenda had been on my mind a lot lately, and I still missed her. I guess I was a hopeless romantic.

* * *

At lunchtime, I found Circe waiting for me with a smile painted on her face and an extra chair pulled up to our small table.

"Are you expecting someone else to sit with us?" I asked.

"Yes, I told you. Surprise! My sister is joining us today," she said.

"Irene's sitting with us?" I asked. "Irene? Sitting with me? Why are you springing this on me all of a sudden? I could have combed my hair."

"You have a brush cut, what's to comb? You look fine."

Regardless, I ran a hand through my bristly hair.

"Look, both of us know you're dying for my older sister to simply notice you. Now you get your wish. Be good and don't make a big deal out of it. If I told you earlier you'd probably have pooped your pants. One more thing... Don't ask her any silly questions."

I felt like a little boy putting cookies and milk out for Santa Claus, and then being told to hide behind the sofa and not look. However, like that proverbial little boy, I was extremely nervous about what was to take place. And it seemed to please Circe that I was a combination of excited and scared to death.

"Just settle down, Alex. If you don't behave, I'll embarrass you to no end."

I nodded and tried to relax.

"Is this chair for me, Circe?"

I looked up at the sound of Irene's voice as she slipped into the seat between us and glanced over at me.

"Thanks, Alex. Circe's raved about your sandwiches," she said, helping herself to mine. "So you're in love with me, huh?"

Circe poked my ankle with the toe of her shoe. "Would you close your mouth and be less of a geek by getting us some milk?"

"Yes, me too, please?" Irene added.

I walked in a daze, retrieved cartons for all of us and returned. I was very conscious of the entire lunchroom watching me. I thought the topic of everyone's conversations for days would be — How did that dorky Alex get the prettiest girl in school to sit with him at lunch?

I handed a milk carton and straw to each girl, then sat down on the other side of the table.

I looked from Irene to Circe. "You're actually sisters?"

"Yes, Circe and I really are sisters," Irene said softly. "Not the way you think of that, though. We weren't born so in this life, but we're Eternal sisters."

I stared at her. Circe had used that term too. *What the heck was an Eternal sister?*

"Circe told you she and I were born on Earth at the dawn of your current civilization," Irene explained. "She as Lachesis and I as Atropos. She and I have stayed close ever since. Ergo, we're Eternal sisters.

Circe then looked to her sister. "He doesn't believe any of what I tell him. Look at that face, read that mind. He's hopeless."

"Stop, Circe," Irene said. "Decima said he's important, and we're assigned to protect him until she can piece this together. Give him some space. It is a lot for him to swallow at this time. He hasn't got his memories back yet."

"How long will this take?" I asked.

"All you have to know at this time is there are a few other Eternals here in your school, too. It's quite unusual that Iris is here. Not to mention the quiet one. Those two are Eternal sisters, too."

"Who is Iris?" I asked. "And...the quiet one?"

"I think Circe told you that Susan Stage is actually an Eternal. She's Iris, one of my dearest friends, but in this lifetime we're not close. I don't know her reason for being here...at this school. She's an Eternal sister with Celaeno, the quiet one. You know her as Patty. I just want to warn you, though; she may not be friendly to you."

"Ha," I laughed, surprising myself. "Are you saying the two of *you* are friendly? Circe's been putting me down since she got here."

Irene snapped her eyes at me. "Circe has actually been nicer than I would have been, had I gotten the job. You're lucky Decima stood up for you, else I wouldn't even be talking to the likes of you. And, for your information, Circe only puts down people she really likes. It's her way."

Circe bobbed her head in agreement, but I thought they must have a different definition of the term nice.

"Do you understand you were not really supposed to die the other night?" Irene said with a serious look on her face. "That someone tried to end your days early?"

I nodded. "At least that's what both of you have told me."

"Listen to us. If you're not who the Parcae think you are, they've got to create a new life for you so you don't upset the future. Why they don't just shift you into another dimension, I don't understand. In the meantime, Circe feels sorry for you, so she's trying to fit you into ours. Unbelievably, she even made herself your girlfriend. She's an Eternal. I'd have just let you suffer."

Circe stopped her by taking one of Irene's hands into hers. "It's okay. I told you. He's an Eternal."

"But he's so clueless!" Irene wailed.

CHAPTER 7
MEETING IN THE WOODS

I didn't know what was worse, going to school feeling like a loser, or staying home and listening to my parents berate me as one. So, after school that day, fed up with their constant haranguing, I took off for a walk to the woods.

My self-planning sessions for my future had not been going well. Of course, losing my job was kind of a setback. In just a few days, my only option seemed to be living at home with mom and dad. I contemplated many things, including joining the Navy, but I knew I'd never make the cut. I felt doomed to mediocrity.

* * *

I walked along Central Avenue, then took a smaller trail down deeper into the forest preserve. It led down to a stream that ran through the center of the woods. When I got to the small creek, I found Circe sitting on an old tree stump, waiting, apparently, for me. She was dressed in black jean shorts and a silver, metallic looking shirt studded with different colored gemstones. She wore black sandals on bare feet and her hair was meticulously combed.

She hopped off the stump, ran up to me, and took my hand in hers. "Ready for our walk?"

I'm sure my face showed the shock I felt at seeing her there, in the woods. "I didn't expect to find you..."

"Yeah, sorry about that. I told you I read your mind the other day, now I'm attuned to it. Listening to you scold Irene and me at lunch yesterday, I began to feel a little guilty for making you out to be so dense."

"That's okay," I said. "After being belittled by the two of you, I got to be ragged on by my folks. All in a day's work. One of my days, anyway."

"Yeah, sorry that Irene and I gave you the business. Not good days, huh? Would a hug help?

I hunched my shoulders in a show of non-committal.

Before I could say anything, she hugged me quickly, then tugged on my arm, dragging me further into the woods. I hurried along behind her, until she suddenly stopped at the shoreline of the stream.

"Follow me," she said.

She released her grip and jumped over the narrow ribbon of water. I imitated her and easily cleared the little stream. As if she knew exactly where she was going, she proceeded up the rise, while I tried to keep up behind her. I could not understand how she moved so quickly and gracefully. She was wearing sandals, and rather than follow a well-used trail through the forest, she blazed her own. I had to dodge branches and stickweed plants, while she breezed right past them in shorts. Branches smacked into her calves and shins, but when she finally stopped in a clearing, I saw not a mark on her. I had little scratches and cuts from thorns, and seeds from stickweed were stuck all over me.

"Sorry," she said. "I'm sorta immune to who you term Mother Nature." She then proceeded to help me pull the little seeds off my clothes. When we finished that task, she took my scratched up hand in hers and looked at me with puckered lips. "Want Circe to kiss your little boo-boos and make them better?" she asked.

"Are you making fun of me again?"

In answer she smiled and said, "Watch, and then tell me what you think."

"No," I said. "For some strange reason, I believe you mean well. But really, did you bring some sort of first aid kit?"

"Just this," she said. She brought my hand to her lips and gently licked several red cuts. When she released my hand, the scratches were gone.

She smiled at my dazed expression. "There is something in our system that allows saliva to instantly heal scratches and nicks. Didn't my sister take care of some cuts you had the other day?"

So that's how she did it. I nodded. "She just traced over them with her finger."

"That works too, but that's kind of boring. Our skin is impervious to little cuts and scrapes," Circe continued. "The stickers don't embed in my clothes because not only are the materials something you won't find on Earth, they're also treated with a chemical I picked up on another planet in a previous existence. Let me lick those other scratches and heal them too. Irene will kill me if you get bloodstains in her car. When I arranged this, I didn't tell her where I was going to—"

"What did you mean, you arranged this?"

Circe's luscious red lips curled back and her amber eyes joined them in a smile. "I was wondering if you caught that. Glad my new Earth boyfriend's not a complete ignoramus. You know, I've been reading your thoughts, and you're finally becoming convinced. What I'm telling you must be true. Correct?"

I nodded, because she was correct. I had completely accepted her as who she professed to be, Lachesis, an ancient Greek goddess.

She kissed me on the nose and giggled. "I only say that I'm a goddess because it's the easiest way to put your mind back in ancient Greece. In actuality, it was the people living there at the time that thought we were gods. I might have been a little more advanced than them, but I was still just a girl. A woman, actually."

"I read a little bit of Greek mythology in the library--"

"It's mostly bullshit," she said. "And it's not my mythology, it's yours. What a bunch of crap they wrote about us. I told you some stuff, but I thought the best way to bring you up to speed is using my term paper. I was inspired to write it in a kind of letter format. To you. I had to turn it in to Mr. Marlowe, but even if he reads it, he'll be left with no knowledge of what it says. I made sure of that. You'll get a copy from me later. You'll see."

Her astonishing eyes seemed to soften as she leaned in close to me. "Irene thinks I must be going soft, taking the time to write out some of our history for some Earth geek."

"I still don't understand what your part is in all of this," I said.

"My part?" she laughed. "You think this is some kind of play? Irene and I are still trying to decide what's going on. Apparently, the quest specifics are spread out among a group of Eternals, and the Parcae are involved in putting it all together. I covered what I know up till now in the letter, as well as gave you a short history of the others."

"Who are the others?" I was scarcely even keeping up with the players now.

"I'm sure various other characters, besides those you've already met, will manifest themselves over time. So far you've just met my sister and Eris—you still call her Miss Heldebride, don't you? In this life she's with some of the nasty ones."

She giggled again. "How old do you think Jocelyn is, anyway?"

"I don't know women's ages that well. Twenty-five to thirty?"

"In this life, Jocelyn was born in 1898. She grew up in Vienna, Austria."

"That's impossible," I said. "That would make her in her early 60s."

Circe smiled and gripped my arm. "You really need to read my letter before we go on about this. Maybe we'll get to discuss it at some later date."

My mind spinning, I nodded and shook my head.

Circe yanked on my arm to regain my attention, then pointed at a tree that had fallen in a recent storm. The trunk was now wedged horizontally, about four feet off the ground, between two other trees like a natural bench. "Come on, Alex. Let's sit. Can you boost me up there?"

I could see why she'd have a hard time getting up by herself. Goddess or not, she was only about five feet plus an inch or so tall. I nodded, put my hands on her waist and easily picked her up. She put her hands on my shoulders to steady herself, and when I looked into her sparkling, now fully amber-colored eyes, framed by rich black hair, I got weak in the knees and froze. I was so grateful for this time alone with her. After all, she had to be one of the most beautiful women on the planet.

"Um, could...you put me down?"

"Sorry," I said. "You're just so beautiful." I couldn't believe I'd just said that. Out loud. I set her down and focused on the ground. I was embarrassed.

"Thanks," she said. Again, her eyes momentarily flashed. Sensing my uneasiness, she bent her head down and tried to look at my face. "What's wrong? Wait a minute. Are you that shy? Is this the first time you've paid a compliment to a girl?"

Recalling Brenda, I shook my head and spoke, but my eyes remained focused on the soil of the forest floor. "You're not just some girl. You're a goddess."

She gripped my shoulder, squeezed and said, "My sister would say, a goddess that ought to have her head examined. Pick your head up and come sit next to me. I won't bite you."

I sat where she indicated with a pat of her hand. When I finally got the courage to look back at her, she was smiling at me.

"You are one strange boy. Jocelyn and Irene are right: you're just so innocent." She tousled my short hair, making me even more ill at ease. "Sorry, I'm embarrassing you. It's refreshing for me to get involved with someone like you. All the other male Eternals have such huge egos." She then took my hand in hers. "Listen. Those dreams you've had with me as Veronique? They were of a past life we had together on a planet we Eternals remember as Trivane. In Earth years that happened about ten million years ago."

"Ten million years ago! That's impossible. I was born in 1939."

"Yeah, keep trying to squelch the truth." She grinned wickedly. "You were reborn for the zillionth time in 1939. Ten million years ago, for a couple of months anyway, you and I had some wild sex on the beach on Trivane. I lost my virginity, in that lifetime, to you. You and me. Quite a coincidence, eh? By the way, when either of us leaves this area, your remembrances of that life should end. Temporarily, at least. Since you are an Eternal, they'll return when you reach age." She paused and looked up into the trees.

"Where is Trivane?" I asked. That was the least of my questions after what she had just said, but I wanted some time to process.

"At night you can see it from here on Earth."

"I can? I can only see a couple of planets, like Venus and Mars. Are you talking about seeing the star it orbits?"

"It orbits this star, you ninny, your sun. You call it Mars now, but back then we called it Trivane."

"Mars? People live on Mars?"

"They used to. Now there are other types of beings there, but no humans, as it no longer has a breathable atmosphere. There's been a lot of changes since you knew me back then."

"The orange-colored ocean?"

"Gone. It was at the base of a very high mountain that burst out into a volcano about ten million years ago. It got that color from all the iron on the planet. Earth still calls Mars the red planet, but it's more orangey to me. I miss Trivane. If I have to leave here, I'll miss Earth in some ways, too. Regardless of what is decided, now that some plan is in effect, I'll be leaving this area soon."

"I'll miss you," I nodded.

She looked at me with a twinkle in her eye and said, "Don't get all mushy on me, lover boy. You need to avoid mentioning this to anyone until I've gone. I want you to be successful on your quest. Don't let me down."

"I haven't mentioned the dream experiences to anyone except you, and I won't."

"It's not like they'd believe you, anyway, and it's simple to twist their minds if they suspected anything, but..."

"But what?"

"I don't want people to think you're a wacko."

For a moment, I looked down at the remnants of leaves from last fall, then back up to her. "I'd have thought, after I messed up your plans to be with your sister and complicated your life, that you'd just want me gone, out of it," I finally admitted. "Why would someone like you care what people think of me anyway?"

"We better end this and leave before I tell you something I'm not supposed to," she said. "Help me down?"

I jumped off the log and turned to face her. She suddenly pushed my extended arms away and jumped off herself, then stumbled. "Oww," she exclaimed. "I twisted my ankle."

"You should have let me..."

"Shush," she said. "Can I just lean on you and—"

"No," I insisted. "You'll just aggravate the injury. Maybe I should carry you back."

For a long moment our eyes locked. I don't know why I had turned so forceful with her. Normally, I would do whatever she asked. I gave her a little smile, trying to lighten her predicament.

Her frown gradually changed to a smirk. "You're enjoying this, aren't you?" she asked.

"Yes, I am." I smiled. For once I felt I had the upper hand in this impossible relationship.

"Okay, you can carry me, but don't you drop me."

I bent down and put one arm behind her knees and the other around the small of her back, easily lifting her as her small hands locked behind my neck. "I don't understand you," I said. "At times you're kinda sweet and nice; other times you're rather cold and condescending."

"Careful with that word," she said.

I shifted her body slightly in my arms. Was it even possible that someone could smell so good?

"That's my natural scent, no perfumes. Am I getting heavy?" she asked.

"You could never be heavy," I replied. It was true; she weighed nothing in my arms, and she felt like nothing I could describe. She was simply intoxicating.

"To answer your analysis of me, though, I'm really rather like you," she said. "Only you try to always show your sweet side and not the confused, the shy side and not the bold. You need to merge the two into something mellow. It's okay to be appealing on occasion and then sometimes distant. I'm sure girls like your introverted trait, but they'd like to see the confident you, too. Show them those other characteristics, and they'll surely show you theirs."

One warm hand then came around and touched my cheek, sending pulses racing through my body. She turned my face to hers. "I know right now your life is bittersweet, for me having come into it and told you things that can be hard to hear. And now I'll be going away, leaving you with no idea of your future. Don't fret, though. Decima will step in and guide you. And, some day, you'll experience the love you seek, just not with me."

With me still carrying her, she guided me out of the forest, and we stopped at what she said was Irene's car. I was totally unprepared. It was a car I'd dreamed of owning, if I was ever able to afford one: a 1955 Studebaker Speedster. The body was lemon yellow and the roof looked almost gold, but I knew it was a lime shade of green. It was the most beautiful car I had ever seen.

"How long are we going to stand here, Alex?" Circe urged.

While still holding her, I opened the door to bright yellow leather seats. "How are you going to drive with a twisted ankle?" I asked.

"Oh, that," she said. She unexpectedly hopped out of my arms and stood at the side of the car. "Sorry, just kidding about the twisted ankle. I wanted to see what you'd do if...I needed help."

"You were testing me?"

"Yeah, but don't worry, I had to tweak your bold side, get you to carry me, but you passed with flying colors." She looked out to the road, then back at me. "Look, your case is special to me. I don't tell everyone that I'm their girlfriend. In addition to you starting some quest planned long ago, the Parcae are trying to figure out who tried to interfere in your life cycle back in that railyard and why. You might get to stick around a few more days, but I've been told I have to leave. Very soon. It means you'll have to deal with Irene for a change."

"I don't think she likes me."

"Irene and I were scheduled to meet in a few months in California. Why that had to change kind of occupies her mind right now. But you're right, she doesn't like Earthies. But now that she knows you're an Eternal, she should be nicer."

I nodded.

"I don't quite understand all of this Eternal stuff," I said.

"Read the letter."

"Can I ask you one more thing?"

She nodded.

"The other guys in school go crazy over Irene, but they seem to ignore you. You are just as pretty, if not more so, than her. Why is that?"

"Oooh, don't tell my sister that. However, only you can see the real me. To everyone else, I appear to be what you call a 'plain Jane.' Guys in your school have enough trouble coping with Irene, without adding me to the mix. So I instituted a shimmer cloud around me."

"Shimmer cloud?"

"Yes. I set an image of another person in my mind, and it broadcasts that into the mind of anyone who looks at me. They see the image I project and not the real me. Sometimes it's set for invisibility, and they see nothing. Right now it's set to show the shimmer image to anyone except you, Irene and other Eternals like Eris. Actually, Celaeno—oops, Patty to you—wears one too, as Pleiads are quite different looking since they keep their off-world appearance. When you look at Patty, you're seeing an illusion. Eris, Iris and Irene, you're seeing in the flesh."

74

I nodded, though I was still a little overwhelmed by it all. I think I was getting used to that feeling, though. I took a steadying breath and looked again admiringly at the car I'd never get to own.

She nudged me against the vehicle, then looked out on the road. Her hand came up in a gesture for me to not talk.

"Hey, want to come with me?" she said suddenly and gripped my hand in hers. "Irene just contacted me, and wants me to check something out. And, since you are sort of my boyfriend...you can be my assistant."

"I'd go with you anywhere," I said. "What does your assistant do?" Of course, by then, I was so in love with this girl that she didn't have to ask me twice.

With that, she slipped off her sandals and handed them to me. "Hold these. I prefer to drive barefoot." We got in the car and she drove off.

"Where are we going?" I asked as I examined the yellow leather.

"Your railyard," she announced. "Irene said someone else got killed there, and she was wondering—"

"Someone else? Do you know who?"

"She didn't say and I didn't ask. She thinks it was somehow connected to your close call. She had originally assumed the other night was just your scheduled day to die, but after talking to Decima, she's sure that's not the case now. Decima said someone arranged your accident, and then someone else saved you. I'm the clue gatherer, so we'll see if maybe you and I can figure out if you were supposed to die on schedule, or if someone tried to hasten things up a bit for you."

"Does Irene or this Decima know something?"

"Maybe. Irene picked up something from you when she signed your yearbook. That might lead us to who wanted to see you dead."

CHAPTER 8
RAILYARD AND REVELATIONS

Thirty minutes later, Circe and I were parked on the street that paralleled the far end of the railroad classification yard, where I'd had my brush with death.

"We can't just go into the yard," I said as we got out of the sleek little car.

"Why not? You said you'd go with me anywhere. 'I'd go with you anywhere,' those were your exact words."

"And I would, but this is... It's against the rules! No one but railroad employees are allowed in the yard. We'll be arrested."

"Rules, smules," Circe muttered. She puckered her lips at me and pinched my cheek with her fingers. "Listen, if you're going to be my boyfriend assistant and do stuff with me, you've got to start living a little dangerously." Her smile at the end of that statement filled me with courage I didn't know I had.

"Do you really think of me as your boyfriend?"

"Of course. Maybe I'll prove it to you later. Right now we have to investigate. Now, hand me my thongs."

* * *

Five minutes later, we walked along Track Eight.

"Are you scared?" she asked.

"No," I said. But truth be told, it was not one of my rare moments of confidence.

"You're lying," she said. "Mind reader, remember? Here, take my hand."

She reached over and gripped my hand in hers. Courage flowed through me.

"We should have done this while that freight car that started all of this was still here," Circe announced. "I'm feeling nothing unusual."

"Are we looking for a body?" I asked.

"No," she said. "The police were already here and gone. So is the dead guy. I might be able to find something they missed."

That's when a sudden breeze stirred up dust along the tracks, rustling her black hair. Then a stronger wind pushed me back and tugged at her silver blouse, causing it to billow slightly, then pull free of her jeans. Pieces of paper, including discarded waybills and other debris, began to fly around as the winds continued to pummel us. The air seemed filled with a mixture of coal and gravel dust. It was like we were caught in a miniature tornado.

"Crap," Circe muttered.

"It's gonna storm," I said.

"It'll storm in a way," she replied.

"What do you mean?" I asked, while trying to keep the grit out of my eyes.

"Come on, Alex, that boxcar's door is open. Let's get inside. Quickly."

We ran to the opening and I easily boosted her up into the empty car. I followed her into the darkness, where we sat, our backs against the interior plywood sheeting of the old freight car. Outside, the first heavy drops of rain began to drum against the metal sides. High winds rocked the freight car on its trucks.

"I didn't know it was going to rain today," I said.

"It's not a normal rain, it's Aello," she replied. "She is trying to scare us away from here. I've got to tell Irene about this right now. I'm going to grip your shoulder so you'll be able to listen to our mental conversation. It should be evident which of us is talking."

Before I could ask one of a dozen questions popping up in my head, she said, "No questions and don't you dare interrupt. Irene will be mad enough when she figures out I brought you with me and I'm letting you listen."

She started the mental discussion almost immediately.

Irene, I'm at the railyard. I think we have a problem. Circe's words echoed in my mind.

What is it? came the familiar voice of Irene. *Did you do something to my car? And just why do you have the little geek tuned into this conversation? Eeeww, you let him ride in my car?*

Yes, I brought him with, and no, we did nothing to your precious car. And watch what you say, the geek's my boyfriend and I think I know why he didn't die here in the yard. He's got to be the one involved in Decima's plan. I think someone else wants him eliminated, Circe answered, looking at me.

Who? Irene said softly. There was mental silence for a few seconds.

We'll figure that out later. Right now, we're caught in one of Aello's tricks. That means at least one of the Harpy sisters is in this thing, too. Circe transmitted.

Those little snots are always causing problems. Hades. I should scan your little boy tart again; maybe I can find out if he definitely is the one Decima expects, Irene continued. *For someone to step in and attempt to change his destiny...and yet another to save him...*

Irene was silent for a moment. Finally, she said, *He has that block...okay, I need to scan him again. It's too dangerous for you to bring him directly here, so pass him off to me. Just drop him in the forest preserve along Central Avenue and get the car back to me. Have him wait there until I return to pick him up. And you stay away from home tonight. Use the safe apartment. If this is some kind of trap, we won't both get caught. See if you can contact Ocypete, then check back with me later tonight. One more thing—first get your boy toy off the link.*

Circe let her hand slide off my shoulder, breaking my connection while Irene apparently sent a final message she didn't want me to hear.

"Bad news, Alex," Circe gripped my hand. "Irene said the police think the guy that got killed was a friend of yours. She picked up his name in your mind when she scanned you that day after school by the buses."

"Who?" I asked.

"Mark Wallen."

"No!" I exclaimed. "How?"

"From what she could gather, the police identified him from his jacket and papers in it. They think he was accidentally hit by a moving freight car while walking down the tracks a couple of days ago. No one knew when it happened, because his body was under the freight car. They found him when they moved the car."

"No way," I said. "Mark taught me to be extra careful at night in the yard, and he knew I almost got run over. He was very cautious." I wished then that I had gone back and looked for Mark after he didn't show up that night. Now I wondered if my telling him what had happened somehow got him involved in all this.

"I'm sure it's hard to hear, but we have our own troubles. This storm that Harpy Aello has cooked up isn't going anywhere, and it'll take a while to get back to the car. So I guess we're gonna get a little wet." She grinned, then turned sober. "I really am sorry, if it's true about your friend."

"You and Irene seem to know what's going on, but you're not telling me much. You said I was the one. One what? Who are the Harpy sisters, and why are people trying to kill me? And what if Mark's death is a part of all this?"

"You've got some of that backwards. For some reason, someone wanted you dead and tried to kill you, yes, but someone else stepped in and saved you for a reason of their own. Since only a descendant of one of the original Greek Gods or Goddesses can do either of those things, we have to proceed carefully. The Harpy sisters are Iris's sisters, and their names are Aello, Ocypete and Celaeno. We're friends with Ocypete, but not the others."

"But Iris and Irene are friends," I wailed, completely confused by this whole array of people who seemed to not be who they were a week ago.

"Iris is usually on our side, but her sisters are touch and go. Look, Alex, my sister and I are not included long-term in this little mess. We're trying to find out what's going on, but we're not supposed to be this involved."

"What about Mark?" I asked.

"I don't know if he was a part of this, or a separate accident. Irene is much better at this stuff than I am. Ask her. I'll meet with you at her apartment tomorrow morning and after school, if I'm still around."

"Wait a minute. You want me to stay the night at...I can't do that. My folks will have a cow."

"I'm sure Irene will appreciate the fact that you questioned spending the night alone with her. Anyway, it's already taken care of. Irene has already contacted your home and mentally planted the memory in your parents of you being home with them. They'll go to sleep tonight thinking you're there and wake up to you having left early for school."

"Why does she want me to stay the night?"

"I never question Irene. Don't worry, Alex, she won't hurt you. You're my boyfriend. "

"I...I'm not worried. I just don't know what she thinks I know."

"Well, you probably know nothing, but we have to be sure. She'll enter your mind while you're sleeping and trace your lives back. That's all. So are you ready to get wet?"

It was raining pretty heavily when I jumped down out of the boxcar, but I caught a flash of color out of the corner of my eye. Glancing over, I was shocked to see a girl with bright orange hair and beautiful blue eyes standing not five feet away. Before I could react, she reached out and, with one hand, gripped my shirt under my chin, lifted me off the ground, and slammed me into the side of the boxcar. As I struggled to get free, she brought her other hand around and punched me hard in the stomach, and I bent over from the blow. She capped off her attack by kicking me directly in my privates, causing me blinding pain and silencing a scream still in my throat.

"Next time, if there has to be one, I'll beat you senseless," she said, then gripped my cheeks together viselike in her hand.

"Aello! He's my boyfriend!" Circe yelled as she now jumped out of the boxcar.

"This piece of Earth trash?" my attacker replied, while waving me from side to side like I was made out of paper. "He's a freakin' Earthie!"

"Fate business," Circe said. "We think he's an Eternal who hasn't come of age."

Aello released me and I fell onto the hard ballast, my head striking the wheel of the boxcar. Aello added to the stars I saw from that by kicking me yet again in the privates. As I rolled on the ground in pain, I heard her say, "I don't understand your taste, Lachesis. You get weirder and weirder." Then she walked away in the rain.

Circe got on her knees next to me and asked, "Where does it hurt?"

"Uh...everywhere?"

She laughed at me, which got me mad.

"You said, 'No one will bother us, my little chicken boy. Take my word.' Those were your exact words." I moaned the last part.

"Come on, she really didn't do any lasting damage. Are you going to complain 'cause you got beaten up by a girl?"

"I don't think I'll be able to have kids," I pleaded. "Does that tell you anything? Besides, she wasn't just some girl. She was a goddess, like you, wasn't she?"

She nodded as, at that instant, the wind blew Circe's top out and up, revealing to my widening eyes that she was not into bras.

"Damn you, Aello!" She snickered at me, then pointed to her head. "She said that was for you, to make up for the beating she gave you. She loved that you recognized her as a goddess. Satisfied? Was it worth it?"

"It sure was, but I do hurt all over."

"Sorry, I'm not getting involved with you down there," she said as she pulled her top back down. "I'm sure your head hurts from hitting the wheel, and I can do something about your headache." She reached over and slid her hand through my hair, instantly taking the pain away. "Can you run?" she asked. "I'd like to get out of the rain and wind."

After I struggled to my feet, I hobbled after Circe as she ran down the tracks and over to the field that bordered the yard. A big blast of wind struck at our backs and, as the gust of air got under her silver top and bloused it out, I saw her bare back. She just giggled as the wind pulled her jewel-studded blouse up almost over her head. When she looked back to see if I was keeping up, I once again saw her perfect breasts.

By the time we got to the car, we were soaked. We got inside, and Circe started it and turned on the heater to dry us off. The silver top stuck to her like cling wrap, accentuating that amazing figure underneath.

"What?" she said when she noticed me staring. She then glanced down at her chest where the wet top draped around her breasts. "I think Aello wanted to make up for pounding the crap out of you. She kept blowing my top up to give you a thrill. Her bod is just as nice as mine; all the Harpies are lookers. I think she likes you, so if she makes another appearance you should make the most of it. Want a better look?" With that, she pulled the top off and tossed it in the back seat.

I shook my head, too embarrassed to speak after she had caught me peeking.

"Don't be embarrassed, Alex," she teased. "It's okay to look. Isn't that what boyfriends are supposed to do?"

"You are so not like your sister. Are you going to drive naked?"

"I'm not naked. All you can see are my breasts, and I've mentally blocked that vision from the people on the road. Shimmer, remember? As far as Irene, there you're wrong. You don't know the real girl. Why do you think she doesn't use a shimmer? She loves that guys drool over her. She has to be careful, though, because she tends to go for a guy head over heels. That hasn't happened in centuries, though. However, she knows you're now off limits since you're taken."

"Taken?"

"Yeah, have you already forgotten you're with me now?"

One thing Circe was great at was pumping me up.

"I mentally met with her the night before I came to your school," she continued. "We talked about you, and she said you were one of the few guys she hadn't gotten a rise out of yet, but she was working on it. Shy is a huge challenge for her. I think she actually has a secret boyfriend, though."

I declined to comment, and with that, she made a U-turn and drove toward Central Avenue. We drove in silence for a few minutes, during which I marveled at how the moonlight framed Circe's pretty face. As she leaned forward, I tried to keep from staring at her bare breasts—but I didn't try very hard.

She slowed down and suddenly turned, studying my face. "We're here. Irene will be back to pick you up in a few minutes." She then made another U-turn in the little car, pulled off the road, stopped, and glanced down at her nakedness.

"Sure you don't want a closer peek? Maybe a touch?" she asked, giggling at her success embarrassing me. "Come on. How about a feel? You deserve something after..."

"No," I said, but it came out sort of as a squeak. "Who is Aello, anyway? Why did she attack me?" I asked, desperate to change the subject.

"What a boyfriend I picked," she said, but smiled. "Okay, I'll stop teasing you. All of those who are descendants of Eternals have powers that Earthlings do not. You already know some of mine and my sister's. The three Harpy sisters can create storms at will. Each creates a different kind of storm. Their storms are usually spawned to cover kidnapping someone, but I think my being with you prevented that. The one we were in came from Aello. She was probably going to incapacitate you and then carry you off, but aborted her attempt when she saw me. We Moirae have a truce with the Harpy girls, but they might try again. It only applies when one of us is present, so don't go anywhere without me. I don't think it was the Parcae who wanted you taken. They will want one of us to stay with you until they know what's going on here. Aello was doing it for someone else. Nothing personal. That's what the Harpies do. I'm sure the others, especially Celaeno, would love to pound up on someone they think is an Earthie."

"Celaeno? Patty?"

"Wrong Celaeno. I told you Patty is a Pleiad. Pleiads don't get caught up in these shenanigans. This one is called Dark, and you don't want to meet her. If you continue to have a torch for Patty the Pleiad, you're wasting this Earth life."

"Are all of the Greek Gods still on Earth?"

"No. My sisters and I, The Seven Sisters, Iris and her sisters, the Harpies, plus a few others, are kind of outcasts from the world we come from. Some of us are definitely on one side or the other, and some alternate sides in each lifetime. And there are those, like the Seven Sisters, that is, Patty and her Pleiad sisters, who emigrated here from other worlds and don't usually get involved."

"Who are the main sides?" I asked.

"Why, Zeus and Hera's of course. Sometimes there's another side."

"Why are there sides at all? What does each side want, and whose side are we on?

"We? I'm flattered, Alex. Zeus and Hera were always fighting, and my mom was involved with Zeus, so that put her on his side. Hera never knew about us three girls. They've kept that battle going even after they left Earth and we were abandoned here. Then, when Zeus disappeared on his last voyage, Hera kept the feud going as if he were still here. There's always persisted this tale that Zeus and Poseidon laid plans for a future exploration to follow them. Rescue them, I guess, or maybe join them. I don't know. The fact that they never returned fueled those rumors. Now Decima thinks there may have been some truth in the tales. If it's true, Hera would definitely want any mission stopped. She's the 'It' girl on Aldebaran now and would want the status quo to stay that way. My sisters and I keep out of it so Hera doesn't find out we're Zeus's offspring and take it out on us. So you may want to make sure whose side you're on."

"Of course I'd be on your side. After all, I'm your boyfriend. So, whose side does that put me on in relation to the other Eternals here?"

"I'm quite sure Eris is definitely on the other side. Right now, I have no side. I don't even know for sure what's going on. If you're truly part of that plan, your side is all laid out by others."

"I'm definitely on your side if you have one. But, if this involves the people of your world and they can create storms, they can surely find us, can't they?"

"You're with me, so you're safe."

"How do I know I can trust Irene?"

"She's my sister! Stop being such a scaredy-cat. Irene is really very nice. If she ever let her hair down with you, you'd be surprised how pleasant she can be. The girl is a seductress at heart. She might even try to steal you from me. Now get out."

I was puzzled by the whole incident, but I got out of the car.

Circe leaned over and said, "See you tomorrow." She then puckered her lips to me and said, "I'd have let you kiss me if you tried. I might have—no, I definitely would have—let you do... other things." She then took a deep breath and thrust her bare breasts forward. "Too bad you're so timid."

Then she drove off.

CHAPTER 9
ANOTHER DREAM, MORE REVELATIONS

Minutes after Circe dropped me off, a blaring car horn shook me out of my mental distress. I looked up to a car pulling off the road in front of me. However, it was not Irene's little Studebaker, but an even smaller sports car I recognized from our school parking lot.

Susan's beautiful face appeared out of the Austin Healy 100-6's tiny side window opening, and she called out, "Hi Alex, you're early. It's not Saturday, is it?"

"Uh, I'm waiting for someone to pick me up," I said, untrusting because of Circe's comments about her as Iris.

I walked up on the passenger side. "What are you doing here late at night?"

"I'm just doing what's expected of me for a friend. You know, the Moirae would not appreciate you walking right up to my car like that. Even on the opposite side from me. After the conversation you just had with Circe, you should be more cautious of who I am. But relax, I'm on your side."

"You're with Circe and Irene?"

"I didn't say that. You see, there's more than two or even three sides in all of this. I'm not allowed to tell you who's on which side: let's just say there's an Alex's side, and that's where I am, along with Circe, who still does not realize that I'm involved. I was sent here to reiterate her warning for you to be very careful. There are Eternals out to see you terminated." She leaned over toward where I stood.

"Not you too, with all this Eternals stuff and me being terminated." It was not lost on me that she said Circe was on my side, but did not mention Irene. "You don't understand. I'm supposed to get—"

"Picked up by Irene. I know, but I wanted to talk to you first. I did not mean for you to think I consider Irene the enemy. Far from it. She's just not involved to the level that others are. Yet. She and Circe are not the source of my warning," she whispered loudly. "I serve another."

"But..." I was confused. "I don't really know why you—"

"I can't take definitive sides in any Moirae problem, as I'm also a close friend of your Jocelyn Heldebride, among others. That's why Irene and Circe find it hard to put me on one side or the other. Ergo, there's...your side. Come on, get in the car."

"You're a friend of Eris?"

"Yes, she and I are close friends. I've known her since Troy."

I stared at her through the lowered passenger side window. "Troy? Are we talking the lost city? Like in Helen of Troy? Are you saying she was Helen of Troy?"

"She? Don't you think my face could be the one that launched a thousand ships and burnt the topless towers of Ilium? The towers of Ilium were not quite topless though, just tall." She smiled and presented me with a profile. "Of course, my hair was different then; it was a more yellowish shade of blonde. Longer. Very curly. Eris's has always been black as night. In Troy, she was more behind the scenes."

"I don't think there's any limit to the number of ships that would sail for you. But, are you..." I stumbled over the words, "uh...saying that you really were Helen of Troy?"

"That's better. Thank you, Alex, you can be so sweet. And yes, I was Helen. Read the whole poem if you get the chance, then forget it. Someday, I'll tell you the real story. However, right now you just need to listen. Please, get in the car."

I could not resist her order. I opened the door and sat down. She motioned for me to come closer so that our faces were at the same level. When I did, she put her hand on the top of my head.

* * *

I was immediately transported away, as if in a dream. I walked in some mountains, but where they were located was not immediately apparent.

My mind reeled with questions and facts. I was aware of being the captain of a ship, sent to rescue my countrymen from a city that was to be the scene of a battle. Having been apparently told they were in a cave a short distance from the city that was under siege, I entered the opening that looked out on what I somehow knew was the Aegean Sea.

One of the women who was being aided by me grabbed my arm. "Admiral Idomeneus, can we take our mistress to Kaptara?"

I knew now that what I was seeking was my sister, from whom I had been separated for a long time. Was it really many years?

"Who is your mistress?" I asked.

"She is Helen, who was brought here to Ilium by Alexandros. She desires to be rescued."

In my mind, it resonated. Helen, who this war was being fought over, was said to be the most beautiful..."

* * *

Gentle fingers stroked my hair, and I turned to see a girl sitting next to me in the car.

"Did you have any other questions?" Iris asked. "Whenever they need someone of unparalleled beauty..."

"You get the call." The words tumbled out of my mouth.

"Does that satisfy your curiosity?" she smiled.

"Who was Idomeneus?" I asked.

"Who do you think? Who was Sylvane?"

I nodded, though I was still baffled by the idea of having lived lives I had no memory of.

She just smiled, then said, "They're going to have to move you away from here, but don't worry. A friend will always be nearby."

A blaring car horn caused us both to jump then look back. Even in the dark, by its size I recognized Irene's Speedster.

"Get out, I've gotta go," Susan said. "You should have met me on Saturday, and I could have told you all this and more."

As soon as I had exited the car, she turned the wheel and stepped on the gas pedal. I barely got out of the way as it sideswiped me and sped off, knocking me down the embankment. Moments later, Irene was kneeling over and looking down at me.

"Are you okay, Alex?" she asked.

I nodded. "Did a friend of yours just try to kill me?"

"I doubt any friend of mine would try to kill you, and despite what Iris may have told you, she is not really a close friend of mine...in this lifetime. Although she and I go way, way back, she is close and forever loyal to only one person that I know of, and that is her original father, Zeus. However, I don't think her intention tonight was to kill you. She's probably working with her eternal sisters, the Harpies. And after Aello bungled the job, they may have convinced her to kidnap you so that we wouldn't learn what the heck is going on. No, I think when she saw me, she just wanted to get away, and probably counted on you being smart enough to move out of her car's path."

When I tried to tell her that Iris had said she was warning me, the words lodged in my throat and would not come out. Then, I tried to simply tell her that Iris was not on the Harpies' side, but stopped when Iris's face, shaking in a negative fashion, appeared in my head. Deep down, I knew that she had not just tried to kill me. And, kidnap me? I had gotten willingly in her car, so she could have driven off at any time. Plus when Irene appeared, Iris had insisted I get out of the car. I knew that Iris, alias Susan, was on my side.

The incident with Iris seemed to have caused a change in Irene. While she drove, she actually talked to me and stressed that, while I was with her, I needed to relax and not think about our past school relationship. I found this version of Irene surprisingly easy to talk to. As she conversed non-stop in her car, she also mentioned, as had Circe, that Jocelyn Heldebride, in this life, had started off being born in Austria.

"After World War II," Irene explained, "She immigrated to the United States, attended Georgia Southern University, and earned a degree in English Literature." She stopped talking briefly to concentrate on driving.

I found this all hard to contemplate.

"Circe said you knew the guy killed in the train yard." Irene's voice brought me back to her in the car. "I've kept out of your private thoughts and memories that weren't relevant to the situation. Would you tell me what Mark told you?"

I relayed Mark's story of his pursuit of a group of female German mystics and German UFOs.

"Yes, that was true," she said. "Uh... Did Mark ever tell you where he was from?"

"What do you mean, that was true? How could you know that?"

"Just answer my question. Please."

While I was curious how she could know what Germany was up to during the war, I answered instead, "He told me he was from New Mexico."

"No more?"

"Nope. I guess he was still in pursuit of those mystics. I don't understand how you could be involved in that? Maybe Eris got to him and—"

"Don't jump to any conclusions; no one made you a detective," Irene said, and parked in front of a luxury apartment building. "Look, you better realize this is not a game being played. You need to understand that I am somewhat on your side. We're here, though, so no more explanations or questions. For now."

I was drawn to her eyes, which had turned completely violet.

"Relax, Alex," she said, as if she knew I was uneasy. "What I'm going to do won't hurt a bit."

When we got to her apartment, she gave me a brief little tour that included pointing out the closed door to the guest room that Circe now occupied. Then she stopped in front of what I assumed was her bedroom.

"I lived here alone till Circe showed up, but no one knows that. I also have a safe house address I use for school. The woman that lives there is a trusted Eternal who pretends to be my mom for school functions. While Circe is here, she's living with me, but the Parcae indicate she will be allowed to return to her home in California shortly. You okay with this so far?" Her reddish brown hair kind of swirled around her cheeks as she talked. It drew me back into those intriguing eyes. "Alex? Stop staring at me like some lovesick puppy dog."

I nodded. "I still don't know who the Parcae are, but whatever you say, Irene."

She let out another long sigh. "Let's get on with the reason you're here. Circe told you I require you to stay over, did she not?"

"Yes," I nodded. "She said when I'm sleeping you would trace back my lives."

"Right, but she probably didn't tell you that I have to be in the same room. I need to touch your head to do it." She nodded toward the king-sized bed in her room. "I'm going to have you go to sleep, and later I'll slip in and sit in the chair in the corner. When I'm sure you're in a deep sleep, I'll join you and trace you back. Maybe I can get past that block. Is that okay?"

"Yes," I said, still nervous, but more relaxed.

"Come, then." Silently, she glided into her room and I quietly followed her. "There's the bathroom if you need it." She pointed toward an open door on one wall.

"Do I—" Was I supposed to undress?

"You can just lie on the bed," she snapped, obviously having read my mind. "There's no need to undress for this. I'm not interested in your body. All you need to do is get comfortable and get to sleep. Not under the sheets, please. When I'm sure you're asleep, I'll mentally join with you and trace back through your lives and see where that takes us. It won't be like what you've shared with Circe. You'll experience nothing and remember nothing, but I will. I'll explain more tomorrow morning."

* * *

When I awoke the next morning, Irene was sitting on the bed in a bright red bathrobe, legs tucked under her and staring down at me. I was covered by the bedsheet.

"Is he stirring yet?" Circe's voice came from the direction of the oversized black chair.

When I looked over, I saw her. Seeing me awake, Circe hopped out of the chair and bounded over. She jumped up on the opposite side of the bed and sat next to my head, then stretched her legs out in front of her.

"What happened?" I asked, and looked to Irene. "What's Circe doing here? Why isn't she at the safe house?"

"She just got here," Irene said. "Listen, this is important. Did you in any way touch that freight car that almost hit you?"

"Uh…" My mind searched back. Having these two women near me while I was in bed, in my undershorts, covered just by a sheet, really unnerved me.

"I could find out by going back into your—" she started.

"No, I remember," I said. I'd had enough people in my head for a while. I recalled for Irene the night I walked down the tracks, touched the car, and everything going quiet.

"That's how it's tracking him," she said to Circe.

"It's lucky we arranged this, and you found the alarm," Circe added.

Irene looked back to me. "Did you get a weird feeling when you touched it?"

"Yeah, I felt a cold shudder pass through me."

"They are clever," Irene said. "What I couldn't understand before was why they'd go through all that trouble for—"

"What's going on?" I asked. "Did you find out something?"

"Answer my questions first, I've just got one more. Do you have any idea of where that freight car was headed?"

"Probably for some bakery in Chicago to be unloaded. That's probably done though, and it's—"

"It's what?" she interrupted. "I don't need its day to day history, just what happens to the car afterwards?"

"Well, normally it would just go into a pool of empty cars in the area, available to be used anywhere, but that car was a specialized boxcar modified for grain loading, so they probably returned it to the owner."

"Who is?" she insisted.

I recalled the words stenciled on the freight car. "The Great Northern Railroad in Grand Forks."

"Where the hell is that?" Irene scowled.

"North Dakota."

"Why me?" Irene looked to Circe for an answer, but she just smiled.

"Decima and Pollux know best," Circe grinned.

"What's going on?" I asked. "Will someone clue me in?"

Irene hopped off the bed, walked over to the chair that Circe had sat in previously and pulled it over next to the bed. After seating herself comfortably in it, she made a show of making sure she was covered by the robe, then leaned back and looked at me.

"You've got a tracking spell inside you. To find out who put it there, and get it turned off, we need to examine the boxcar. We must go to North Dakota and find it. *We* means you and me."

"I can't go to North Dakota," I wailed.

"Yes, you can and yes, you will. Did you hear me?" She punctuated that by pushing against my side with her feet. "I have to go with you! Do you think *I* want to go there?" She poked harder with the heel of her foot.

"Stop kicking my boyfriend." Circe pushed her foot away.

"Sorry!" Irene said. "Look, Alex. I can get a mental image of it out of your head, but you're the only one that knows for sure which boxcar. Not to mention, the spell would probably only materialize in your presence."

"I have school. I'm graduating..."

"We're going right after graduation," Irene said matter-of-factly.

"Tell the poor guy more than that," Circe urged. "Tell him everything."

"You and Decima like him so much, you tell him," Irene barked at Circe. Then she got up and left.

"Sometimes my sister can be difficult," Circe explained.

"Ya think?" I said.

"Okay, here is the scoop, Alex. We know who saved you, but not who tried to speed up the process of your dying."

"Who saved me?" I asked.

"Decima," Circe said. "At least indirectly, we know she was involved. We got this story from Ocypete, who I trust. The day before that freight car almost made you a permanent part of Earth, Iris detected multiple brain waves around you outside of school. You may not have noticed, as the person could have been wearing a shimmer. That's usually associated with Eternals. One of them wasn't the wave of someone in your school, so when you came in for school that day, Decima had Iris put a little alarm on you. That mental buzzer would signal her if anyone messed with you."

I now recalled the previous day, when Susan—that is, Iris—came along and briefly bumped against me...

"Yes, and that same night, someone checked your location, then proceeded to tweak the minds of the train crew and cause that freight car to be routed down the wrong track, the one you were on. When that someone checked on your location, however, it sent a signal to Iris, who had planned to somehow warn you. But she discovered that the sensitivity of your hearing had already been turned up and you were alerted."

"By who?"

"I thought, Decima. But she said she didn't do it. Maybe you have more guardians."

"And why would Susan get involved in the first place?"

"Let's keep in mind that my sister and I are not deeply involved in this, so we don't know all that's going on. It appears you have Iris as some kind of a guardian angel watching over you. Irene's monitored you, and based on all the mental attention you're being given, she and I are sure you're an Eternal, but we won't know who until you turn eighteen. Normally she could just go back in your mind and trace back your past lives, which would answer that question. But not even she could get past the mental block you have."

"Sorry," Irene broke in. She had reentered the room with a cup of coffee. "I lost my cool, Alex. Would you like some coffee?"

I nodded.

"Get him some, Circe. I'll take over."

"You be nice," Circe said to her and left.

Irene set her cup on the nightstand and hopped up on the bed. "I don't get it, but for some reason, Decima, Iris and Circe really like you, and since you're a Lemurian, I'll try to be friendlier."

"I'm a what?"

"Oh yes, that's the other thing I stumbled on. Part of your history points back to Lemuria. I forgot Earthies are ignorant of their own past. Lemuria was an Earth island located in the lower part of what you call the Pacific Ocean. Or it could have been the Indian Ocean, I'm not into borders. It existed until about twelve thousand years ago. Well, that's not entirely true. Parts of it are still left as smaller islands. It was destroyed when there was the unlikely combination of the glaciers melting and a huge increase in volcanism caused by a passing comet, parts of which crashed into Earth's oceans. A large piece hit the Pacific and ended the existence of Lemuria, while another slightly smaller fragment caused the extinction of what ancient Earth historians called Atlantis in the Atlantic Ocean. I do believe your current historians claim they never existed. Typical. Anyway, back then was not a good time to be living on this planet, because other rising civilizations also perished. A lot of what was land became seas. As for you, many of your lives were apparently spent in Lemuria, but they have a mental block on them that prevents me from finding out who you were and what you did. That generally means you were an Eternal, but not one of the Greek kind, like Circe and me. My guess is you might have been an Eternal on Aotearoa or Terra Australis. You know them as New Zealand and Australia."

She then moved over so that she was lying next to me on top of the sheets and blanket. "You," she poked me in the chest, "must therefore stop staring at me like some love-sick cow, because we're equals. Besides, you're Circe's boyfriend. She really likes you, and she hasn't had a real boyfriend in quite a few years."

"I thought she had lots of them."

"She's had lots of lovers, but very few boyfriends—emphasis on the *friend*. She's very hard to get close to. So there must be something to you, after all," she teased. "Here's the bottom line, Alex. We've been in contact with the Fate Council—that's the Parcae—and Decima thinks we might get a clue about who's involved on the other side by examining that boxcar. So, you and I are going to North Dakota, and from there to California."

"I can't go to California! I already told you I couldn't go to North Dakota. My parents will be upset."

"Decima's already fixed that," she explained. "She's mentally implanted in your parents the idea that Jocelyn Heldebride, your English teacher, arranged for a scholarship to Antelope Valley College in California. It includes a train ticket there, but you're not taking the train."

"Isn't Jocelyn Eris? Isn't she the enemy?"

"Eris is on the other side, but there are no enemies here. Decima thought it was a good idea, but you're not taking any scholarship. It's just a way to get you where you are needed."

"Do I get to graduate Friday?"

"You and I will graduate..." She then grew quiet, and when I looked over she appeared to be in some sort of trance. Finally she snapped out of it and continued. "Decima just communicated to me that I will pick you up after graduation to supposedly take you to the train station. Instead, you're driving with me to North Dakota so you can interact with the tracking device. Decima can intercept its reading and defuse it, especially if it means you or the mission harm. She will also see to it that your folks are at ease by mentally appearing to them before graduation. Satisfied?"

"What about Circe? Is she coming with us?"

"No. She's leaving early tomorrow morning to return to California. She's taking a faster route. One of our planet hoppers will pick her up in a farm field outside of town."

"Did I hear my name?" Circe appeared in the bedroom doorway, holding two cups of coffee. She handed one to me.

"I was filling your lover boy in on what he needs to know," Irene smiled at Circe. "Decima really liked the letter idea. Could you include the stuff about us in Germany?"

"I'm already telling him about us in Greece," Circe said in a pleading voice. "It'll include your history and I'll cover all the minor characters. Now you want me to add that shit in Germany?"

"It's not that much to add, and some is relevant. I told you what I found. Please?"

"Okay," Circe replied.

"I know the part about Germany," I said, "and where Jocelyn was born...in Vienna—"

"Hush!" Circe hissed.

I had intended to save Irene some time, but all it got me was the wrath of Circe. I took a sip of coffee to hide my exasperation.

"There are a great many more things you don't know, Mr. Smarty Pants," Circe scolded. "I'm trying to get you the whole story, so be quiet."

"Sorry," I said.

"Thanks, Circe," Irene said, then returned to the story. "Eris was born in this life as Leona. Circe's letter will explain more of that. Her family moved to Paris six months after she was born. She went to school and, in 1915, the year she graduated from high school, recalled that she was Eris. Then, for reasons we haven't quite figured out yet, and she won't tell us, she contacted Aldebaran. To do that we must go into a trance-like state and project thought patterns. When we do that, the transmission can also be picked up by other Eternals. Her message was intercepted by Eternals who were in a high position of the German war machine."

"Don't leave anything out," Circe interrupted. "Tell him who it was."

"Decima told me not to."

"He deserves to know who and what we're possibly up against."

"I promised her. You can tell him in your *Real History of the Greek Gods,* if you so desire."

"I will, then. I don't have to do everything that Decima says."

Irene smirked at her, then continued.

"At the time, the Germans, who had attempted to create a mighty war machine to conquer Earth, were losing the first of what you call World Wars. After the 1918 Armistice agreement ended that war, the surviving Eternals that aided Germany appealed to Aldebaran to supply them with plans for an airborne weapon which would make them victorious in the next war. Not wanting to interfere any further with Earth's development, the ruling council refused their request. But Germany's Eternals were able to convince friends on Aldebaran to let them have a planet hopper that had crashed in a dense mountain forest of Germany. Since parts of the hopper were completely destroyed, including the power plant, the council assumed that made it useless to them, so they agreed.

"However, the same Eternal that had previously intercepted Leona's communications schemed to have a sympathizer on Aldebaran attach the blueprints for the power plant to a message being sent to... " She paused, apparently not wanting to name names.

"You know," Circe interrupted again, "dancing around the names is not very helpful. You're just confusing him and me with your attempts to follow Decima's wishes."

"I'm not telling," Irene insisted.

"You are a drone," Circe said to Irene, then turned to me. "We have three particularly evil sisters, the Keres. Not much is written about the Keres in your mythology books, but they were given birth by Nyx, our mother, before we were. They are not like us, the daughters of Zeus. Your mythology books say their birth was by parthenogenesis."

"What's that?" I asked.

Irene took a deep breath and explained. "Parthenogenesis is a process where a creature is born without any kind of a relationship with the opposite sex. But in this case, the mythology books are incorrect, because our sisters do have a father. Mother had a romance with someone else before she settled down with Zeus. It lasted several years actually, and out of it were born three other girls. They are usually older than us, but we rarely meet them in any of our lives. Except for Circe's friendship with one of them, they don't like us, and the feeling is mutual."

Circe took up the tale. "Your books are murky here and get things mixed up. Different people called them and us by different names. To some we are the Fates, to others the Moirae, and so on. Our three half-sisters go by different titles also. Collectively they were the Keres, although your mythology does not name Achylys, Anaplekte, and Stygere as such. Some of your writings also call them the Fates, but they are the Fates of Death and Destruction. It was Achylys who conjured up the idea to have plans for the hopper added to Eris' message, and got her involved with what was to be the rebirth of Germany's efforts to take over your world."

"But why—" I started to ask.

"No questions yet," Irene insisted. Circe glowered, but did not move.

"I don't want to get too much into this, as Circe will cover the relevant history for you in her letter. I'd rather answer your questions after you've read it. Circe does want you to be aware of the people involved, though, and how we got to here, in your town, today.

I nodded, and decided to do my best to keep up.

"As I've already said," Irene continued. "When a planet hopper disk malfunctioned and crashed in the German forest, one of the Keres convinced Aldebaran to let the Germans have the disk in the hopes they could salvage Germany's destiny. Aldebaran agreed, thinking that giving them the craft would be useless without knowledge of its inner workings. In the early 1920s, the three of us Moirae, along with one of our friends, met on vacation in Berlin and became re-acquainted with Eris and the Harpies and Keres. One of the Keres, along with several of the German High Command, were close by when Eris received a message from Aldebaran, upon which had been piggybacked the diagrams for the planet hopper. Those plans were coded in an ancient Earth language used by very early planetary explorers who had visited Earth. It was hoped Aldebaran would not notice the encrypted blueprints, or would ignore them as space chatter.

"Unaware of its full contents, Eris picked up the message and, by previous arrangement, the plans were deciphered by the Keres. Once the Nazi inner circle of Earthlings knew of Eris's talents, they pulled her into their war planning. It was either help them or be shot as a traitor. In her defense, Eris tried to convince them that planet hoppers could not be armed and make war, as their design prohibited the mounting of weapons.

"As work continued on building the craft," Irene went on, "the German Luftwaffe selected a young pilot, Herman Kort, to fly the initial version. It was finished in 1926, and Herman flew the first, and last, test hop in 1929. It crashed in a forest and Herman was killed.

"Heike, an Eternal who was a member of Eris's group, was heartbroken. She had fallen in love with him. Heike blamed Aldebaran for Herman's death because they had supplied the Germans with the plans for the hoppers, and herself for not telling him something Eris and all of her Eternal friends knew: The Germans had not understood the power source for the craft, so they had tried to adapt one of their new jet engines. The engineers on Aldebaran had said it would never work, and they were right, in a way. The engine failed, and Herman was killed.

"So, Heike appealed to Eris to find out when and where Herman would be reborn, since lives are recycled at ten year intervals. Eris used her considerable influence with our Reincarnation Group to find out that Herman would be reborn in 1939, in the USA. Of course, by that time, Europe was moving toward all-out war, and Germany was to be embroiled in it. Heike came up with a plan where she would die in a staged accident and be reborn in the USA, in 1939, when her Herman would be reincarnated. So she should now be close to eighteen, like you."

"Oh my Zeus," Circe said and grabbed Irene's foot. For a moment they stared at one another. "Could this be someone at the school? It's the right age."

"But we don't know who all were born here or who came over from Germany and Europe," Irene pointed out.

"You're right," Circe replied. "But it all fits."

Irene shook off Circe's stare and continued. "In 1945, with Germany losing the war, we made plans to get out of there. Eris planted the false story with us and her friends that she was to return to Aldebaran, but instead, like us, she fled with most of her group of Eternals to the United States, where they scattered.

"What she had not counted on was the resourcefulness of Mark, who never gave up keeping track of her. In Germany he found a dying SS soldier who had overheard Eris and her followers discussing their plans. The soldier didn't know where the other women were going, only that Eris was going to a place called Georgia in the USA. Mark followed her there, and then here."

"What? Wait. How do you know that stuff about Mark?"

"He loaned Moe his jacket that night," Irene continued, ignoring me. "That's how the mistake happened. That boxcar was meant for Mark, and he suspected a tracking device was placed into it."

"How...? How do you know this?" I asked, dumbfounded. "Circe told me Mark was—"

"Dead?" Irene said as she jumped off the bed and walked about the bedroom. "No, that was Moe. The police should be just finding that out about now."

"Mark is alive?" I said stupidly.

"Yes, sorry, Alex," Irene said. "We haven't been entirely honest with you. Mark is an Eternal, like us, sent by Aldebaran to make sure that our technology doesn't again fall into the wrong hands on Earth. He is following Eris to make sure there isn't a repeat. Mark never told you who he really was, so I will. His Eternal name is Pollux. He's a problem solver. We work with him at times."

"So he's the one who saved me that night?"

"Don't jump to conclusions," Irene snapped. "I told you before, you're not a detective. When I told you we had not found out for sure who saved you, I also said we're not sure who tried to end your life either, remember?"

"Yes, but who do you suspect?" I asked. I had been afraid to ask earlier.

"We're not sure, but we think it might be Eris. It matches her style and she's in tight with her siblings. She's another of Nyx's forgettable offspring."

"This is a lot to take in at once," I said.

"We don't know who tried to end your days as Alex," Irene continued. "But Mark was not the one who sent the signal Iris picked up that night you almost died. However, Iris might have thought he was."

"He was going to help you the night of your close call," Circe added. "But he's not the one who saved you by ratcheting up your hearing, so that you could actually hear that relatively silent, rolling box car."

"Days later, Mark gave Moe his jacket, which allowed Eris to think she was tracking Mark. That's what she does. She probably thought it was a safe way to have Mark killed. Luckily, he was one step ahead of her."

"I still don't understand my involvement with all of you." I looked from Circe to Irene.

Circe smiled brightly. "You are so dense, it's cute. Irene's given you enough clues. We think you must have been Herman! Someone was saving Heike's lost love."

All I could do was stare from Irene to Circe. I was born in 1939, ten years after Herman died, and in 1960 I would turn twenty-one. It all fit in.

"That part is true. I confirmed it when I did my scan of your past lives," Irene added. "During your more recent life times, I was only able to go back as far as parts of your last life, and there you were: Herman Kort, virile young German pilot. Now you're just a gangly geek. How fitting." She ended with a giggle.

"Irene!" Circe said loudly. "That was mean. You know there are reasons for a person's characteristics in each life. Besides, he really is an Eternal. Not to mention he's my boyfriend. But what's this quest that Decima talks about?"

"Decima is mum about the quest. I'm sorry." Irene looked at me and shrugged.

"What happens now?" I asked, ignoring her geek remark.

"Eris filed a request with the ruling council to have you live out this life under her guidance," Circe said.

"Ruling council?" I asked. "Her guidance? But I'm not dead, why can't my life just go on? Why should I go with her? And isn't she possibly the one that tried to kill me?"

"Episodes like yours, where you dodge death early, happen now and then," Circe started.

"I'll handle this, Circe," Irene interrupted. "Decima put me in charge. When something like this happens, you escaping death, normally it's the ruling council of Fates, currently headed by Decima, who get to decide what to do with you. However, this wasn't a scheduled death, and Eris stepped in and asked the ruling council of Aldebaran for disposition. While we suspect Eris is responsible for the attempt to end your current life, there is an air of uncertainty. The council passed it back to Decima who ruled that for now, since you're an unknown Eternal, and those of us at school are now personally involved with you, none of us get to be part of your destiny. She has to be very careful, as she can't reveal to the other Eternals that you might be involved in the long-rumored mission to find Zeus. The Parcae will decide your fate, in time."

"But what happens until then?" I asked.

"I suggested to Decima that we leave you on your own, but she and the Parcae ruled you are to leave Illinois immediately. Since Eris wanted responsibility for you, it raised an air of suspicion in us. Circe thinks she wants you for Heike, whoever she is, so I said let her have you. However, Circe wouldn't hear of casting you aside, even though I likened you to a loose bolt of lightning. So..." she looked over at Circe. "We asked the Parcae to get custody of you on the basis of you being Circe's boyfriend. Until they find out who you really are, we're—make that I'm—stuck with you."

"Will someone just tell me what happens to me in plain English?"

"The Parcae decreed that we have to get you to California and they'll take over," Irene said, matter of fact. "The council ordered me to protect you until your Eternal identity is known and they've made their final decision. I already told you we're going by way of North Dakota."

"But you hate me."

"I don't hate you. It's just that...never mind. I must do what is decreed."

"Why can't Circe take me?"

"I volunteered," Circe said. "However, Decima said I was already too involved with you. Actually, she lectured me on who my boyfriends should be, and told me I was late enough getting back to where I should be. Sorry, she ruled that effective tomorrow morning, I could no longer be your girlfriend. I must leave very early tomorrow."

"You and I get to graduate tomorrow afternoon, and then we leave," Irene added. "Decima thought it was wise for us to go ahead with the graduation; she thought you were owed that. I hate the graduation ceremonies. I usually ditch them. Smack me with a dead fish, this whole thing sucks. Regardless, you and I leave right after the ceremony."

"But my mom and dad! What will they think of me leaving?"

"Eris managed to get you that scholarship, remember?" Irene pointed out. "Right after graduation, your parents expect you to leave for California. Everyone's memory of your graduation will be kind of a sad one: Alex never even got a party. He could have had so much fun. Boo hoo."

"But what will I do in California? Where will I live?" I asked.

"It will all be arranged," Irene said shortly. "Look, the alternative was everyone thinks you actually got killed by that boxcar. Would you rather that?"

I simply shook my head.

She then turned back to me. "However, there are rules when you're with me. I'll explain more when we're on the road. Know this, though. Those that are pursuing you probably don't follow rules. We must be careful. I want to reunite with my sisters. Until I do, Decima says my future is also subject to revision. That means I could actually die early."

"Why can't I just go off on my own?" I asked.

"Absolutely unacceptable," Irene said emphatically. "Here are your new ID cards. Decima said you could keep your first name but she picked a new surname for you."

"Winters? I'm Alex Winters?"

"I had a hand in picking it, so don't knock it," Circe grinned. "Right now, I'm the only one on your side, and that's tenuous."

"Look, geek," Irene interrupted. "You're going on a road trip with an Eternal who can either make life interesting or unbearable. I wouldn't be complaining."

"I'm beginning to think I'm going on a road trip with a stuck-up wench."

Irene immediately swung an open hand at me, which delivered a loud smack when she struck my cheek. Before she could follow through and pummel me further, Circe grabbed her by the wrists and pushed her back.

"You promised Decima," Circe warned her.

"He called me a wench. You know I hate that word," Irene struggled to get free. "Just let me kick his ass."

Circe gave her one final shove back away and whirled on me. "You jerk. You have no idea how hard this is on her. It'll be awhile before we get a clue as to where our sister actually is in California. Because of you, Irene has to pick up stakes months early and go there. With you along, she can't be herself. And now she'll probably have to deal with the very people we've avoided getting involved with the last thirty thousand or so years."

Circe turned around and hugged Irene. "Sorry, Sis, but you know Decima will be furious if you cripple him." She then turned back on me and said, "I think we all need a break. Go outside, please, Alex. We need to talk alone for a little while."

And with that, she fairly shoved me out the door.

* * *

Not really knowing where I was, and too proud to ask for forgiveness, I made my way downstairs and out of the apartment complex. I walked down the street looking for a telephone to use to call my parents. If I was to be leaving soon, maybe I should spend some time with them. Or maybe I just didn't know where else to go.

"Are you lost?"

"Yeah, I don't really know where I'm—" I said as I turned around at the sound of a voice.

A girl, casually dressed with one lock of brown hair dipped over her left eye, said, "My name is April Sunshine, and I have a car problem. Can you help me?"

"You're kidding, aren't you? I mean, about your name?"

"No. What's wrong with my name?"

"Uh, nothing," I said. "It's unusual, but has a nice ring to it."

"My car?" she asked.

"I don't know much about fixing cars," I said. "I don't even have one."

She grabbed my hand and said, "Come on, cutie, it's a simple problem I'm sure you can help. My brake pedal seems stuck. If you could just pull it up for me."

She led me over to an early 1950s Chevrolet Fleetline and settled into the driver's seat while I got in the passenger side. I leaned my head down and tried her brake pedal, which seemed to operate normally. Before I could say anything, she kicked me in the face, started the car and sped off. When I tried to get up, she slammed my head against the dash and I saw stars.

"Just sit still, honey, I've got something to show you."

When she got abreast of the forest preserve on Central Avenue not far from my home, she pulled over and stopped, then reached across the seat and gripped my shoulder. "Just stay there, Alex. Someone wants to see you."

"See me? Who? Just who the heck are you, anyway? How did you know my name?"

"My real name is Apate. Don't worry, I won't hurt you as long as you keep quiet."

I tried to open the door and get out, but she seemed to be able to create an odd wind that pinned me in the seat.

"I can create any kind of wind necessary to keep you here," she said. "Don't resist further. As I said, you won't be hurt, but only if you keep still. Otherwise, I'll give the crows around here something to pick at. I was told that if I couldn't catch you alive, I could finish the job from the other night."

"Finish the job?" I asked.

"You know, your constant questions are boring me," she said. She reached down to the floor and picked up a roll of strange-looking tape. "This tape will someday be popular in your world. It's great for taping noisy boys' mouths closed." She pulled off a six-inch piece and slapped it over my mouth, finishing the job by patting all sides of it tightly to my skin. Her strange wind kept me pinned in the seat, helpless to oppose her.

"In fact..." She started to open her door, but then twisted herself out of her seat instead and knelt on my legs. Smiling down at me, she said, "I was just told my sister no longer has time for the likes of you, and she told me to dispose of you. So now you're all mine."

With that she proceeded to dig her knees into my thighs, sending shooting pains in both directions.

"That'll cause you to hobble. I can't risk you running away. Luckily, you were too dumb to know that April Sunshine is a shimmer cloud," she said. "But since I'm going to be the last person you see, I've decided to do away with the shimmer and let you see the real me."

Her hair, with the curl still positioned over her eye, changed to lilac as her eye color shifted to match. Her face lost its common look, and her clothes were replaced by ones that I instantly knew were not of Earth. I gasped, as she was every bit as beautiful as the other Eternals.

"You should be thrilled. Not many can say they saw Apate in the flesh. Well, not in her naked flesh, but I only go so far. Now, let's you and I take a walk in the woods, Alex." She flipped the door open, kneed me in a very vulnerable spot, and hopped out of the car.

While I was doubled over in extreme pain, unable to cry out with my mouth taped, she reached in and pulled me out of the car by my belt. Once clear of the car, she literally lifted me up off the ground. I was surprised at her strength.

"Eternal," she said into my face, and pushed me ahead of her into the forest.

I did my best to walk, but pain still wracked me.

"Just keep limping straight," she said. "It is permissible for you to steer around the big trees, though." With that, she chuckled to herself as if she had told me a joke. "Angle yourself down towards the stream," she said. "I'm thinking you're going for a moonlight swim."

My thighs burning with pain from her knees and my privates still aching, I crept forward and stopped a few feet shy of the stream. It was then that I noticed that here, at the base of where the drainage pipe ran under the road, the stream had been dammed and had backed up to a much higher depth than normal. In fact, it was probably eight or more feet deep.

"I know you think you're in pain." Apate spat the words out. "However, let's give you a little more to compare it to." She grabbed my shirt and pulled me backwards so that she now stood in front of me. Then she kicked me in the stomach, knocking the wind out of me. While I doubled over in pain, she again brought her knee up into my manhood and at the same time slapped me so hard across the face, I thought my teeth rattled.

"Now you have something to really cry about before you die." She put one foot on my back and shoved me toward the creek, where I fell just shy of the water.

As she drew one leg back in preparation to kick me yet again, obviously into the water, I realized that this girl actually meant to finish what was started in the railyard. She was going to boot me into the swollen creek and drown me. It took all my remaining strength to put the pain aside as I rolled my body away from her. Her foot missed me completely and, now off balance, she unceremoniously fell on her backside as one of her slippers flew off. It landed with a splash in the creek.

"You son of a cyclops," she muttered, kicking me several times in the side of my head with her now bare foot. "That shoe came from Coorrydon."

"That's enough, Apate," Circe's voice came from behind us. "He's an unknown Eternal, so you can't kill him. He probably deserved a little pummeling though. Since you're a friend and relative, I'm overlooking the beating you're giving him."

"What?" I tried to mutter through the tape. I had just got beaten to a pulp, and she'll overlook it?

"He's not exempt from killing until his Eternal self appears," Apate said to Circe.

"Please?" Circe said. "He's important."

"This Earth trash?" Apate knelt down next to me and gripped me by the neck, drawing my face up to hers. "Okay," she said to Circe as she stared into my eyes. "We're family, so I'll give him back to you. But first he retrieves my shoe and apologizes for my duress. You know you can't find decent shoes on this shithole planet." With that she ripped the tape from my mouth.

"Your duress?" I gasped, after taking in a lungful of air.

"You'll do what you're told, Earth boy," Apate spat at me, and slapped me yet again across my face. "Get my shoe, apologize for tricking me, and maybe I'll call it even."

"You need to follow her orders, Alex," Circe said. "Rules of Eternals. I can't interfere with her request because she's a relative. Besides, she's correct about fashion on this planet. Hard to get decent stuff. Give him a few minutes, Apate. Let him get his strength back."

Seeing no way out of the situation, and grateful to still be alive, I took a deep breath and walked into the cold water. Luckily, her slipper still floated on the surface, and I grabbed it and waded back to shore.

Apate, with a look of cool disdain, held her foot out for me. While Circe couldn't do anything, I thought I was free from any such rule, so I drew my hand back, intending to smack her with the shoe. Before I could do that, her arm shot out and she gripped my wrist. She twisted my arm behind my back and drew me to her.

"I claim privilege with your boyfriend," she said to Circe, who merely nodded.

Apate then pulled me even closer and wrenched my arm high, nearly dislocating my shoulder.

"Now would you like to reconsider?" Her lips were poised over mine, like she was about to kiss me—or bite me. "Show repentance by putting my shoe back on my foot?"

Still unable to talk from the pain, I nodded.

"Wise choice, Earth boy. How about you get down and put my shoe on, and then we're even," she said. She took the shoe from me and blew on the slipper. Water mist flew in all directions. With a triumphant look, she handed the dry shoe to me, and I got down and slipped it on.

"Stepsister?" Circe said quietly.

"Oh, what the Hades," Apate said, and blew that wind in my direction. In seconds, I was completely dry as well.

"*Now* the two of you are even," Circe said.

* * *

"You idiot," Circe wailed at me when we were in the car. "Next time I tell you to wait outside, don't you dare move from the spot."

"How did you find me?"

"I told you I was mentally connected to you. Eris told me where Apate probably took you. My stepsister wasn't told you're an Eternal, which would have protected you." She was quiet for a few seconds, then asked, "Are you hurt anywhere?"

"I'm sore all over. That girl was ruthless. What's this privilege thing?"

"She bested you in battle. It gives her the right to do whatever she felt appropriate, short of killing you, and I couldn't interfere. Don't be embarrassed that she wiped the ground with you. Apate is a warrior and a damn good one. If you had reached age, she might not have been able to best you. You're lucky it wasn't her Keres sisters. Achylys wouldn't have been so gentle. But, my stepsisters and I are very close no matter what your books say of us. We're usually on different sides, like now, but we don't let that interfere with our personal relationships. Apate and I have been born as twins several times and we love each other very much. That's why she let you off so easily. Heck, she even rewarded you."

"Huh?" I asked. "What reward?"

"She let you see the real Apate."

* * *

Irene looked me up and down when we walked back into her apartment, then laughed. "Apate had all the fun," she teased.

"Why don't you both try to get along until you get to California," Circe replied. "Then you'll go your separate ways."

"When are you leaving?" I asked Circe.

"Before dawn, tomorrow. I didn't bring much stuff when I came, so packing should be simple."

"What about me?" I asked. "Am I supposed to live the next however long in these clothes?"

"Relax," Irene said. "Circe picked up your stuff while you were sleeping last night."

"You went to my house? Saw my folks?"

"They never knew I was there." Circe smiled.

"I still don't understand how my almost dying got me involved with the two of you?" I asked.

"Toward the end of each lifetime, the three of us Moirae make arrangements for our next life," Circe explained. "Who will be born when and where, how we'll get together, and where we'll eventually live. When you failed to get killed by the boxcar, you were caught up in a catch routine that automatically transferred you back into a past life in which one of us designated as Fates was nearby. Ironically, it was the one with me on Trivane. As part of being the Fates, we pick up any signal on the world we're presently living if something in the process of death and rebirth has gone wrong. I was mentally recalled to that time on Trivane when I lived as Veronique and found you in Sylvane. He was one of your predecessors, and one of my multitudes of lovers during that lifetime.

"It was surprising enough that one of us actually lived a life with you. Now, finding out you also were with Heike, who was also an Eternal, in your last life is uncanny. Makes me wonder who the hell you really are? Anyway, because they were living this life with you, Eris and Irene couldn't get physically involved and Clotho hasn't surfaced yet, so the council ordered me to come here to see what the problem was."

Circe continued. "When I got here and found you still in school and not at the local morgue, I knew something was up. My mental scan of the immediate area for others from Aldebaran revealed that not only were Eris, as Jocelyn, and my sister, Irene, close by, but also Iris, as Susan, and several others too, including several of my stepsisters. This many Eternals together is more than coincidence, but all Decima would say is, 'it's part of some plan.'

"Iris is usually involved with some scheme of our original dad, Zeus. But he disappeared on a mission thirty thousand years ago, so what she's doing here we're not sure. The only thing Iris has done was try to pick you up on the road last night."

"At school she asked me to meet her in those woods," I said.

"What?" Irene asked.

I described the morning when Susan had cornered me at my locker with the Walk-in-the-Woods request and about the Get-a-Date-with-a-Geek note.

"That sounds like something she'd do, but it's strange it wasn't in your memories when I scanned you," Irene said. "This is a new twist."

"You think it could be her?" Circe asked with a strange face. "Was she Heike?"

"It's possible. She was being oddly nice to him. However, she doesn't know he's an Eternal. Or does she?"

"She said she was doing it for someone else," I said. "Where in California is your remaining sister?" I asked, not mentioning the dream Iris caused me to have that evening.

"We're not supposed to know that," Circe answered. "Here is the paper I wrote for American History. It will start to answer your questions."

CHAPTER 10
THE FIRST LETTER

I took the paper from her outstretched hand and glanced at the title: *The Fates and other Greek Gods in America by Lachesis (Circe)*

"I used my Eternal name on your copy," Circe said as she flicked the paper with a finger. "No more questions until you read it. Irene and I have work to do." With that, she grabbed Irene's hand. "Let's go."

After the two of them left, I moved over to the lounge chair, sat down, flipped the title page over and read...

Greek Mythology says that Zeus was the King of the Gods, married to Hera who was the Queen. The truth is, Greek Mythology is a misnomer, because, for one, we weren't Greek, and two, we're not gods. Zeus was a space explorer from the planet Aldebaran, and Hera—that bitch—was from the same place. Zeus, continually fed up with Hera's antics and jealousies, cheated on her frequently. He loved to run off with Nyx, the daughter of one of the geologists in the landing party.

Nyx was also my mother in that lifetime and friend in many others since. She was the original Earth mom to the three of us girls, known on this planet as the Moirae, The Fates. Eventually, Hera, the cow worshiper, found out about Zeus's indiscretions and became extremely jealous of Nyx. And for good reason. Nyx was a looker, and still is absolutely gorgeous; she is probably one of the most beautiful women ever to come to Earth. She originated on the planet Chaos in the Orion

Maelstrom, where she later existed as an advanced spirit. Eventually, she migrated to ZeeWaterize, an Ocean planet near the star, Tau Zeti, as a mermaid.

You'll notice, throughout this document, I will give you origins but not complete lifetimes. Nyx came out of the spirit world 50,000,000 years ago! That's a lot of lives. If you want more of her history, just meet and ask her.

In addition, before I get too involved, we don't always remember every lifetime. Some of the oldest ones are forced back into our memories, but can be recalled if needed. Many of the others are just not worth remembering. I won't go into the mechanics of that 'cause it's boring shit that I never bothered to learn. A case in point is you, Alex, on Trivane. I had to reach way back to actually remember you. I meet a lot of cute guys.

Back on point, the three of us Moirae, by virtue of our first time birth on Earth (we like to call it an introduction), were fortunate to have inherited Nyx's general looks, and she made sure each of us had something of hers that was unique. In my case, the amber eyes and curly black hair, common to ZeeWaterize mermaids. Irene has her stunning long legs and ability to search minds for previous lifetimes, while Clotho, well, you'll see when you meet her.

Greek Mythology should actually be called The History of Aldebaran's Civilization of Earth. Other planets launched similar missions to other parts of Earth, both before and after Aldebaran's. Since Irene (Atropos) discovered your apparent connection to Lemuria, you may have been on a comparable assignment from another world, but Irene and I know little of the work of the other planets. I believe Pleiads were involved, so the Seven Sisters may be able to help you out. I'm not sure that the Sisters were actually there (the Seven came to Greece after us), but they might be able to fill you in. Irene told me that Lemuria goes back over millions of years, so you may have been here on Earth longer than both of us combined. And to think, you and I were intimate little humanoids, struggling to attain Eternal status, millions of years ago on Trivane. That explains a lot to me, because Eternals tend to attract other

Eternals. You'll find that out someday. It might explain my continued attraction to you. And, be assured, my attraction to you is genuine.

As I mentioned, Zeus, my original Earth father, and his party came to this world over 35,000 years ago from Aldebaran, a planet orbiting the star of the same name in the Sirius C System, to help introduce it to civilization. Back on Aldebaran, he desperately wanted the appointment as leader of the Earth exploring and civilizing party, but had to marry Hera the Bitch to get it. From that point on, Hera's sole purpose in life seemed to be to make Zeus miserable.

When the civilizing party arrived in their spacecraft, the savages that then populated the Earth proclaimed them Gods, and Zeus, as leader, became the king. Hera, of course, as his wife, was queen. Ergo, the real Greek Myths.

Over the first twenty years they were there, Zeus had five children by Hera and four by Nyx. Prolific wasn't he? Of Nyx's offspring, Atropos (Irene to you), was the oldest, followed by Lachesis (me, Circe), and then Clotho (I don't know her present name yet) a year later. You'll learn more about the fourth child later.

Nyx was always the center of Zeus's world. While outwardly Hera was in the limelight, Zeus secretly met with Nyx for love. Nyx became known as the Goddess of the Night, not only because of her penchant for black, but also because their meetings were usually in the dead of night. While Nyx was pregnant with a fourth child, Hera discovered Zeus's indiscretions. (Yeah, it took her that long to learn what everyone else had long known. She not only worshipped cows, she was one.)

Hera sought to make Nyx's life miserable, so Nyx took the three of us girls and fled to an island, then called Kaptara. It was an island we'd be born on numerous times. Shortly afterward, the civilizing party, including Zeus and Hera, returned to Aldebaran, leaving the four of us—five, counting Nyx's yet unborn child—behind. Actually, there were others left behind too. Most were on outlying islands, and a few were still mermaids. More on some of them later.

We were all stranded on Earth. While Earth remained a strange world to Nyx, to those of us born there in that lifetime, it was the only world we knew until we recovered our memories. We did not miss our home worlds of long ago. However, each time we reached the age of enlightenment, the three of us Fates discovered what we long suspected was true. We were different from other humanoid inhabitants of Earth. We rarely strayed from our secluded lives together.

We were Eternals. Among other things, those of us descended from the visitors from Aldebaran can recall past lives and determine their next one. You should recall that I actually go way back further than the mere 34,000 or so years since I first came to Earth. Actually, I can trace lives back over 50,000,000 years; you know about our time together on Trivane, one million years ago. Your Earth mythology books talk of specific gods, goddesses, nymphs and the like, but keep in mind there are millions of Eternals scattered around the universe. When you recover your memories of past lives, even though you are an Eternal, we still might not know who you are.

Since Zeus and the others returned to Aldebaran, those of us left behind have chosen to only live in this sector of space, mainly Earth, for the last 34,000 years. With the start of each new existence, except for this one, we have settled into a routine. Atropos is always born first, quickly followed a month or so later by me, and in another year by Clotho.

Nyx alternates lives between us, being alone, and her other offspring. In this existence she is alone. I told you that jemales recover their memories of past lives on our seventeenth birthday. If you really are an Eternal, as a male you'll recover that knowledge on your eighteenth birthday.

On Trivane, when we were having that fling? Well, truth be known, you were only seventeen. That's why I didn't know you were an Eternal then.

While books of Greek Mythology attribute all kinds of powers over mankind to the Fates, in actuality, during our worldly existences, we are only involved in situations like this. There are, in fact, ten sets of Fate goddesses. What we in reality do is not fit knowledge for any male. Your mythology books list the various Fates as being different names for the same three daughters; however, each set is unique. For instance, Roman mythology says the Parcae, our cousins, Nona, Decima and Morta, are just another name for us, the Moirae, the Fates of Greek lore. But our dear cousins are not only different, they are the ones deciding your current fate.

You see, we get to live nine normal, Eternal lives, and then must live one where we serve as the Fate Council. Our distant cousins, the Norns, are next in line. We Moirae have six lives to live before it's again our turn to perform that task. Most Fates consist of groups of three or four, except for the Pleiads, who number seven, and Nyx, who occasionally serves herself. Talk about sisters who stick together. The Pleiads are kind of pseudo-fates though, and not all seven serve when it is their turn.

We are all female. The male species is neither trustworthy nor impartial enough to fulfill the role.

Nyx's last child, Moros, was a boy, but we've never really known much of who he was. Hera knew Nyx was pregnant with child, and the rumor was she had left some of her minions to hunt down Nyx. Most didn't know what she looked like, just that she would have a newborn. So she was forced to give him away to be raised, and he was never instructed in the ways of how we are reborn together, or involved in reincarnation. Nyx was afraid Hera would somehow find him, and in so doing, discover us, her three daughters by Zeus. She kept us hidden in isolated areas, which is why many of our existences were on Kaptara and neighboring Kalliste islands now called Crete and Santorini.

The existence of the Moirae was never known to Hera, even when she learned Nyx was pregnant with child before she left. She keeps track of Eternals, so she knows we exist, but she has no idea that the three of us are from Nyx. Hera, through others, has mainly pursued Nyx and Moros, but I don't know what ever happened to him. After his initial life, my sisters and I don't even remember his Earthly name. I assume he has existed like any other Earth inhabitant. The ironic thing about the boy was he was not the son of Zeus. Nyx had broken away from Zeus when, during one lifetime, he temporarily let the idea of being a God go to his head. Nyx never told us who the father of the boy was.

We tend to stay away from Earth, primarily because of fear that Hera monitors this planet for Moros, but we love being born here occasionally, as it holds many good memories of those years with Nyx. In her current existence, Nyx was born in Russia, but left there in the 1920s for somewhere on the east coast of the United States. Our last contact with her was when we came over here after the war. When we Moirae are born together on Earth, we meet in life. This was one such time, the three of us having all been reborn in France around 1900.

This time, however, our plans went astray. Clotho, who was born in Toulon in 1901, came to Paris as planned in 1918 where we three met as dancers at a nightclub. Four years later, having all recovered our Eternal memories, we moved as planned to Giverny, where we met Iris. Eris contacted us from Berlin about joining her group of Eternals that had become immersed in some scheme with Germany. Clotho went with Iris to see what that was all about, and we didn't see Iris again until she surfaced at your school in the United States. Despite Atropos' requests, Iris won't talk about those years, except to say she'd been reborn after dying in Germany. All we know of what happened to Clotho was that she died with Iris and was to be found in California in her next life. We don't even know where she was to be reborn, except that it was in the United States. This is why my sister and I were to meet in California after she finished school here, to search for Clotho. Now we've learned that you are supposed to be instrumental in that search.

After the events of the Second World War, we had hoped that leaving Europe and coming to America would give us the obscurity we desired to search for Clotho. But after being forced into involvement in your surfacing, we now wonder, can—or will—Hera somehow find that Nyx is living in the United States? While we have dealt with Eris and her minions, none have ever betrayed the secret of our existence to Hera.

However, does she now know about us and is trying to break up our lives together? Irene and I are searching to find out.

Decima prefers I don't tell you anything at all about who the others are, but I disagree. You should know the dangers you face and who you can count on for help. As I mentioned above, we were not the only ones left behind when Zeus and the exploration party returned to Aldebaran. A number of the other party members despised Hera, and in that we were in agreement. But some were Hera's offspring or sympathizers, left to create chaos among the sons and daughters of Zeus and other Eternals not born of Hera, especially those who came from Nyx. Ironically, some of Nyx's early offspring are the ones we now face.

While I can tell you who some of these individuals are by their long ago 'Greek' names, I don't know all of their current ones. Some of them were with Eris in Germany and managed to also escape to America. That group includes the Keres, Anaplekte, Akhylys, and Stygere, wenches that were known to early Earth inhabitants as the Fates of Destruction. The three of them, along with the three Harpies, comprised most of Eris's pack of bitches. You'll have to ask Nyx why she had her girls in groups of three. Eris has other friends that may be about, including Orzys, Momys, Nemesis and Geras.

As you now know, Susan Stage is the reincarnation of the goddess Iris, who your mythology states was the principal messenger of Zeus. Decima won't talk of what happened to her in Germany or her reasons for being here with us, so Iris is a constant mystery to us Fates. At times she is on our side, which seems to lend credence to her being our half-sister, and at other times she appears to take up the cause of Hera. However, that usually doesn't happen, as her loyalty strongly lies with Zeus.

As of now, since all that happened in Europe, plus Zeus's disappearance those many years ago, we are not sure who Iris represents in this battle. We still await the event in which it will be clear which side she is on. Irene still thinks she meant to kidnap you on the road last night, but Mark Wallen urged us not to jump to conclusions.

As you have now discovered, your friend Mark is, in reality, on our side and is an Eternal named Pollux. If you look up the mythology about him as Pollux, you'll find a lot of hokum. The reality is simple. He is the son of Zeus by Leda. Pollux has requested that I tell you little of his history, as he feels he owes you an explanation of why he has not told you himself. What I can tell you is that he and Iris are kind of eternal brother and sister. If you read the mythology, one of the few correct things in it is that Helen of Troy was his sister. And, as I think you already know, Susan Stage is Iris and Iris was Helen of Troy. She is a cute little thing, isn't she?

The twin Harpies, Aello and Ocypete, are two sisters like us, but they vary in their allegiance. They are the sisters of Iris, but don't always embrace her cause as she is usually on Zeus's side in everything. You already had that run-in with Aello, but I'm sure we'll hear from them again in one way or the other. Irene thinks that Iris will be the one that we'll have to deal with somewhere along the road.

And there is that third Harpy, Celaeno, who is very secretive. We only occasionally encounter Celaeno. When we scan that life of yours as Herman, any encounters you might have had with any Eternal, including us, are blocked.

Hopefully, the Harpies don't throw in with Eris and the Keres, as they'd be much more formidable. You'll recall that Aello caused that little storm we encountered in the railyard, but it may have been her doing Eris's bidding. Ocypete is definitely on our side in this, and she told me she didn't know who the instigator was. I believe her, as, though we frequently find ourselves on different sides, she has always been honest with me. As you've already witnessed, I have a good rapport with some of them, in particular Apate and Ocypete.

Apate is one of the few single offspring of Nyx. She won't talk of her father, they never got along. She said he was a womanizer and she hated him. She's a very dear sister to me. She told you her shimmer name that she uses is April Sunshine.

I told you that when we reach adulthood (that's about age twenty-five), we stop aging. So, provided we live that long, we all look pretty much the same when we're one hundred fifty. Unfortunately, so do the Fates of Destruction and the Harpies.

By the time we've aged to the century mark we'll have relocated several times. Since we do retain a memory of past lives, we naturally collect things from each existence. We have a special off-world company that stores our things and makes sure it gets to us on different planets when we reach that age where we recall who we are. Seventeen, remember?

The Pleiads I know little about, as I've had little to do with them. They don't appear like one of the Greek Eternals, but use a shimmer cloud that is almost impossible to detect. Pleiads didn't come to Earth at the time of Zeus, but appeared here much earlier in other places first, mainly the west of North America and the South Pacific Ocean. They tend to stick together and not associate with any other Eternals. If you are a Lemurian, you'll probably recall them when you gain your memories. There supposedly was one in Germany, and at first I thought she might be your classmate, Patty. But Apate told me the one in Germany was much more outgoing. My sister said Patty's basically a snob. That's funny, coming from the Eternal who is quite a snob herself.

Aldebaran and the known council of planets have lots of political intrigue, but they abhor war. That's why Earth is not a member. As we told you, Germany could not get the disk ship to fly, nor, for their purposes, figure out how to arm it. Its flight characteristics were such that weapons were hard to integrate into it. Planet hoppers were not designed for that objective. In Germany's haste to turn the tide of the war, they tried shortcuts, including trying to install a jet engine for a power plant. That resulted in the crash of the prototype, killing the test pilot.

You now know that was you, living as Herman. They never really recovered from that. When the war was seen as surely lost, Eris and her band of Eternals planted the story they had returned to their home in the stars, when in reality they secretly intended to come here to the United States and continue their lives.

End of Part I.

Alex: You are not to read further until, once on the road to California, Irene so instructs you.

I stopped at that part of the document, then went back and read it twice. Then I closed my eyes and sat back, trying to think it all through.

At some point, I fell asleep.

* * *

It was wintertime and I was out on an enormous bridge. However, it was like no bridge on Earth. For one, it was probably ten times bigger than any bridge I'd ever seen. It was simply gigantic.

I was in an icy wind, clinging to the framework of the bridge and looking down. The bridge didn't have the usual roadway or path. It was constructed of an open latticework, like a decorative fence that extended out toward the far-away horizon.

There were five levels of latticework, the first beginning perhaps three hundred feet above the water's surface to the top one I clung to, towering about a thousand feet over the waves below. Looking way down at the water below me, I could see something floating that looked like huge blocks of ice. Watching them bobbing in the water, shrouded in haze, I tried to figure out what the bridge traversed. But as far as I could see there was only water and the bridge. In the end, I decided it didn't matter. Both the bridge and the body of water it spanned were just too big to comprehend.

As I clung precariously to the framework, I realized my hands were freezing cold. The bridge didn't have a solid walkway, just pieces of open trellis-like metal connected together. Stuck out on the icy grating, I was afraid to move for fear I would slide off.

I heard no sounds save a whistling noise every now and then. The noise was similar to what I'd heard in war movies, when bullets are zinging by. Every so often, I'd see a flash from way down amidst the huge floating ice blocks.

Occasionally, there'd be sparks and the ping of something hitting the bridge. From my height, though, I could not make out any details.

Then suddenly everything seemed to go dark, and I had the sensation I was falling.

* * *

I awoke to the door opening as Circe waltzed in while humming a tune. She actually waltzed in, as if she had a dance partner.

"So, do you have any questions?" she asked as she two-stepped her way in my direction.

"Why are you so happy?" I asked.

"Little ole' me is leaving tomorrow morning bright and early for the Golden State. Wouldn't that make you want to dance?"

"Maybe, if I was going with you. Can I just join you in a non-complicated life? One where you're in it as my girlfriend?"

"That was so sweet. Move over," she said, and waltzed back my way. I did the best I could to make room on the lounge chair, which wasn't that big to start with. When Circe reached the chair, she ignored the space I made for her. Instead, she jumped onto my lap. "Oops, I didn't hurt you, did I?" she laughed.

"You don't weigh enough to hurt anyone," I said, smiling. "You can't weigh more than a hundred pounds."

"Actually, I'm always four-foot-eleven and usually weigh ninety-four pounds. But… I have curves in all the right places. You should know that. Listen. I know you've been hit with a lot of information at once. But I hope the letter helped clear things up. If you still have any questions, just ask."

I heard the door close, and seconds later, Irene appeared.

"Get out of his lap," her voice almost boomed. "No PDAs, Circe. Come on, we've got lots to do before you leave tomorrow morning." With that she stomped off toward her bedroom.

"No PDAs?" I asked, as Circe stood up.

"Public displays of affection. Irene hates when I'm openly friendly with guys."

"I have a question," I said. "I just had a dream about some huge bridge. Does that ring a bell? Was there such a bridge on Mars?"

"No, I don't remember any bridge. Your mind is really out there, searching. You could ask Irene, but I doubt she can help you since she couldn't see any deeper earlier. Do you remember the dream details like you do the ones from Trivane?"

I nodded.

"You do? That means you lived it. Funny that another life is surfacing. That's usually caused by you meeting someone from that life. I'll ask Decima if she knows anything."

"Circe, let's move our ass," Irene's hollered command drifted out of her room. "We have a lot to do before we leave."

"Oops, duty calls. I'll contact Decima later."

* * *

By early evening they had completed their packing and arrangements to have Irene's things shipped to a location in California. I wanted to help them pack the car, but Irene insisted I stay in the apartment. When they finished, Circe quietly went to her room while Irene came over to me.

"Look, you can't be seen anywhere around here. That's why I insisted you remain in the apartment. I'll give you more freedom once we're on the road and far away from here."

"I don't understand the need for such secrecy. Who would be looking for me?"

"Shouldn't two beatings be enough for you? Did you not understand that someone saved your ass a few nights ago from someone else who tried to give you an early death? That someone else knows you escaped death twice now, so we have to assume they will either try again to kill you or pry you away from us somehow. There is no shortage of assassins available among the Eternals."

"But there's four of us and—"

"Four? Who are you counting on? Circe leaves in the morning, we don't until late tomorrow night. Mark wasn't cleared by the Parcae to go with us. So it's just the two of us and any number of them. Face facts—you're not much help. At least the opposition is one less. Apate dropped out when she realized you were a boy toy of Circe. However, if you meet the others, they could care less. Until you reach age, you're fair game."

Chapter 11

A Night with Circe

"What would you like to do?" Circe asked. We were alone in her room.

I didn't answer at first, too taken in by what I saw. "The paintings on your walls," I said. "I've never seen anything like them before. The colors are... I'm at a loss for words." The colors actually changed shades in the light, as if the objects were real.

"That's the Irene Sea, from Trivane," Circe said, looking over at the painting. "You should know it from your dreams."

"They named the sea after Irene?"

"Not quite. Irene took her present name from the sea. It was her favorite spot when she lived there. Now it's a dust bowl. We all miss Trivane."

"In my dreams I remembered it as the Orange Ocean."

"Yeah, you have quite the imagination. And that painting shows the Triluna."

She was pointing to a painting of the three moons over Trivane. The moons glittered in beautiful life-like colors while the waves seemed to wash up on the shore of the Irene Sea.

"I thought Mars only had two moons," I said.

"It does now," she replied, with a sigh. "Millions of years ago, I can't be specific, one of the asteroids in what you call the Asteroid Belt, collided with one of the moons. It is now part of the belt." She looked sad, and I decided not to press her any further.

I looked over at the bed, draped with a canopy of shimmering blue fabric. The bed covering was the color of deep water, like a pool under a waterfall. I walked over to it and slid my hand over its surface. It felt very smooth to the touch and cool, but was not wet. I pulled back suddenly when my fingers seemed to disappear into it.

Circe chuckled. "It's jacka, from a plant on Loton. Loton is a world in the Alpha Centauri system. It's made of a special grass grown in the fields of Waazzii, near the star LHS 292. The grass is super soft; it feels like floating on air. We can burrow down into it and be supported but not feel at all constrained. Come on, dive into the pool."

"Dive into the pool?"

"The jacka will actually part when you jump on it, like water. That's why your fingers were disappearing into it. It's like being in water without getting wet. You'll love it. Turn your head."

I did, and I could sense Circe wriggling out of her clothes.

"Okay, it's your turn," she said from behind me. I turned and saw just her head sticking up from the surface of the bed. It was like she was in a pool.

I just stood there. The prospect of disrobing in front of this girl who possessed a perfectly shaped body was unnerving.

"You need to stop being so timid around me," Circe laughed. "I won't bite you. If you'd prefer, go in my bathroom and change. There is a pair of shorts there for you to wear to bed." She was still reading my mind.

The bed had a padded step running the length of it on both sides and at its base. After I changed, she goaded me to step up on the satiny material and jump into the middle of the bed, which I finally did. My feet seemed to go right through the material without displacing any. There was no sensation or splash, and when it reached midway up my thighs, I felt my body sliding under the jacka and into sort of a sitting position. There was no sensation of either sinking or even being held.

Circe positioned herself with her head next to mine. I felt a slight pressure on my back and realized it was her hand.

"Keep your body steady until you get the feel of the way it reacts to the material," she instructed me.

I did as she said and quickly felt comfortable in the strange bed.

"When you sleep in a bed like this, you only need about three hours of sleep a night," she said softly. "When you're with someone else, it leaves lots of time for fun and games. Turn your head to face me so I can kiss you."

"Kiss me?" I wavered.

"You're still my boyfriend," she said, turning my head to face her and planting her deep red lips to mine. I was barely conscious of her hands moving first on my thighs, and then slipping all over my body, massaging me. I started to sink further into the bed, and then things went blank.

Chapter 12

Life goes on... Or does it?

I became aware of a hand roughly shaking my shoulder.

"Get up. We only have about twenty minutes to get you on your way. You have to get ready for graduation."

"What are you doing here? Where's Circe?"

"It's morning, she's gone. This is our schedule for the day. I'll drop you off at the forest preserve where I picked you up so you can spend your last morning at home. I've got much to do today, like get this stuff ready for the movers and finish packing my car for our departure tonight. So, after I drop you off, I won't see you until this afternoon at school."

"Do you want me to help you?"

"No, that's sweet of you, but there is really nothing for you to do. We have a specialized mover do our transporting, and they will take charge. I don't have that much to pack, and they will finish loading my car for me. Except for my bed, most of this furniture stays behind. Thanks for offering to help, but enjoy your last hours at home."

She was being unusually nice, so I decided to ask her something that had been on my mind. "If I'm an Eternal like you all are, why do I look like a geek?"

"Some of us change as we age. Others started out looking as we do now, still others morphed into their looks. I suspect you'll lose that geeky look as you get older."

"Did you…?"

"Change? No, I always look this way. So does Circe and the Pleiads. Their blueness doesn't return until they reach age. You'll have to ask them about that. When you look at Pleiads, you see their human shimmer. No, that's not fair. They do look human except for the blueness. You may never see one, though. In the flesh that is. They're very shy. Anyway, I'm just as cute at five as I am at fifty-five."

I nodded, hoping she was right about change. It seemed to me that I had a long way to go.

"Now let's get moving," she said. "I'm behind already."

Irene was quiet on the drive and, when I got in the house, my parents acted like I'd been there all the time. Of course, I couldn't tell them anything, and before long it was time to go to school. My Dad dropped me off for the rehearsal with the words, "We'll see you later."

At noon, all of us graduates gathered in the cafeteria in our caps and gowns to await the ritual. Many, including me, brought yearbooks for last-minute signatures. I sat down on the floor in a small corner and opened to where Irene's warning note had been on the first page, recalling once again how inane I was. Not only was it gone, but the personal message that she had written had disappeared also.

I broke out of staring at the empty page when the bottom of a high-heeled shoe pressed my hand to the floor. At the time I was glad it wasn't the spiked heel.

"Hey, boyfriend!"

I looked up to Irene, standing over me with her yearbook outstretched. She was a vision, dressed in a white dress trimmed in gold that came just above her knee and made her long legs appear even more glorious. Irene had several jewels embedded in her meticulously done hair, while her green eyes shone as if they were lit from within. When she smiled at me, her eyes flashed with violet. She really looked like a Greek Goddess.

"I thought you might want to try this again," she said as her toes, peeking out of a sparkly white and gold-strapped high-heeled shoe, nudged my leg.

Her calling me boyfriend had been a shocking revelation to others nearby, and looks of amazement spread over most of the kids standing around us. With a smile, I took her book and handed her mine. She knelt down next to me and opened my yearbook.

I figured maybe if I was complimentary in my note, she might be friendlier on our trip.

```
Dear Irene,

You are by far the most beautiful girl I
have ever known. Good luck in California
and I'm sure our upcoming road trip will
be the highlight of this life. Your
allure and charm enchant me.


Love,

Alex
```

I looked up to see Irene, holding my book out to me. We traded books and she winked again, then leaned over and kissed me lightly on the cheek.

"Liar," she whispered. "I know you think Circe is prettier. And that's okay, you're not my type. But wait until you meet our baby sister."

She left while I opened to the first page and there, right where her previous message had been, was the new one.

Dearest Alex,

Our time, you and me, will come in another life. But now, in this one, Circe and I need you. Somewhere out there is Clotho, our baby sister. Apparently you are the key to determining who she is in this life. Without you, I am told, we are lost. All will be explained on the way to California. You have to help us find her. Please! I will be eternally grateful.

Lots of Love,

Your new girlfriend (Promised Circe!),
Irene

* * *

I took one final look around as my high school years came to a close. Before meeting the Eternals, this final year had seemed a waste of time. I had only the slight inclination to work on the railroad. No thoughts of college or some other job. Now, I think I knew why. Not only had my status as an Eternal been blocked, but any desire to function in the Earth world had been as well.

My immediate task lay before me. I had to find the third Moirae, Clotho, in California. Then, maybe that would open up the real quest I faced. For the first time, I didn't feel like some kind of interloper. Looking over to where Irene now stood with Susan and Patty, I realized I had just been looking for friends in the wrong place.

"Alex, this is Decima," a quiet female voice came into my head. "You should now be calling them by their Eternal names, Atropos, Iris and Celaeno. You will learn your true identity when you find Clotho."

"Isn't anything ever easy, Decima?" I thought. I knew who she was immediately.

"If it was easy, we wouldn't need you," she answered.

When I looked up to where the three Eternals stood, I saw they were staring at me.

* * *

My parents had given me a watch for graduation, which I promised to always keep set to Central Standard Time. It would remind me of home. I realized they would wake up the next day thinking that I would be coming home for visits, but somehow I knew that I would probably not. I guess I was a little emotional in my goodnights, and they seemed puzzled at that. After they retired to their room, I slipped out the front door and walked down the driveway to the road that led to the forest preserve.

As I walked to meet Irene, I noted headlights of a car about two blocks behind me. It appeared to be parked at the top of a rise in the road. After I walked about a block to where the road took a sharp turn right, the car slowly began to descend the rise and follow me, still keeping its distance.

About a block directly ahead of me, in a flash of lights from a passing car, I saw the bright yellow of Irene's car. I hurried to it. When I got in, Irene smiled over and said, "Ready?"

"I think someone is following me," I gushed out.

"Yeah," she said. "That would be Eris. We're going to stop for some breakfast in the morning, and she'll probably join us."

"What? Isn't she...?" I was completely confused.

"The opposition? Yeah, in a way, but she has the ear of the Parcae, too. She's trying to get them to remand you to her. Decima can't show favorites among Eternals, so she approved of Eris following us to make sure I take you to North Dakota and then California."

"But she tried to kill me. I don't understand!"

"She never touched you, and we have no proof that Apate was acting on Eris's orders. Bottom line is that she's possibly the one wanting you dead, but we respect each other. Among Eternals, it's the civilized thing to do."

As she talked, I noted that the car behind had made the left turn onto the road we were on, and had pulled off the road behind us and turned off the headlights. I became conscious that, even though she finished talking, Irene had made no motion that signaled we were starting on our trip.

"Why aren't we driving away?" I asked. "Should we be sitting here?"

"This trip ought to be fun," Irene muttered in mock seriousness. "Look, Alex. I told you, Eris is following us, but don't worry, I'll protect you from her and any other bad, beautiful women should they come after you." She shook her head, causing that gorgeous hair to tumble around her eyes. "The deal is, she can't do anything to you while you're with me on the road, so don't leave my sight, understand?"

I nodded, but I was not satisfied.

"I promised Circe I'd be extra nice to you. I think I would anyway, because you still have that little crush on me," Irene smiled. "You are kind of cute for a Lemurian. Not that I know anything about Lemurians. But right now, the three of us should be on our way."

"Three of us?" I asked.

"Yep," she said. "You, me, and Eris behind us in her car."

She turned the key and the engine rumbled to life. When she pulled out onto the road, I looked back, and the headlights of Eris's car snapped on as it followed us onto the highway.

As Irene drove north she was mostly quiet. "Cars are the best part of this world," she said. "I love driving. You do drive don't you?"

"Well, I don't have a license..."

"I asked if you drove, not if you had a piece of paper. Stupid Earth rule."

"Yes," I said. "I know how to drive."

She pulled over to the side of the road and stopped. "Good," she replied. "Then go in the back and get some sleep, 'cause when we get to Madison, Wisconsin, I'm stopping for gas and I'll want you to take over and get us to the western end of the state, around LaCrosse."

I slipped out of the door and checked behind to see that Eris had also pulled over. I got in back and settled the best I could into the cramped seat, watching the car slowly follow us as Irene pulled onto the road.

* * *

It was morning when Irene physically shook me awake. "Come on Alex, wake up."

I sat up with a start. "Where are we?"

"Madison, you genius. It's your turn to drive."

"I've never driven in Wisconsin or to LaCrosse," I said.

"I've already implanted the route in your brain. You'll instinctively know the right way to go," she said. "Oh, and Alex?"

"Yes?" I said as I put my shoes on.

"I like my privacy. Keep your eyes forward, understand?"

I got in the front seat and ignored her sarcasm while, in the soft glow of the early hours of morning, I slipped the car in drive and pulled out onto the highway.

* * *

As the skies gradually brightened, I drove along easily. Irene was right, I seemed to know the right roads to take as if by instinct. Before long I was passing a sign that said we were close to La Crosse.

"Ten miles to La Crosse," I hollered out. "Wake up, sleepy head."

"I am awake. Stop your yelling," she said, and then her head appeared over the seat. "Stop the car momentarily so I can get in the front seat and explain some things. I don't like talking to the back of your head."

I did as she asked. We were on a fairly deserted road, except for our tail. I now could plainly see that Eris's car was a light blue 1957 Thunderbird.

"Stop staring at Eris and get us moving." Irene's voice came from my right. When I looked over, I gasped. The sun was bringing out the beautiful shades of brown and red in her hair, and her skin seemed to glow, even though she'd been sleeping in a car all night.

"Oh. My. Gosh." I managed to get out. "You really are beautiful."

She smiled at me in an odd, but friendly, way. "Let's get going, loverboy."

That triggered something, I'm not sure what. I felt like she was tolerant of me and yet, I was supposedly the one who possessed the hidden knowledge to find her sister. "First," I said. "We need to get something straight." Courage seemed to flow through me from somewhere. "If I'm to be in charge of some upcoming quest, even though you may not be involved in it, I think you're supposed to be helping me, not vice versa."

Where that came from, I just don't know, I mean, I didn't really even know much about the quest at that time. As I stared, she brought her small bare feet up and positioned them together on the edge of the leather seat, then tilted her head forward so that it rested on her knees. All the while she stared over at me with violet eyes. *Now what?*

"Whatever you say, Alex," she said. "Tell me what we're to do, 'cause I'm flying blind here. Don't forget I can read your mind, so I hope you back the words up with action." Her head came up and she stared, first at me with a slight smile, then forward out the front windshield, onto the highway that stretched before us. "Why are we sitting here? If you're the boss, get us moving. I can listen to your orders just as well with you driving as parked. Let's go. Impress me."

I slipped the car in gear and pulled back out on the road. I saw the Thunderbird, in the rearview mirror, follow us. All the while, I thought I had misspoken and searched for a way out of this predicament.

"By the way, not everything you think you know is fact," Irene announced. "Things are subject to change. Eris will explain the 'facts' as she envisions them to you when we stop at the restaurant. Once you and I are back in my car and on our way to North Dakota, I'll try to correct her inaccuracies and answer any questions you may have. Let's face it. You're out of your element here, especially in dealing with Eris, so despite your little speech back there, I suggest you let me help by sharing the responsibilities. I mean, as long as I'm along for the ride? You'll be in charge of this quest when I'm gone. Right now, I'm the one with the powers, and I do want to use them to help you. Okay?" She ended that with a genuine smile and a wink.

I nodded while continuing to glance over at her. Somehow she just let me off the hook without making me feel like a total loser.

"Let's start with keeping your eyes on the road, Alex. Why do you keep looking over at me?"

"Because you're the most beautiful thing I've ever seen."

"Thank you. Circe's right, you do have redeeming qualities."

As soon as we entered the outskirts of La Crosse, she pointed to a small diner on the left.

"There, Suzy's Diner," she said. "I suggest you pull in, and let's let Eris add to your education and get me something to eat."

I watched in the outside mirror as the T-Bird followed us in. This, I thought, should be interesting.

CHAPTER 13
ERIS... REVISITED

After we both parked, Eris, the woman I knew as Jocelyn Heldebride, my English teacher, jumped from her car and embraced Irene as she got out.

"Aren't you bringing any others along too?" Irene exclaimed. "Don't you always travel with your little band of assassins?"

"Watch your mouth, Atropos," Eris exclaimed with a wicked look. "I don't control other Eternals who are my friends. Besides, your sister seems to have convinced those in Illinois that he's an unknown Eternal, and they backed away. Luckily, I have a good supply of friends. So be careful on the road, my dear. Let's just say that my followers will see to it that all things are kept fair." Just as quickly, her mood switched and she winked at me. "So, now he's Circe's boyfriend? And you think he was a Lemurian? I thought of that... They have a certain...style. Not suited to Circe, though, my dear."

Eris stared at me intently. "No," she finally said. "I don't see him with either of you."

Eris came around as I, hoping it was safe, got out of the car. Eris walked right up to me and kissed me full on the lips. I stepped back, but not before catching a snicker from Irene. I'm not sure who it was directed at, though.

"Hello, Alex," she said. "I trust you had an interesting trip with our Irene." She didn't even wait for a reply as she pushed past me and joined Irene as she headed toward the door.

Once inside, we were seated at a small round table.

"Should we tell Alex what he's up against?" Eris asked with a big smile as her fingertips positioned themselves on the coffee cup in front of her.

"I think he knows enough."

Let's just eat and get back on the road," Irene said. "We've a long way to go, so we need to keep moving."

"Agreed." Eris was quiet for the rest of the meal.

* * *

"I thought you said Eris was to give me some explanation for what is going on?" I said when we returned to the car.

"That was the plan before you said 'I'm in charge' back in the car," Irene replied. "So, after I suggested you knew what you needed to, she'll cry to Decima and Decima will probably throw her a bone—"

"Throw her a bone?" I said.

"Put her in charge of something non-consequential, you know, so she shuts her trap," Irene said. She stopped talking when I laid my open hand on her arm.

"If it comes to Decima being forced to decide who I go with, tell Decima I'll continue with you," I said. "After all, we were just becoming acquainted. Besides, I love your car."

Irene's eyes turned violet and she smiled back at me. "You're still not my type, so you'd better stick to Circe if you get a chance with her again. And remember, it's my car. It goes with me when I go. Okay, Alex?"

"As you wish," I replied.

"Now that that's settled," Irene continued. "It's time we got back on the road. Ready, Alex?"

I nodded as Irene tromped on the gas pedal and the little car surged forward. After she fishtailed onto the highway she glanced over at me. "We'll continue this at the next stop, which will be for dinner."

* * *

Thirty minutes later, I looked over at Irene. "Eris didn't seem so terribly bad. From what I can figure out—"

"Shut the Hades up," she barked. "There's only one right side in this struggle, and Eris is not on it," she continued in a lower voice, but still louder than necessary in the small car. "For some reason, she means to have you killed early, and I have to find out why. What she doesn't know is that Decima and I have had our own discussions, and I'm the trusted one here. That's why you're with me. Decima agrees that Eris needs to go. We need some Eternal reason to send Eris on her way without her getting suspicious. I don't think you yet realize the importance of this quest."

"Why is it important?" I asked.

"How the Hades should I know? I'm just a chauffeur here. I do what Decima tells me. In the meantime, to avoid Eris and her playmates, you must stay under my protection. Hopefully, if we can examine that boxcar that almost caused your early death, I can determine if a spell is still gripping you now. That is why it is important to get to North Dakota, where you said that freight car would probably go. Only you can trigger contact with the actual boxcar. After that you'll get your wish as far as I'm concerned and you can take charge. Of yourself."

Her voice finally came down a few decibels. "I've been given a very important assignment in getting you safely there. And that is what I intend to do, understand?"

"You need not be so loud," I said. "I was just saying I thought Eris was nice to me."

"Look, Alex. Eris is a raving beauty, and I know she's very desirable to you, but she's one of the bad guys. They never mean well. After all, she had both Aello and Apate beat the crap out of you. They'll tell you anything to get you to their side. You must resist them. And don't buy Eris's bullshit." Irene paused. "And especially don't surprise me with agreeing to anything she says."

"Okay, okay. I trust you," I replied.

"Do you think I'm stuck up?"

"No," I replied quickly, wondering where that question had come from. "You are who you are. I was in love with you in high school even though you never knew I existed."

"Oh, I knew you existed. You were the only boy who never pestered me for a date. Then, when Circe showed up and displayed her usual aggressive boy pursuit..."

"Aggressive?"

"Yeah," she laughed. "Circe is an extreme boy hound. Did she not start after you right away?"

"She said she did that to do a scan on me..."

"Scan? I don't think she knows how. Rather than sit by me as she normally does when we're in school together, she took a seat behind you and immediately started flirting. I've long ago reconciled with her ways, though. It's the only thing my sisters and I argue about."

"So, you're not a boy hound?"

She glanced over, violet eyes sparkling, then once again fixed her eyes to the road ahead. "Nope, I'm a one guy girl. And, as I've said several times, you're not it. Circe and most of her Eternal girl friends are crazy over boys. I'm surprised Apate didn't seduce you first and beat you up after."

"But they're goddesses..."

"Goddesses is a term invented by early Earth inhabitants for Eternals. Besides, they're still females. Some of us, though, are much more reserved. I like my loves to be long affairs of the heart. So does my baby sister, Clotho. When Clotho found a guy she liked, she would wait for him forever."

"Would I asking you out have made a difference?" I grilled her. "You wouldn't give me the time of day even if I had talked to you in school anyway, would you?"

"No," she said and laughed. "No, I wouldn't. I had an image to uphold." Irene was quiet for a few moments. When a **Rest Stop 1 Mile** sign appeared, she said quickly, "I have to pee. We're pulling off here."

"Okay," I said, as she took the exit road.

After she pulled into a parking space, she turned to me and tugged my arm. "Come here, Alex. I owe you something."

Cautiously, I leaned over, and was pleasantly surprised when she kissed me. It was a totally unexpected, soft kiss on the lips, and I was suddenly conscious that my road trip partner smelled wonderful.

"That's for, I don't know. I just felt I owed you something. This trip has not been so bad. Whenever you want to overrule any decisions I make, just tell me. I'll consider it. Let me handle Eris, though. You'll be pleased to know that Decima agrees you should be in charge. Of your quest. At some time in the future."

She then slid out of the car and joined Eris, who waited on the sidewalk in front of the car. As they walked away, Eris turned and blew me a kiss.

I made a decision. While she had not acknowledged me the leader, I was determined to show Irene that I could take charge.

* * *

When she returned, I was sitting in the driver's seat. "Hop in back," I said as firmly as I could. "You didn't get much sleep, and I want to be able to talk to you when we stop for the night."

"You want me awake to...talk?" She grinned like a Cheshire cat. "I hope you don't think you can get more from where that kiss came from," she warned as she opened the passenger side door and crawled into the back seat. "I have to follow the edicts of the Parcae."

"No, I didn't mean that. I really do want to talk to you," I said, but felt my confidence wavering. "I need to know more of what the hell is going on."

As I pulled out of the parking space, her fingers softly stroked the back of my neck. "Taking over driving was a nice touch. Thanks, Alex. I am very tired."

"Good," I called back, my eyes focused on the road ahead. "Now go to sleep."

"So, now you're giving me orders?"

"Sorry," I said. "I guess I got carried away."

"Well, you're the first male who, in quite a few recent lifetimes, I've let tell me what to do. Thank you, Alex. I will do as you command. At least in this situation. By the way, you know as much about 'what is going on' as I do."

Chapter 14
Eris's Revelations

Before we left La Crosse, Eris had suggested she assume the lead car, and proposed our little caravan meander across southern Minnesota, stopping somewhere shy of the border with the Dakotas for the night. Irene agreed, and I held out hope that if my traveling partner got some sleep, she would be even better company that night. However, my thoughts that she would simply nap for a short time, then keep me company, were dashed. She slept soundly until Eris pulled into a restaurant/motel in a town called Granite Falls.

"Wake up sleepy head," I said loudly. "Time for dinner."

Once inside the restaurant portion of the motel, the three of us settled at a table that was away from the few other guests.

"Okay, Alex," Eris started. "Despite Irene's objections, I was going to give you additional background information, but Decima convinced me that we should wait until after we have examined that boxcar. So, for now just enjoy your dinner."

With that settled, Irene was much more relaxed during the meal, and she actually joked with Eris. It was a side of her I hadn't seen, but much enjoyed. For most of the meal, the two women discussed arrangements that had been made for them in California. My repeated plea of, "What about me?" was usually answered by Eris with a simple, "I assume Decima will tell you at the right time."

After dinner, as Irene and I walked outside to our room, she poked me and said, "When we get to our room, the first thing you must do is read the next part of the document that was written for you by Circe. That will explain some additional things to you. If you have any questions, ask me, not Eris. I need to shower, so you get to reading." She punctuated that with a finger pointing to the paper on the nightstand.

While she retired to the bathroom, I grabbed the paper she had left out for me and jumped up on the nearest bed.

I thumbed through to the spot I had left off, and on the next page, it said:

Restart here.

When the three of us Moirae were teenagers in ancient Greece, Nyx and Zeus came up with a plan to throw Hera off the trail of finding us. Zeus took up with Themis, who was Nyx's cousin.

It was hoped the more public affair with Themis would cause Hera to overlook Nyx and us Moirae. Of course, many of your mythology books took off on that and incorrectly credit Themis with being our mother. Don't you believe it! Themis supposedly had two children with Zeus: one was a boy and the other a girl.

Most of us descended from Zeus have the ability to recall our past lives, but the boy does not. His sister, however, is able to recall her past lives at the age of seventeen, just like my sisters and I.

This is where it gets strange; she was not actually BORN of Themis. Zeus took her in to shield her from prying eyes, and she was treated as his daughter. Where she came from originally is uncertain, but we now know that she was a Pleiad. She was in Germany at the same time as we were, but we never had personal contact with her. She was one of the seven sisters but she was using a shimmer, and the name Nicolette Green. This was after Zeus convinced the Seven Sisters to be born human and revert to their natural blue when they recover their memories.

And she was also taken with you when you were the German pilot killed in the crash of their prototype planet hopper. She died back then, but unlike Heike, Nicolette's passion for you as Herman did not carry over into her next life.

However, she was instrumental in arranging future passage for us out of Europe. She had made arrangements with a planet hopper pilot. In 1945 he secretly flew us over to the United States. At that time, Irene decided to go to high school, while I moved to California. We arranged to meet in California, not on the day you first met me at your school. As you now know, we do not know where Clotho was to be reborn, but she was to move to somewhere in California as a teenager. None of us know either what Clotho or Nicolette's names are or what they look like in their new lives. However, Nicolette might have arranged some way to contact Clotho or you in California.

I suppose something could trigger in you, I don't know. All I know of Nicolette is she was in love with you when you were the German pilot killed in the crash of their prototype planet hopper.

Eris has no knowledge of Nicolette. In our meeting with the Commission, Eris promised she would not interfere with us bringing you to California. However, Irene and I know that others do her bidding and are probably planning some kind of surprise for the two of you on the road. Be vigilant. The Keres know your whereabouts and, together with the Harpies, will try to capture you as a bargaining chip for Eris. Neither Irene nor I know who they all are today for sure, and you won't until they act. Shimmers make it easy for them to disguise themselves. Remember how easily Apate picked you up?

Stop reading here until you're told to read on. THIS IS IMPORTANT! Do not read any further.

So I stopped. The sound of running water told me that Irene was still showering.

At the sound of a soft knock at the door, I walked over and opened it.

A young girl with very curly, short, orange hair and beautiful blue eyes was standing there. She reminded me of Aello from that night in the railyard.

"No, I'm not Aello, but she's my twin sister."

My mind started spinning. "Am I asleep? Is this like in a dream?"

"Maybe. Who says you aren't?" She smiled and took my hand. "If you prefer to think of this as a dream, you may, but I am very real and you are actually awake. Come with me."

"I'm not supposed to leave," I answered, but then my thought process was interrupted. What was I supposed to be doing? Just why was I here?

"Look, you must trust me," she cautioned and, for some reason, I did. She led me around to the front of the motel and over to an old Kaiser parked in the lot. "Get in," she ordered, and I felt compelled to obey. She started the old car and drove out of the parking area and onto the main highway.

"Wait," I said. "Shouldn't you tell Irene that we're leaving?"

"No," she replied with a shake of her head. Beautiful orange curls flew in all directions. "There's a lesson to be learned here, and Irene will learn it."

"I don't understand," I replied. "Who are you?"

"My current name is Kara Simpson, but my eternal name is Ocypete. I'm sure Circe mentioned me. I was designated to kidnap you, and I must confess I did not believe it would be so easy. But don't worry. I won't harm you, like Aello and Apate did, and you'll be returned to your supposed guardian in the morning."

"I don't understand why you're doing this," I said. I was confused. Why kidnap me and then return me the next morning?

"I'm doing this as a favor for my half-sister, Iris. Would you rather spend this night being killed by those bent on the failure of your mission, or come with me?"

"Who wants to kill me?"

"The same people that tried to do so in the railyard. One of the Kere's sisters, Achylys, and one of my sisters, Celaeno. They work for Eris. I abhor killing when there is an alternate way. Indirectly, I had a part in saving you in the railyard, by telling Iris of their plans. You and I once actually lived together many years ago. You lived as Morpheus back then. Occasionally, I've wondered what happened to you. Anyway, I play just a small part in the recovery of your memories. I wished it was bigger, but all Decima would say is 'we'll see.'"

I felt no urge to resist her. In fact, I felt protected in her custody.

"You trust me for very good reasons, Alex. Now, we are here."

She pulled up to a motel at the edge of town. There were no lights visible beyond the lone structure, just a black highway. I followed her as she led the way to a room on the far end and opened the door.

"You can rest, now Alex. I will stay awake just in case."

"Would you tell me now what the heck is going on?"

"If you had not come with me, others would have killed you five minutes later. Instead they simply found Atropos, alone in the shower."

"Irene? Would they hurt her?"

"No. They are not allowed to harm a known Eternal. When I return you tomorrow, you will find her restrained but uninjured."

"Restrained? Is she okay?"

"They will probably just disable her from spreading the alarm to others and interfering with their search for you. I doubt they would extend the search tonight beyond your hotel, but just in case, I left false clues to lead them away from here."

At that moment the door swung open and Iris, the girl I knew as Susan Stage, entered.

"Thank you, Ocypete," she said. "Would you please leave Alex to me now?"

"Glad I could help, sister."

Iris looked at me and said, "Alex, go to sleep."

She snapped her fingers, and that was all I remembered until I woke up the next morning to find Susan/Iris lying next to me.

"It can't be morning already," I stated the obvious.

"Good, you're awake," she answered. "Did you sleep well?"

I nodded. "What happened to Kara...uh...Ocypete?"

"She did her job and had to leave suddenly."

"She said she was kidnapping me and..."

"Forget her choice of words. Ocypete has a flair for the dramatic. She was only doing me a favor, more like babysitting. You're lucky it was her because, while she is a Harpy, unlike her sister, Aello, she hates to be involved in something where anyone will get hurt. With her help we now have you firmly under the protection of Decima."

"What happened that night in the railyard, Iris? Both the Moirae and Ocypete said you were the one who warned me..."

"I did not warn you. I wanted to, but someone else beat me to it. Decima knows but won't tell me. Now come on, no more questions. We must now return you to your hotel."

* * *

Twenty minutes later, I was dressed and in her car. She drove me back to my motel but refused my request to come to the room I shared with Irene. "She is not to know that it was I who came for you at this time. You will tell her you wandered out and got lost. It's for Irene to find that you are safe and to realize she must be more vigilant."

After I exited the car, Iris drove away and I readied my story of walking the highway alone.

When I entered the room, I found a naked Irene, lying on the bed while bound hand and feet with strips of white cloth and a gag over her mouth.

"What happened?" I asked as I removed the gag.

"Where the hell have you been?" she said angrily. "I...did they find you?"

"I went for a walk and got lost," I said. "No one found me. Who's looking for me? Why are you tied up naked?"

"They grabbed me out of the shower. It was Aello with one of the Keres. Decima will be furious with me when she finds I let my guard down."

I looked down at the strips of cloth holding her arms and legs. They had ripped them from the sheets.

"Instead of staring at me, could you please untie me, Alex?"

"Already doing that," I said as I unbound her feet. "Lean forward and I'll untie your hands. You know," I said as I worked out the knot, "Decima doesn't have to know about this. Why tell her?"

"Are you saying I need not tell her?" Irene asked after she first pulled the bedding around her, then massaged her wrists.

"No, why should you?" I replied while kneading her ankles.

"Because I am supposed to relay to her all that has happened."

"As far as I'm concerned, nothing happened. I went for a walk and now I'm back. Where's the harm?" For a long moment she just stared at me.

"What the Hades possessed you going for a walk anyway? It was good that you did, they'd have killed you if you were here, but how could you know that?"

It was if my mind went blank. At the moment, all remembrance of Ocypete and Iris was gone. "I don't know. I read the letter and then needed some air. I'm sorry they did this to you. I wish I had been here to protect you. As I said, Decima needn't know."

"Thank you, Alex. That is kind of you, but my job is to protect you, not the other way around. However, Decima will know anyway, but...it's late, we must meet Eris for breakfast."

* * *

Back underway, two hours later we were nearing the outskirts of Fargo. My thoughts couldn't get away from the notion that finding that boxcar was a useless venture. I mean, even knowing the serial number, finding the exact one had to be next to impossible. While the freight car had that stencil, directing it to be returned here, I knew that in reality it might have been sent wherever they needed a boxcar of that type.

Irene's voice broke into my negative assessment. "Alex," she said softly. "Are you okay?"

"Actually, I was wondering something," I said, "That note you wrote at graduation—how am I supposed to help you find Clotho? I don't even know her."

"Decima said someone else you both knew would provide you with the opportunity of finding her. That's all I know. Circe thinks that's Nicolette, but none of us know who Nicolette, Heike or Clotho are in this lifetime."

"What I don't understand is, how will I know someone I've never met?"

"You lived with both Nicolette and Heike in Germany. Maybe you will feel an instant recollection of Nicolette. A déjà vu, as

Earthlings call it. Hopefully your experience with Circe will allow you to recall something about Clotho from your other existences. The other possibility is that Nicolette is using a shimmer cloud. You won't know Clotho at all, but she will know Nicolette, who will know Clotho."

I shook my head and lied. "I haven't had any of the dreams since Circe left me with you. Can't you describe anything about Clotho in France or Germany for me?"

"No. Decima said I am not part of this quest and I'm not to interfere. It's her mission, and that Eternal rule I must obey. Now, pull over so I can get into the front seat."

She had piqued my curiosity, but I knew it was useless to press her further. We had entered the town of Whapeton, and I saw railroad-crossing gates lowering ahead as a freight train, coming from the southeast, slowly approached.

"We're stuck here for this train," I pointed out to Irene. "Why don't you use this opportunity to get up front?" Of course, my words were unneeded, as she had already pushed the seat forward and opened the door. Seconds later, she was sitting next to me. As we waited for the train to pass, my gaze took in my passenger. She had dressed in a silky yellow top with black shorts, put her bare feet up on the dashboard, and provocatively shook her butt as she hummed along and silently mouthed the words with Elvis's *Hound Dog* coming from the radio.

"I love this song," she said, obviously aware of my watching.

Unable to observe the sexy spectacle she provided for too long, I stared ahead as the various freight cars rolled by in front of the Speedster. My mind drifted back to the rolling boxcar that had started this whole ordeal. Outside, the train began to slow, and I knew from my railroading experience that it was probably entering a yard area or such, to the west, which would have it running under caution.

Suddenly, with the sound of screeching wheels and slamming couplers echoing through the open windows, the train came to a stop. On my left, my eyes took in the right side of the boxcar, barely visible through branches of shielding trees. It was the exact same type of car that had almost crushed me days earlier. The glacier green paint scheme and huge mountain goat herald of the Great Northern Railroad drew me back to that night. I recalled the legend stenciled on the side: *When Empty Return to the Great Northern Railroad, Grand Forks, North Dakota.* Now, I squinted at the lower part of the car in front of me and saw the same inscription. For a second, the words seemed to glow, and I thought I saw a dark face appear on the side of the car.

With a lurch and the sound of the couplers unslacking, then straining under the massive weight of each car, the train inched forward. As the left half of the car drifted past me, the serial number 27368 caught my eye. I couldn't believe it was the same car being returned. After the last freight car in the train cleared the tracks, Gogi Grant singing *Wayward Wind* replaced the sounds of Elvis and the moving train. Irene still swayed in the seat to my right.

A car horn from behind broke me out of the stupor I was in, and I drove forward across the tracks and pulled over as soon as I could, in front of a drive-in restaurant.

"Lunchtime, Alex?" Irene said. "How thoughtful. And I didn't even have to ask. I'll mentally tell Eris to turn around so she can join us. She beat that train, and last we communicated she was about five miles ahead. Meanwhile, order me a burger, fries and a vanilla shake, sweetie. I have to pee." Before I could interrupt or stop her, she jumped out of the car and ran into the restaurant.

I sat there barely hearing sounds from around me. The radio had switched to a less hectic Elvis song, *Love Me Tender,* but the whole train incident kept rolling through my head.

"Pretty car. What can I get you, sir?"

I looked up at a young girl with curly blonde hair, dressed in a bright pink halter top and skimpy black shorts, poised on roller skates at the car door. All I could think of was the 'When Empty' stencil on the freight car.

"Sir?" the girl asked again.

"Hey Alex, stop staring at her," Irene said as she returned from her pit stop. The girl on roller skates was visibly taken aback by this barefoot girl who had jumped into the car.

After glancing at the girl's nametag, Irene said, "Hey Cindy. Sorry about his staring, but what can I say? My boyfriend is flawed. I'm hungry, though, so why don't you skate your tight little ass out of here and bring us each a cheeseburger with fries and vanilla shakes. Thanks."

Cindy's eyes narrowed, and as she skated away, Irene slid closer to me. "What's up, Alex? That little blonde wasn't that pretty, was she?"

"I need to tell you something," I interrupted her. For once, she listened as I told her of seeing the ominous dark face on the boxcar. For a moment it was quiet.

"Okay, I just communicated that to Eris," she finally said. "She said it's about fifty miles to Fargo and one hundred and thirty to Grand Forks. She's going on ahead and skipping lunch. After we eat, we're going to follow and stop in Grand Forks for the night. Tomorrow we'll see if we can find that boxcar."

Four hours later, we were in Grand Forks. Irene was strangely quiet for the balance of the trip. She had even stopped her seat dancing to the music from the radio.

After we found Eris's T-Bird in a restaurant parking lot, Irene said, "During the ride here, Eris and I were having a mental parlay with Decima and the other Parcae. Despite my objections, Decima has ruled Eris has an equal say in this, and since you came with me, you must go with her to the railyard. It's the Eternal way. We can't prove anything about Eris's role in the attacks on you. Plus, Eris insists on going tonight, and without me. I think Decima is disappointed in me. Eris probably told her about last night."

"What do you mean?" I asked. "I'd rather be with you. Eris would probably just as soon kill me."

"She won't try anything in the freight yard, she'll be afraid Decima is listening and watching. Decima will decide after you find the freight car."

"I don't want to go with Eris…"

"No, it's for the best," she said. "However, once we find out what forces are at play here, Decima might reschedule the balance of your trip to California. I think she might replace me."

"What about us…?" I asked.

"Sorry," she said, opened the door and scooted out.

Crestfallen yet again, I followed her into the restaurant. Eris already sat in a booth. Irene hurried over and we sat across from Eris.

"Irene told you of Decima's decision that you and I go to the railyard tonight, Alex," Eris said. "Irene will stay in her room." She then looked to my driving partner. "Actually, Decima thinks you've done well, Irene. You're not still upset, are you?"

Irene looked up at me and shrugged. "Just doing my job. You know I tried to follow Decima's orders. We're hardly halfway there, though. We still have the balance of the trip."

"Yes, well, we'll discuss that after we find that boxcar and Decima decides what's best," Eris replied, looking from Irene to me.

After dinner, Eris selected a hotel two blocks from the rail classification yard of the Great Northern Railroad. We checked into adjoining rooms on the second floor of the hotel. As soon as we got off the elevator, Irene headed quickly down the corridor towards the room I had hoped we were to share.

Eris stopped me from following with a tight grip on my wrist. "For now you can go to Irene. It'll be dark in two hours. Meet me in the lobby after I signal you by knocking twice on the door between our rooms."

I nodded, but Eris still held my arm. "Wait, Alex. Before you join Irene, come to my room."

She pulled me ahead, opening the door and handing me the small black suitcase she had been carrying. "What's your deal, Eris?" I asked.

"My deal?"

"Yes, what are you the goddess of? Who's your..."

"That is none of your business. You need to change into dark clothes, Alex. Less chance of being seen in the railyard. That Moirae is clueless, but I packed some for you in this suitcase." She tapped on the small black bag that I now held.

"If you don't mind I'll...uh...change in Irene's room," I said nervously.

Her snickers were musical. "Whatever you say, Alex."

When I came into the room, Irene asked, "What did she want?"

"She just gave me clothes to wear," I replied, and went inside the bathroom. I quickly changed into the clothes Eris had given me. I didn't know what to make of Eris. I was even more nervous about going with her than I had been with Irene.

When I came out of the small bathroom, I saw that Irene's clothes had been thrown about and she had nestled herself under the covers.

"Irene?" I called out.

"I may as well get some sleep while you're gone. Wake me and tell me what happened when you return."

Two sharp raps on the adjoining door told me it was time to meet Eris.

Irene popped up in bed and looked at me seriously. "Be careful, Alex."

"I wish that it was you going with me."

"Don't worry, you will be safe with Eris."

Eris was waiting for me when I got to the lobby. She was dressed in a black pullover top with a charcoal grey skirt. I had on a pair of black cords with a black t-shirt.

"Minimum talking would be best, Alex," she whispered as she pulled me through the door.

I followed behind as she moved quickly down the street, until we found ourselves looking down on the Great Northern Railroad's freight yard. It seemed to stretch endlessly in both directions.

"I think it best if we split up," Eris whispered. "If you find yourself in difficulty, just think my name and I will come to you. You go to the left and I'll go to the right. Remember, we're looking for a green freight car with a picture of the mountain goat and..."

"The serial number 27368," I said sharply. "I should know."

The outside line of freight cars I was facing were all orange Western Fruit Express refrigerator cars. After walking past perhaps ten of them, I looked back and noted that Eris was no longer in sight. I stepped up on the coupler of the next car and jumped down to the inside row of cars. Looking in both directions, I saw no one. However, a glance up and down this line of cars showed me, even in the feeble light of the yard, that they were mostly black or red hopper cars. On some, a telltale mound of coal peeked over the top, while others appeared empty.

I could see no green boxcar interspersed, so I again stepped up on a coupler and jumped down to the next row. Here, barely any illumination entered from the yard light towers. When I looked to my left, I was shocked to see Iris, dressed in a short yellow dress, leaning against a tank car walkway. Even though it was a dark night, I could see her clearly.

A breeze caused the dress to billow around her, exposing bare legs.

"Susan," I said. "What are you doing here?"

"Iris. Susan was just a school name. Didn't Decima tell you it's Iris now? Why am I here? Saving you some time," she whispered. "Keep your voice down. Eris is not that far off."

"She's tuned to my mind," I whispered. "I'm sure she knows I'm talking to you."

"She knows nothing of me. I have control of your mind right now. I have the ability to mask you and not make her suspicious. Come, I will lead you to what you seek and then leave so you may summon her."

I followed as she hopped over couplers and moved quickly through the lines of freight cars. I almost collided with her as she stopped in front of a green boxcar, which I instinctively knew was the one we sought.

"Don't touch the freight car, and do not mention to anyone that I was here and helped you. If you attempt to, I will interfere and freeze your voice," she said. She hurried into the darkness, and was gone. I summoned Eris mentally, then heard her voice in my mind say she got my message and was on her way.

"Good work, Alex," she said moments later, as she joined me. "You didn't touch it, did you?"

I shook my head. Nodding, she gripped my wrist and reached out with her other hand. Even before she touched the green boxcar, I saw sparks leap from her fingers to the freight car. My body tingled slightly, and I felt as if a weight had been lifted from me.

"Is that you, Dark?" Eris said softly. "Still following Hera's whims? Oh! I thought..."

She paused as if she was listening to an answer, yet I could hear no other voice.

Her eyes widened in disbelief, and she took in a quick breath as if startled. "I understand," she finally said.

She broke contact with the car and pulled on my hand. "Come, Alex, I must be prepared to leave early tomorrow."

"What happened?" I asked. "Who were you listening to?"

"Hurry. Now is not the time or place to educate you. I am behind schedule already."

She pulled me through the railyard and then up onto the street. After she led the way back to the hotel, she paused only to say plans had changed and I was to return to Irene's room. No other explanation was given.

When I entered the room it was dark and quiet. I sat on the edge of the bed to remove my shoes and was surprised by Irene's softly spoken words.

"Decima contacted me, Alex. I'm to stay with you tonight and tomorrow, but only until we reach Devils Lake, which is about ninety miles west of here. Someone else will take over for the balance of the trip. Get some sleep, five a.m. comes awful early." She then rolled over to the far side of the bed.

"What of Eris? What the hell happened in that railyard?" I asked. "Why is everything a damn secret?"

Irene pushed herself up with one hand holding up her head. With the other she brushed back a reddish brown curl that had drooped across one violet eye. "Eris has also been ordered to leave. I can't tell you much else, Alex. Decima lost confidence in us. She told me to be prepared to leave very early in the morning as she wants you in safer hands. Unlike you, I follow orders and don't ask questions. Did anyone appear to you and tell you anything?"

I instinctively knew better than to betray my meeting with Iris. "No. Eris talked to someone she called Dark. However, she seemed shocked. Then she pulled me out of there and didn't say anything except she had to be prepared to leave early."

"Dark is Celaeno; she's the one who was probably tasked to kill you in the railyard. She's the Harpy sister of Ocypete and Aello, who created that windstorm when you were with Circe in the railyard back home. Those Harpies seem to have developed an affinity for trains. Ocypete tends to side with us while Celaeno is usually, but not always, on the side of Hera. Eris slipped up by saying Dark's name, and Decima stepped in and stopped their plans."

Irene looked at me as I struggled with this news. "Circe told you that there are two different Celaenos. Both are very mysterious. There is the harpy Celaeno, and the one who came from a star in the Pleiades, who is also called Celaeno. The harpy named Celaeno is called the Dark. She has that name because she appears as a shadow and always leaves people in the dark about her loyalty. The Pleiad you knew as Patty was called the Hidden One by Earthlings because they could usually not see her star with their naked eye. Looking from Earth, there are seven bright main stars in the Pleiades cluster, but hers, the seventh one, is very dim. *That* Celaeno came here to Earth with her sisters as nymphs from various worlds in the Pleiades; she is from a world that encircles the star Celaeno. You might also have known her when you were Herman in Germany."

"I don't remember anything in Germany or elsewhere. How do *you* know?"

"When I scanned your life as Herman back then, I saw that one of the Pleiads was your girlfriend in high school, and you were living with her when you met Heike. They all have various shimmer appearances rather than show you their blue form. Maybe she still has a torch for you. Are you sure you didn't talk to anyone else in the railyard?"

I again thought of Iris, but quickly blocked the image from my mind. "No," I said. "I saw no one else. Could Patty, uh...Celaeno, have been Nicolette Green?"

"I don't know which Pleiad was Nicolette. However, I doubt it was Celaeno. Celaeno is very shy, and from what we saw of Nicolette she was a party girl."

"Why are you being replaced?"

"It was Dark that Eris plotted with. Eris got specific instructions to leave from Decima, who interrupted their plotting. I think they might have been planning to create some mayhem, and Decima probably blamed me for not seeing that. So both of us have been told to leave. Anyway, I thought you'd be glad you're not stuck with me for the rest of the trip."

"On the contrary," I replied as I crawled in bed opposite her. "I was really very pleased to be with you." I then duplicated her pose by putting a hand under my head and met her eyes. We stared at one another for a long moment.

"I've been in love with you forever," I admitted.

"You are so delusional," she smirked. "You don't know what forever is. You keep forgetting that you're supposed to be with someone else this lifetime. However, I have enjoyed being with you...get over here."

"I've enjoyed it too," I said as I cozied up to her warm body.

* * *

The next morning, as we had a quick breakfast, she informed me that Eris had left earlier. She got behind the wheel and we headed towards the town of Devils Lake.

I had planned to make the most of my last hours with her, but still tired from the night in the railyard, I fell asleep.

* * *

I found myself in a dream. I was on a cliff similar to the one where I first saw Veronique. There were rock-like steps leading down the precipice, and several other people were near me, but for some reason I could not see them clearly. When I would look over, faces would appear to blur, yet I was conscious of their presence.

To add to that mystery, I was terrified that I was going to fall into the darkness below me. I couldn't see what was down there, yet somehow I sensed it was a long way down.

The steps were far apart, at least five or six feet. Was this a place of giants?

Unlike the dreams in which Sylvane was involved, I was unable to get any answers to my questions by thinking of them. The co-inhabitant of this body was undoubtedly unaware of my presence and didn't pick up on my thoughts.

I accompanied the group down the cliff to an outlook that presented a view of a scenic valley. Why could I not see my companion? I was conscious of strange, blue-leafed trees, and many small birds filled the air. I had never seen any of these birds before. Most plentiful was a small, golden yellow bird with dark blue zebra striping.

Like the bridge, this dream was different from my previous experiences on Trivane, yet the feeling that this was something I had experienced in the past was compelling. Was this also on Trivane, or somewhere else?

I was awakened by Irene, to whom I immediately said, "I had a strange dream."

"They should have stopped by now with Circe gone," Irene replied. "Unless they were instigated by some other Eternal."

"They weren't on Trivane," I said. "It was like the bridge one I told Circe about."

"Circe mentioned that, and she told Decima, who had no comment. It might be something relative to your quest. Possibly, somewhere else in a past life. Maybe your memories are coming through. You are one weird Eternal."

I shook off the experience and forgot about it.

CHAPTER 15
A NEW PARTNER – ON TO CALIFORNIA

We had reached Devils Lake, and the Devil's Café, in the midst of a rainstorm. While I waited, Irene seemed to take her sweet time gathering things in the back seat.

"Damn," she finally exclaimed. "Sorry to be so slow. I wanted to wear my black slippers, but I think they're in the bag in the trunk. I didn't want these red ones to get wet. But they'll have to do." She punctuated that with an elaborate smile. "Let's go."

"I'll get your black ones," I said.

"Don't be ridiculous, it's pouring rain."

"A little rain never hurt anyone," I said.

* * *

I was thoroughly soaked after I had fished out her black slip-on shoes. For that, she awarded me a big smile and stepped out of the car. Just before we reached the door, she slipped; one foot plunging into a deep puddle. As she quickly stepped back, her other foot likewise disappeared into a stream of running water from a misplaced gutter downspout. "Oops," was her only comment as she gripped the door handle to go inside.

I was surprised, but Irene wasn't, when we entered the small restaurant and found Mark Wallen sitting in a booth, waiting for us.

"I hoped it would be you," Irene said. As he rose, she hurried over to him. I was shocked when she practically leaped on him and kissed him. Hard.

"Sorry for my exuberance," she looked to me as she spoke. "Really, my apologies, Alex, but I haven't mentioned that Mark's my actual boyfriend. We fell in love in Germany. That's partly why I wouldn't give guys at our school the time of day."

I guess my temporary silence at the news stood out.

"Don't be upset, Alex," Irene continued. "Mark will confirm what we've been trying to convince you of all along. You will eventually belong to someone else. Sit down and we'll explain."

"I took the liberty of ordering us breakfast," Mark said. A waitress came over and poured Irene and me coffee.

"I told him what you like," Irene added, in an aside to me after the waitress left.

"You're together?" I finally managed to croak out the obvious.

Irene smiled. "Mark and I have been in love before ... let's see, I think this is love affair number fifteen. Circe's been with him three or four times."

"Circe's only in love with Circe," Mark explained. "But she's a terror in bed."

"So the me being your boyfriend thing was..." I looked to Irene.

"Actually, I was honest with you before," she replied. "However, just so you know, Circe did petition to be the one you end up with, and it apparently did her no good. Not sure who Decima is so adamant about being with you. But, Decima probably has a good reason to exclude her."

The waitress returned with our breakfast, and I was quiet as we ate. I watched Irene as she obviously enjoyed her reunion with Mark.

Finally, as we had a last cup of coffee, she said, "Alex likes my Speedster. Can we trade cars, Mark?"

"Sure," he replied. "I love that car too."

"Hey, I get it back, after you drop him off and come back to me," she added.

"Of course." He smiled and looked to me. "Ready to go, Alex?"

* * *

Outside, the rain had stopped, and after Irene transferred her things to Mark's car, she kissed him and said, "You know where to find me." He nodded and she walked over to me.

"I'm really going to miss you, Alex. I know I was kind of a bitch at first, but you're okay."

With that she kissed me on the forehead, crunching that gorgeous body into mine. My shirt was still damp from the rain, and I could feel her warmth pressing into my chest. "As soon as you're on the road, read the third part of Circe's letter," she said. And after a final, "Take care of him, Mark," she left.

Mark and I watched her drive off, then he said, "I should get my jacket before we hit the road. Don't go anywhere, Alex." He ended that with a laugh.

After he walked back into the restaurant, I reached for the car door handle but never made it. A strong hand seized mine, while another gripped my mouth tightly so I could not utter a sound. I was conscious of being dragged toward a black car. As I was pulled abreast of it, the back door flew open and someone gripped me by my throat and pulled me in. While I struggled to get free, I saw that it was the April Sunshine version of Apate. My other assailant, who I didn't know, leaped into the driver's seat, and in a screech of rubber we pulled out onto the highway.

"April," I said loudly. "I thought we were friends."

"Surprise!" she said with a wicked leer.

"Will you do something to shut the Earthie up," the driver said.

Seconds later my mouth was sealed by the same tape she had used before.

"Don't fret, Achylys, his lips are sealed."

"What does...the boss...want with this puny Earthie anyway?" Achylys asked.

"Good, you remembered to not use her name. She wants to interrogate him to see what he's being used for. She talked about some sort of plan he's involved in."

"I say we smash his head with a rock and throw him into the lake," Achylys suggested. "Why drive all the way back to Grand Forks?"

"We can't do that, they'll know he was murdered."

"Not if we had grabbed Atropos too. They'd think they went swimming, hit their heads and drowned."

"You know we promised the boss to keep him for her," April replied. "Plus we can't hurt Atropos, she's an Eternal. Why do you hate her so much?"

"I just do."

"We stick to the plan. She's letting us have him for fun afterwards."

"It's over ninety miles back to the railyard," Achylys moaned. "Why couldn't she just come here?"

"We don't question her motives," April replied. "Okay, Alex, you've gotten stronger, but you know we both are still tougher than you, and my partner would like nothing better than to end your days. So will you cooperate and be docile, or must we do this the hard way? Just shake your head yes or no."

I saw no way out, so I nodded yes.

"Good little boy," April smiled, then dropped her shimmer. I was now looking at Apate in her glorious self.

"Lean forward and put your hands behind your back," Apate said as she struck me hard across the back of my head. I did so, and I could feel her tying my hands together. When she was finished, she grabbed me by my ears and yanked me back in the seat. "Our boss promised us that we'd both have our way with you when she's finished. I get you first," she sneered at me. "It'll be fun at first, then...well, you won't like then. My partner here then gets to do with you what she wants. I think she's stuck on that lake thing."

Achylys laughed in the front seat. "Just twenty more miles," she smirked.

I couldn't believe they talked so casually about killing me.

* * *

A half-hour later, Achylys pulled over in an open field above the railyard. "We need Aello," she said. "Agreed?" She looked to Apate.

"Aello," Apate ordered aloud, then continued. "I was thinking very windy, blinding rainstorm, to cover us getting him down there. Then, once we have him secured, cover the area with a pea soup fog. Oh, and maybe..." Apate stared at me and smiled. "Make it a cold rain, like forty degrees."

"Great idea." Achylys agreed. "That'll keep him helpless while covering us and the boss. We should shimmer while Aello gets busy."

Apate became April again, while Achylys took on the appearance of a normal girl with straight, shoulder-length black hair and deep blue eyes. "My shimmer name is May Storms," she told me.

I saw it had become very windy outside, and dark clouds had moved in. Suddenly there was a torrential downpour, and May opened the rear door and pulled me out into the freezing cold rain.

"Sorry," April laughed behind me. "You're gonna get a little wet. And cold." With that, she used her foot to kick me hard in the backside. I fell forward into the grass alongside the road. May put a foot on my neck, pinning me to the ground.

"Hold him down until I get out of the car," April ordered. "We don't want him running off."

April laughed as she slowly slid out of the car. "Now get your ass up!" she yelled, and kicked me again. Although it was difficult getting up in the wet grass, with my hands tied behind me, I struggled to my feet.

"Wait." May put what looked like a dog collar around my neck and attached a long leash. "Now he surely won't run off." She yanked hard on the leash and ordered, "Move it." With her pulling on the leash, I was practically dragged down to the lines of freight cars. I could only see a few feet in the blinding rain, and I struggled to keep my eyes open in the icy downpour while they laughed at my pain and dragged me up to the couplers of two adjoining cars. May lifted me over to the next line of cars and dropped me, causing me to tumble on the unyielding ballast.

April then dragged me a few feet by the leash. When she stopped, she put a foot on my head. "How's that rain temperature?" she asked. "Frosty enough?"

Both snickered and giggled at my predicament. Finally, May used her foot to push the side of my face into the ballast, then kicked me hard and urged me up. This lifting, dropping, dragging, lying in the rain and kicking was repeated several times until they finally got to their destination.

We had stopped in front of the green boxcar that started all of this. I found myself standing with cuts and scratches all over from being dragged over the ballast. I was sure I was frostbitten. My shirt was now completely soaked, and my wet pants hung low on my hips.

"What do you think?" May asked April with a kick to my backside. "She wanted him docile. Think he's cold, tired and wet enough?"

"Yep," she replied. "He's spent." She then doubled me over with a well-placed kick in my privates. "That should do him one better. He won't give her any trouble. Let's get him into the boxcar and seal it up."

May reached up and slid the boxcar door open. She then lifted me up and tossed me into the freight car like a sack of potatoes. Despite all the manhandling, it was good to be out of the freezing, blinding rain.

They both then climbed up into the car after me. April first replaced the tape over my mouth, then pulled something out of the front of her short skirt.

"Close your eyes, Alex," April commanded. When I did as ordered, she wrapped the scarf over my eyes and tied it tight behind my head.

"She said to attach the leash to one of these loading hooks so he can't get out," I heard April mumble. "Just attach it anyplace for now." Someone tugged hard on the leash, and I was conscious of my head being pulled back.

"Not so hard," April said. "You don't want to choke him. On your knees, Alex." She shoved me hard to the ground, and I got to my knees.

"Tie his feet and connect them to that hook," April said.

My feet were icy cold, and I barely felt the tugging of the rope being tied around my ankles. When they were finished, I couldn't move. I was tied kneeling, and cold water still dribbled from my hair down my back and chest.

"Good," April said. "Now take the leash and loop the end over that highest hook up there. I can't reach it."

My head was pulled taut by the leash, making any movement difficult.

"Good job, May," April gushed. "She'll love her present."

"Seems like a lot of trouble for one Earthie," May mumbled, then one of them kicked me in the privates. My scream came out muffled by the tape.

The next thing I heard was the two of them apparently jumping out of the car. Someone began sliding the door closed. Then it stopped.

"Wow, it's really foggy," April's voice drifted over to me. "Good job on that, Aello. Keep it icy cold and foggy for about three hours, until all of us have had our turn."

"She better hurry before he dries off," I heard May mutter.

"Good thinking," April chuckled. "I left the door open for a reason. Let's wet him down once more. Aello? A little crosswind?"

Suddenly the cold rain swept into the car from the open door, and I was again freezing from a torrential downpour. "Come on, Achylys," April continued to chuckle. "Let's go wait in the car until the boss arrives. She'll contact us when she is finished."

With that, the rain stopped, the door, making a loud screeching as it rolled in its tracks, was closed, and then it was quiet. I struggled for a short time in an attempt to get free, but I could barely move my icy arms and legs since I was not only tied up, but leashed to the car's side. I was frozen through. Water continued to drip down my body and I ached all over.

The quiet was suddenly broken by the shrieking sound made by the sliding open of the car door. I tensed, expecting to hear Eris's voice. All their talk of 'the boss' didn't fool me. Who else could it be?

"Another mess you've gotten yourself into, I see." It was not Eris. The scarf over my eyes was pulled off.

Ocypete. Why would she want to hurt me?

"Apate did a sweet job, just as we planned." She pulled the tape off my mouth.

"Huh?" I said. "You're in league with them? You're the boss?"

"No, stupid. Remember, I'm on your side. Decima learned of Eris's plan to grab you to see if you know anything of the many tales of some quest. Eris trusts Apate, so Iris had her get the assignment to kidnap you and bring you here, where I could rescue you again."

"What kind of quest am I supposed to lead? Why don't I know anything about it?"

"Hey, simmer down," she said. "There has always been this rumor of a great quest. Since Zeus disappeared so many years ago, it's assumed it has something to do with him. With your sudden appearance, it's come back to the forefront. Eris figured you were a part of it and planned to kill you, in hopes it would upset the mission, after she got any information out of you. Eris is in deep with Hera, who would not want any plan that involved Zeus to be instigated. Now shush, I need to get you out of here before Eris shows up."

Ocypete quickly untied me from the car walls and took the leash off my neck. In response to her touch, all the little cuts and scrapes went away. When I looked at her in wonderment, she merely said, "Eternal," and pulled me to the car door. We dropped to the tracks below and hurried away.

* * *

Twenty minutes later, the two of us safe with Iris in her old car, drove past the spot where Achylys and Apate stood next to their car, looking toward the railyard. They were obviously waiting for Eris to signal them that it was their time to dispatch me. I could swear that Apate looked over and smiled at us as we sped by.

"It was hard for Apate to agree once again to beat you," Iris joked.

"She seemed to be enjoying herself," I replied, wrapped in a blanket in the back seat.

"Actually, she toned down what Achylys wanted to do. If she'd have had her way, we wouldn't be talking now."

"How did you know they were going to do this?" I asked.

"That was Ocypete here."

Ocypete turned around in the front passenger seat and waved back at me as Iris explained.

"Ocy talked to Eris before she left, and picked up that Eris planned a surprise for you and Irene. She just didn't know where. Decima was in that boxcar when you and Eris got there, and she scanned Eris to learn of her plans for them to return with you to Grand Forks."

"So that's why Eris was called off driving with us," I interjected.

"Correct, and Decima decided to replace Irene with Pollux, but he fumbled the ball by leaving you alone. She had also called me and Ocypete into it as a backup, because of Ocypete's close relationship with Apate, to get her to take the mission of transporting you back to Grand Forks and that boxcar. We had a little trouble there; but in the end, she was pleased to do it. Apate convinced Eris that Achylys was not to be trusted alone with you, as she was vicious."

"Apate was no different. What was Eris going to do?"

"Let's just say that you would not have gotten out of that boxcar alive."

"If you knew all of this in advance, why didn't you just prevent it? Tell Pollux to be more vigilant. Stop them from grabbing me in Devils Lake."

"That was Decima's original plan, but I overruled it."

"What? You wanted them to beat the crap out of me?"

"Yes, as it would be the only way Eris would still trust Apate. Apate is the only ears we have on what Eris plans."

"I still can't get over how ruthless Apate was with me. I still ache from her kicks. Not to mention, she requested Aello to make the rain be cold."

"The cold rain was actually my idea," Ocypete added. "I didn't want Eris to suspect Apate really works with us. Eris knows Apate loves to inflict pain. She had to make it look good. No lasting damage."

"Besides," Iris interrupted. "You need to toughen up."

"Easy for you to say. What happens now?"

"Decima said it's too late to replace Pollux, so he'll meet us in Devils Lake and take you to Needles as planned. However, knowing Decima, she might have someone else replace him somewhere along the way. I suggest you try to keep warm and get some rest. We'll be there in an hour."

* * *

Later, after I met up with Mark and we headed out from Devils Lake, I pulled out the folded letter and opened it to where I had previously left off.

Part III starts here.

There is no new information to give you except, at this point, I wanted to remind you of two things. By now, people have told you of rumors of a great quest. We now know they are not rumors and you ARE the leader. For some reason, Clotho's reemergence as an Eternal is tied to yours and this mission of yours. Decima tells me all will be made clear if you can successfully complete this trip to California and find my sister. When you find her, you find yourself.

Mark Wallen (Pollux) is taking you to Needles, California. He might be replaced along the way if Decima can get someone in position to do so. Once in Needles, Decima has selected someone else to take you to a secret location where you'll be until your birthday. This change of plan has been necessary because Decima thinks Eris, the Harpies, and Keres still mean to kill you despite the ruling of the Parcae that you be left alone until it is clear who you are. Ocypete told me that Eris is again shopping for assassins, and, though they bungled the last job, she might go back to Apate and Achlys. Be vigilant!

Finally, don't forget, it's up to you to request their history from whomever you come across. Most will willingly share it with you, but only if you ask. As I've told you before, most of the Greek mythology shit is just that, so much bullshit. Irene was instructed to tell you to read this, the third and last part of my history, when you are approximately two days from California. I hope you arrive safely within the next week. Until then, if you have any additional questions, direct them to Mark. I will keep you updated about any threats through Mark.

Mark glanced over as I folded the letter up, but remained quiet. For a long moment, I thought of Irene, Circe and all that was happening to me. Fearing some kind of an emotional breakdown, I covered my face with one hand. I was exhausted, and had been running on adrenaline for the past several hours.

I feared another attempt to end my life, but Mark put that to rest, telling me that our continuous traveling to my final destination in California should prevent any attempts. Of course, once I got there, it would be open season on Alex Winters. Until my eighteenth birthday anyway, which was coming up.

I needed out of that 'Woe is me' mood. I recalled the end of Circe's letter and her telling me I had to ask for a person's history.

"What's the story of you as an eternal?" I said to Mark. "You're Pollux?"

"I came to Earth from a planet called Meiran, near the star that Earth calls Pollux. I left when the star was not unlike your own star you call Sol. It has since evolved into an orange giant."

"I don't understand that part," I interrupted. "You left...how do you leave? I thought Earth scientists said it was impossible to travel from star to star, something to do with the speed of light?"

"I can't reveal to you anything not known to Earth, Alex. However, Earth's interpretation of the laws of nature is faulty. You'll find out for yourself when you recover your Eternal memories. But Circe told you things she wasn't supposed to, and I have assured Decima I will not reveal anything to you before it is time.

"Most highly advanced life on far-off planets exists in various forms, mostly spirits. Spirits are not bound by what Earth scientists call the rules of nature. Millions of years ago, there was a call through the inhabited universe to populate the planets in several emerging systems, including this one. To do that, spirits needed to revert to a life-form more indigenous to those planets. On most, it's some type of human form. In Sol's System, at the time, Earth was not yet habitable, but the planet we called Trivane was. I think Circe has told you there was a huge catastrophe that rendered Trivane uninhabitable."

"Did that have something to do with the moon being destroyed?" I asked.

Pollux nodded. "Yes, that collision resulted in most of the surface features being sucked off into space. It wasn't instantaneous, though. Many survived. Those life-forms moved elsewhere, including to Earth. Trivane was named Mars by emerging Earth civilizations. Those of us who lived on Trivane, however, usually call it by that name."

"I don't understand the spirit thing," I said.

"Each individual has a consciousness, a spirit, we call it. On many advanced worlds, the individual tires of its body, so it leaves it behind to exist forever as the spirit. However, to some like myself, and possibly you as well, being a spirit gets monotonous, and we seek to return to a more adventurous life. To do so requires a body, so…"

"How do the spirits travel across such great distances?"

"It's a kind of dream process. Many of us came to Trivane as spirits and went through a process in which we re-evolved to a life-form."

"Life-form?"

"Yes. That includes what you know as human, but you don't have to be human. Many of the nymphs—"

"There's another word," I interrupted. "Nymphs. Isn't that a sexual thing?"

"Somehow Earth gave it that connotation; however, no, it's not. Male spirits are known as satyrs and the females are nymphs. Many thousands of nymphs came to Trivane from all over the universe, while the satyrs who came numbered much less."

"They then became human?"

"What you envision as human, yes, most did. But many nymphs chose to live in the sea and became what Earth calls mermaids."

"So you were human if you chose to be on land and a mermaid if it was the sea?"

Mark chuckled. "Actually, you could pick any creature. Many nymphs loved the body of cats, so that's what they chose. Especially when they came directly to Earth rather than by way of Trivane."

"Why was that?"

"Here the oceans were seeded with many carnivorous creatures, so there were only a few who wanted to continue as mermaids or mermen."

"So that's when you came to Earth?"

"No. Before the collision, we on Trivane were warned that the planet would be rendered uninhabitable, and those that wanted to were transferred here to Earth. I elected to return to the spirit world and returned to Aldebaran first, then to my home world. The initial settlings on Earth were on lands much different from today. You might recall them when your Lemurian memories return."

"But you obviously came back."

"Yes, as I mentioned previously, adventure called. I came with a friend, named Castor. In the times of Zeus and the civilization of Earth in Greece, we were born as twins to a human named Leda. Your mythology says we had different fathers, Castor had a human father and mine was Zeus, but that's wrong. We were both born as twins to Leda and Zeus."

"Castor? As in the twins Castor and Pollux?"

"Yes. I'm Pollux, but we aren't always twins."

"Where is Castor now?"

Mark pulled out and passed a slow-moving new Buick, then returned to the right lane. "I was getting to that," he said. "Circe will not be pleased with my telling you, but hopefully, she won't find out."

"I don't understand," I said. "What has Circe to do with this?"

"I told you there were many more female nymphs than there were male satyrs in the settling of Trivane. Circe told me you relived part of that time with her. When you met her on Trivane, she was sixteen and had not yet regained her memories of being an Eternal. She unknowingly was enjoying her second existence as a human, after spending many years as a free spirit roaming Trivane."

"Free spirit?"

"Circe originally came to Trivane as a water nymph from the planet ZeeWaterii in the Tau Zeti System. They live primarily in water; that's why so many choose to be mermaids. Irene and Clotho, who would later become her Eternal sisters, also came over as water nymphs via ZeeWaterii, but from different star systems."

"You mean..."

"A lot of life exists in the vast oceans of various planets. That's where Earth mermaid legends started. Irene originally came from Harnon, a planet near the star Betelgeuse, and Clotho from Varrnall, near Taygete. The three became friends on ZeeWaterii, and after being born as sisters to Nyx on Earth, petitioned to be Eternal sisters. They have been very close ever since. What's really ironic is, I was the one who stole Circe away from you on Trivane. You were with her in their equivalent of high school, and after she graduated and turned seventeen, her memories returned and she sought out Irene and Clotho. I was going with Irene then, but went crazy over Circe when I first met her. You see, each of the sisters has basically the same personality from lifetime to lifetime. You've met Circe, so you know how exciting she is. Irene is a one-man girl. In this current life, Irene and I met in Germany and we've been sort of together since."

"But if Circe is so exciting..."

"You can only take so much of being under Circe's spell, and then you need a break. I've always thought that her wildness was a trait of planets orbiting the star Meissa, in the Orion Belt, where she came from. Irene is a welcome change from trying to keep up with someone who epitomizes the female spirit."

"And Clotho?" I asked.

"What I recall of her is that she is very loyal, soft-spoken and a little like Irene. She represents the nymphs of the Pleiades, who all have those traits. They'd wait for the guy of choice forever. The Seven Sisters are also very close and very selective. Most of them won't even talk to a human or, for that matter, an Eternal that is not one of them. They had special permission from Poseidon and Zeus to retain their Pleiad features when they converted to human. Clotho, however, did the full conversion to what you view as human. Most of the others shimmer now, as they have started to blend into the Eternal society. Actually, I don't really know Clotho, or any Pleiad, so I can't tell you much."

"Do you look the same in every life?"

"Yes, even as a child. I have control of that. Only my name changes. I can make bodily changes, but I usually refuse to do so."

I decided to change the subject just a little, while I considered this new information. "You never explained what happened to your twin brother."

"Oh yes, Castor. Sorry, it involved Circe, and I got off on that tangent. Just before Zeus left, I think Circe told you that Nyx and the girls made themselves scarce so they wouldn't be discovered by Hera. They had planned to flee to what was Egypt at the time. Castor was in love with Circe then, and he wouldn't hear of them making the journey alone. So he escorted them there. While he was gone, Hera insisted to Zeus that we leave for Aldebaran. She knew Castor was Zeus's son by Leda and my brother, but it meant nothing to her that he'd be separated from me.

"I returned two years later to bring him back, only to discover the rumor was he'd been killed on his return journey to Newald, where we lived. I have not been able to find him since."

"But if he's an Eternal..."

"As far as I know, he was not with any other Eternal when he died. We must plan for that so the bond can be made to recover our memories. He had left Nyx and the Moirae, and thought he'd be returning with me to Aldebaran. So he had not bonded with either them or me to guarantee his birth with us in the next lifetime."

"I don't think I understand. Doesn't he know he's an Eternal?"

"If he didn't bond with anyone in that lifetime, he would not recover his memories unless he happened to be with one of us at the hour of his eighteenth birthday. That would trigger his memories back to that fateful day."

"I'm sorry, Mark, I didn't know..."

"Hey, it's old history, Alex. Are you getting hungry? We're coming up on the town of Williston, and we'll shortly be out of North Dakota. After that we'll be steadily angling south and west for California."

I had thought that I'd miss my time with Irene. However, my time with Mark was fabulous. We had a lot in common, and he never tired of showing me the historical sites of the western United States. I suspected he had lived through most of the history, during one of his many lives on Earth.

Following lunch in Williston, he drove down to Miles City, Montana, where we stopped for the night. The next morning he took me on a tour of the Little Bighorn Battlefield, scene of General Custer's Last Stand, where he confessed to having been a young Lakota Sioux lad at the time of the battle. Fifteen years old, and considered too young to fight, his assignment was to protect women and children if the soldiers entered the camp. They didn't, of course, as all the soldiers were massacred in the battle.

Five years later he was killed by a soldier trying to avenge that day. Following that, he was reborn in New Mexico in 1887. That told me that while he looked twenty-five years old, he was now actually seventy.

That afternoon he gave me a detailed tour of Yellowstone National Park, where I discovered the park was actually a giant supervolcano. Mark told me there had been a number of eruptions over the time he'd been in our planetary system, but none since civilizations restarted on Earth 34,000 years ago. He would not tell me what he meant by restarted.

He did say he had lived on Trivane through three huge eruptions of the volcano whose caldera was now under Yellowstone National

Park. The first of those eruptions, he explained, was near the Oregon-Idaho border. Successive eruptions formed what is known as the Snake River Plain, moving the active part of the volcano steadily eastward to its present location, under our feet.

Later, while he drove, he expounded on his tales of Trivane and some of his Earth lifetimes, including one when he had been one of three hundred Greek warriors who defended a mountain pass at a place called Thermopylae.

"Thermopylae?"

"Sorry, I forget you're history deficient. Look it up some time," Mark said. "Anyway, enough about me. You once told me you had a girlfriend back in Chicago. What was she like?"

"I thought you could read my mind about her. Circe seemed to know..."

"I don't do that shit. And, Circe knew nothing. Actually, she's even less snoopy than I am. She finds out some obscure little thing and then gets you to admit stuff. She then pretends as if she knew it all the time. Tell me about your little Earthie."

"Brenda and I were both shy when we started high school in Chicago," I began. I hadn't really talked to anyone about Brenda, not even my parents. Mark was a great listener, and it was nice to talk about something fairly normal for once. "On one of the first days after school started, I was struggling with trying to figure out how to open my locker when some upper class girls pushed this girl out of their way and into me. The girl was so apologetic, while I was equally sorry for being in her way. For a few moments all we did was keep repeating 'I'm sorry' to each other. Luckily she was a little less shy than I was and introduced herself. I was taken back because she was so pretty and I had a hard time accepting that she wanted to be friends with me. It turned out that she had just figured out how to open her own locker, so she helped me with mine.

"All that first year she stuck by me. She'd wait for me in front of the school and we'd have lunch together. When there was a school thing like a dance or other events, she'd know I was too scared to ask, so she'd say something like 'Think we should go?' to make it sound like it was a joint idea. As the year progressed, I stayed pretty much in the same geek strata, while she skyrocketed in popularity. She even became a cheerleader. But despite all that, she remained my friend. She cried when my family moved me to the suburbs."

"Why didn't you go back to visit her?"

"She wanted me to, but I felt it was best for her if we just cut it off. We were from two different worlds. It would never work out. So I never went back, and after a while she stopped writing me. I assume she graduated when I did."

"You know you were an idiot for not pursuing her."

"I wanted to pursue your girlfriend."

"If you have a choice, don't get involved with Eternals, Alex. I usually stick to Earth girls. My only exceptions are the Moirae."

"I thought Earth guys and girls were off limits to Eternals?"

"Since there are so few male Eternals, we get some special privileges. One is we can appeal to make an Earth girl a nymph so she can become an Eternal. Zeus, and his brother, Poseidon, used to do it all the time. However, Eternal girls are not supposed to go with Earth boys. It's a double standard that has gotten Circe and others in big trouble with the ruling council. The council is supposed to keep the ratio equal, but they drag their feet most times and it ends up more like sixty-forty. Eternal girls are fighting to get the ability to elevate Earth males to Eternal status as a way to make it equal. I support their movement, but most Eternal guys don't."

* * *

That evening we stopped in the small town of Afton, Wyoming for the night. Mark had planned to take two days to cover the rest of the trip to Needles on the eastern California border. However, the next morning, he informed me that Decima had decided he should be replaced. I guess she was still miffed that he had left me alone back in Devils Lake, which enabled Eris's gang to grab me. He said his replacement was enroute and should be there within the hour.

"There she is," Mark suddenly said. We were sitting in the hotel's restaurant, and I looked up to see a silver Valiant turn in off the highway.

"I'd rather have you get me there," I pointed out.

"Oh?" he replied. "Watch who comes through the front door and then tell me that."

I looked over and couldn't believe my eyes as the door pushed open and Circe walked in.

She came over to our table, all smiles. "Thanks for butchering the job, Pollux," she said to Mark, then looked to me.

"What are you doing here?" I asked.

"No one else was close by, so Decima's giving me a second chance. It's only to Needles, though. There, someone else will take over. Excited to see me?"

"Very," I replied.

We both bid Mark goodbye. It was bittersweet, as I hated to see Mark go, but was happy to see Circe once again.

Circe took Mark's seat and said, "There is a reason I insisted to Decima that I take this job and see you once again. Apate. Do you hate her now?

"Are you kidding?" I said seriously. "She beat the crap out—what do you expect me to say?"

"I was the one who suggested her to Decima. Apate only did the deed after I told her it was okay. 'Make it look good,'" I told her. "'Eris is no one to mess around with.' I didn't want Apate to compromise herself. So, I told her to beat the hell out of you. Are you mad?"

"Not at you," I said. "I understand. And despite her mopping the floor with me twice now, I guess I can forgive her too."

"Woo hoo! She's gonna love to hear that. Apate is super shy, and she would never expect you to understand her reasons. I had to beg and plead with Decima to use her. She insisted you wouldn't go for being manhandled just so we could convince Eris that Apate was loyal to her. Finally, Decima concurred, and let me do this ride to see if you were up to her using Apate again."

"Yeah," I said after a short contemplation. "I think I'm okay with that. But tell her I want it to be with Apate, not April Sunshine."

"You'll have to be with one of her shimmers at times. In private she'll always be Apate. Now, we better get on the road, Alex," she said, and we left together.

We drove all the next day, through a corner of Idaho, down across Utah and through a piece of Nevada, until we entered Needles that evening. We were both exhausted and went right to sleep.

* * *

I had forgotten that Circe would only drive me this far. The next day I found she was gone, and a strange looking blue girl was sitting on the bed, apparently waiting for me to wake up. Her hair and skin was a light shade of sky blue and her eyes were a very bright blue. She wore a short, yellow dress with sleeves that stopped at her elbows, and light yellow slippers.

"What are you doing here?" I asked. "Where's Circe?"

"That's the greeting I get? What are you doing here? They moved heaven and earth to get me to take this assignment, and you miss Lachesis? She's gone, but you'll see her again, I'm sure. I'm Merope, by the way."

"You're my ride?"

"I wonder how you can be an Eternal?" she smiled. "I've heard you've been pining over the Moirae sisters after you passed up a chance at love with a human, and now you have neither. My sister told me you were uninformed, but I had no idea."

"Your sister?"

"Patty Zerbean, remember her?" She said it with a grin. "Okay so far? I'm not going too fast for you, am I?"

So she was a Pleiad, like I thought. I had read of the Pleiads in high school, the ones that were stars in the constellation Taurus. I was completely unprepared for this tiny blue bundle that now looked questioningly at me. Her eyes shown like starlight from hot blue stars, and she was absolutely stunning.

"I have been put in charge of you until your birthday," she continued.

"What do you mean, in charge of me?"

"In charge of you means just that. You will do exactly as I say. I do not take sides in these nonsensical little squabbles the Greek Eternals love so much, and I'm only doing this at my mother's request and because they agreed to my one condition."

"I don't understand why I need a guardian. When do I find out what this quest is?"

"The current Fate council, the Parcae, knows things we don't. And, we know things *they* don't. This mission appears to have been cleverly hidden in the minds of a number of people. It was concealed in such a way that as one thing becomes known, it triggers something veiled in another. From what Decima has been able to piece together, you are the main catalyst in this unknown operation. It appears that the initial part of your mission is to locate Clotho. She in turn will then reveal something that triggers another, and so on until the mission is laid before us. Why that was set up is a mystery to me, but the so-called Greeks love their mysteries. Regardless, no one has the power to overrule the task that Decima and the Parcae have prescribed for you. My advice is to do what they say. Accept whatever decree they hand down. Locate Clotho, and you'll find out the breadth of your involvement as well as who you are as an Eternal."

I nodded. What else could I do? I felt trapped, and had decided maybe it was best to go along with their plans. And I really wanted to locate Clotho, at least for Circe. Hopefully that would satisfy the other Eternals. Of which I was, supposedly, one.

Merope continued. "I agreed to step into this diversion of the Greek Eternals with the stipulation that I am not to be trifled with. As long as you are with me, you are safe. I wouldn't be much help if someone tried to hurt you, as I do not get involved in violence. We Pleiads are Eternals who also function as Peacekeepers. Hopefully, all parties will respect my involvement, which has been arranged by the Parcae. Is that understood?"

"Yes."

"Any more questions?"

"Where are we going, now?" I asked.

Her voice came into my head. *"I'm planting the knowledge of where we'll actually be in your head, and will shield it from any type of probe. Outwardly, I'm telling you we're going to a remote location in Utah. Whenever you speak or think of it, it'll come out as St. George, Utah. Even Pollux and the Moirae will think that. Only you, the Parcae, my six sisters and I know the truth. You know it unconsciously."*

As she spoke those words, a California map appeared in my head and funneled down to a place called Sequoia National Park, which appeared with a big star next to it. Afterwards, however, all I could think of was St. George, Utah.

"We'd better be going," she said aloud. "It's a long drive to St. George, and I want to be there by nightfall." The map of Sequoia appeared in my head.

In my mind she said, *"I also shimmer as someone named Echo Lake. Outside the car, you will address me by that name. In my shimmer or as a Pleiaa, don't forget, I cannot protect you if you leave my side. I'll discuss this more with Decima for a solution.'*

I hated the position I was in, but was powerless to do anything about it. After driving across desert for what seemed like forever, we arrived in a tiny town called Amboy. She drove right through it, though, then did the same for several other small desert towns.

Finally, we pulled into a small restaurant in the town of Mojave.

"Are you hungry, Alex?" she asked.

When I turned to answer, I was in for a shock. I guess that somewhere, in the last few miles to Mojave—which of course, I thought of as St. George—she had shimmered into Echo Lake. I only knew it was her because the name, Echo Lake, came into my head. Again, the shimmer was of a small girl, barely five feet tall, with short brown hair. Just a normal girl.

In my head, her words appeared. "I need to be forgettable, that's why I chose this disguise. By the way, this isn't *St. George*. We still have a way to go."

With that she opened her door and got out. I followed her lead and we went into the restaurant. I thought Echo rather aloof. She ignored all attempts of mine to make small talk. Almost all of her 'talking' was in my head, where she kept repeating, "We need to hurry. Your birthday is tomorrow. We must be at the right place at the right time."

Merope was quiet after we resumed our journey, now on Route 466. As we skirted the town of Bakersfield and turned north on

Highway 99, she stirred and announced, "I've been in mental communication with Decima, everything is prepared."

"Can you tell me why my birthday is so important?"

"Clotho has the same birthday as you do. Decima has pieced together and told me the story. You have gone through many lives not knowing who you were. Long ago, you were appointed not only the key to her rescue in this lifetime, but to your own as well. The two of your futures as Eternals are tied to each other. You only have a narrow window to find her, the last twenty-four hours before your birthday. In addition, you and a Fate goddess must be with her at the exact moment of both of your eighteenth birthdays. If you do not find her and fulfill this requirement, you will never recover your memories of who you are, and she will be lost to the lives of Eternals forever."

"I don't understand why Irene or Circe can't find her. They should know what she looks like."

"Were you not told Clotho wanted to change her look in this life? None of us knows what she looks like. Besides, the other two Moirae were dismissed from this task."

"Then, how can they expect me, a complete stranger, to know her?"

"It was said you'll be drawn to her, and she to you. Decima provided us with only one clue: she can be found in Sequoia National Park on your birthday. You must scour the park, find her, and be with her at the moment of your birth. We simply need to follow this road until we get to 198 west. Think you can do that?"

"You want me to take over driving?"

"Yes. Decima thought you might subconsciously pick up on something that will lead you to Clotho. At least it'll give you the chance to pick up her trail as we get closer."

* * *

It was now mid-July and warm outside. As I drove, I lowered my window, and the air rushed in. The breeze caused the bottom of Merope's dress to flutter, and revealed her sky blue feet.

She glanced over at me, then reached into the back seat for one of the pillows she had brought. I knew something was amiss. She obviously disliked windy conditions.

"Do you want me to close the window?" I asked.

"No, leave it. You should be comfortable too." She said this with a bit of a smile.

"How about telling me how you, a Pleiad, got involved in all this, including my quest?" I asked, glancing away from her slim, blue ankle.

She leaned back in the seat and smoothed her dress, settling into her story. "In the last lifetime, a way was found which would allow us to have a shimmer identity as a human child. When we reached seventeen, we could recover the ability to transform back to a Pleiad. I was the role model for that. Not content with the shimmer I had in that lifetime, I developed a second shimmer personality, and was born as that into this life.

"When my Eternal memory returned on my seventeenth birthday, I discovered there was a price to pay for the development of the shimmer technology I had pleaded for. I was tasked with a role in aiding your quest."

"What's the object of my quest?"

"No one, not even Decima, knows the whole picture. By the way, the Moirae girls were clueless as to what happened that night you almost died in this life...in the railyard. Actually, there were only two Eternals who understood that minions of Hera were trying to foil plans set in place eons ago. That was Iris and Decima. Pollux figured out some of it, thanks to tweaks from Iris. He was useful in helping to protect you those early days. However, neither of them was the one who actually saved you. As I told you, we each have different parts. When someone executes their part, it sets off a recall of memory in another."

"Who saved me?" I asked.

"Not for me to say. The one who did will tell you at the right time."

I pondered this, thinking, of the small ways Mark had helped—and even protected me—on the job. We drove through Three Rivers, near the park entrance, and I glanced over at Merope, who grew quiet as the breeze through the window shifted and again caused her dress to billow around and up her legs. I could not help looking back over at her. She was simply breathtaking.

She stared intently at me, a smile on her face. "Am I causing you stress?" she asked.

"Do you have any idea how absolutely beautiful you are?" I replied.

"Posh," she scoffed. "I'll bet you say that to all the Eternals. On second thought, it's not often an Eternal compliments a Pleiad. Thank you. I hope you don't mind camping, by the way."

"Camp?" I asked. "We have no camping equipment." I spoke haltingly while navigating the twisting mountain road that led up the final miles to the park.

"I said YOU camp, as in you, Alex, by yourself. I never said anyone else was camping with you."

"This is all so bizarre," I pointed out. "I don't know what Clotho looks like, and I'm sure she won't be waiting with a sign saying, 'I'm Clotho,' at the park entrance. Now you want me to camp out?"

"Decima thinks you should trust your instincts once you're there. As I said, completion of one event seems to lead to clues to another."

We arrived at the park entrance, and I paid the entrance fee and pulled over, waiting for her next instruction. Merope continued to study the park map.

"I thought you knew where we were going," I probed her.

"I do, you smart aleck," she said. "We need to get you to Lodgepole campground, but first I wanted to see General Sherman."

"General Sherman? We're here to see some general? How is he on a map?"

"It's a tree, you ignorant human. The Sequoia trees here are the oldest living things on Earth. I have always wanted to visit them."

With that, she momentarily shimmered back to Echo Lake. "Remember, I'm Echo Lake in public. Circe told me how she set her shimmer for everyone but you, so I'm doing the same now. You will see me as Merope while others see Echo Lake." She directed me to a huge tree, and after I parked, she sprang out of the car and literally waltzed around it. Her yellow sundress billowed out as she danced, barefoot and solo. After one pass around the tree, she grabbed my hand and pulled me along with her.

"Can you waltz?" she asked as she skipped around the giant trunk.

"I never learned," I admitted as I stumbled, but tried to keep up with her.

"Try to follow me," she laughed. She faced me and instructed me in how to strike a dance pose. After twice around, she laughed again as I added a flourish to the steps, spinning her into a low dip.

"I thank you, Alex. Now I can cross that off my 'things to do in a future life' list. Let's get you to the campground, so you can get to where you need to be by nightfall."

* * *

"There," Echo said, and pointed to a large, yellow canvas tent. My eyes, however, were glued to the girl who stood next to it.

"I...I..." was all I managed to get out as I stared at April Sunshine. She retreated into the tent. "What the heck is going on?" I asked Merope.

"We had to pull some strings with Decima, but Apate will take over now," she said. "Be very careful with her."

"Careful? But..."

"You've loved a lot of girls from afar, including my sister, but she's a Pleiad and we don't mix well with humans or non-Pleiad Eternals. However, I thought it only fitting that one of Circe's friends be the one to tell you the rest of the tale. Now, get your ass out of the car so I can get back on my way. My part in this is mostly done."

"I don't want your part to be done."

She stared over at me for long seconds, then said, "Goodbye, Alex. Thanks for the dance."

After I got out, Merope wasted no time in pulling away from the site, leaving me in front of the tent. After several moments, April came out and said, "Hi, Alex. Surprised?"

"Stunned is more like it," I replied. "I thought I'd never see you again..."

"Yeah, Decima doesn't like this, but Circe and the others were adamant they wouldn't cooperate unless I could do this part. Circe had originally planned to be here, I guess. You and I still have unfinished business, so here I am. It's fate. Come on, sweetie. Let's take a hike. We've still got a few hours of daylight, and I want to see the Tokopah Falls."

"We're going sightseeing?"

"Of course. It'll be fun."

"Do you even know how to get there?" I asked.

She waved the park map in my face. "It's not difficult." She led me over to a log bridge where a sign indicated the Tokopah Falls Trail. She pointed to it and said, "See? Even you can follow this."

It was still a bright, sunny day, and as we crossed the bridge, she stopped and looked down into the river below. For a moment we watched the water swirling by. When I turned and looked at her, I saw she was smiling at me.

"What?" I asked.

"Strange," she said. "Being here with you and not to inflict pain. I'm just glad to be out here, in the quiet. I like Earth nature."

The trail followed the riverbank, and as we walked, I marveled at the energy and power of this fork of the Kaweah. The water moved swiftly in among granite boulders, crashing around and over them.

Finally, I decided to ask her the question I had been wondering more recently. "I don't get why Eternals are coming into and out of my life. It's like a number of lives are being twisted to make a point of some kind. I don't have a real say in this, do I? I have to accept whatever you gods want me to? Even some girl that's been chosen for me despite the fact that she beat the crap out of me—twice?"

April abruptly stopped walking, pulling me off balance. "Whoa. Wait a minute. You gods? You've been told before, we're not goddesses. I'm a girl. An Eternal girl, but I do have feelings. You say those words as if you're accusing me of enjoying the position I've been put in. Well, I *am* enjoying this. I'm helping the Moirae get their baby sister back, and if it means giving up on the life I'm currently living, then so be it. Besides, I'm not the one calling the shots in your life. I had no idea back when I picked you up outside Irene's apartment and was told to dispose of you that I was being used, just like you. Once I knew, I volunteered to be this girl in your quest."

"Quest? This is a stupid game. Why do I have to be—?"

"First of all, you jackass, it's not some game. The Moirae sisters and I have existed together for thousands of years, and we want to continue to do so. Losing Clotho forever can't be compared to a little one-time sacrifice you'd have to make. You get to start over your next life. Don't you think the four of us had plans in this life? Irene's gone who knows where and Circe has been dismissed, so now it's just Clotho and me. But first you must find her, otherwise my unique relationship with the Moirae would end here."

We had continued the hike while we talked, and were now at a forested area with the Tokopah Valley in the distance.

"Why do you say that?" I asked. I was mystified. I couldn't imagine how by tomorrow I could possibly find someone I didn't know.

Instead of answering, she reached over and grabbed my hand, squeezing it tightly and pulling me along the trail. "Come on, we're both in the dark here." We walked in silence for a while as she seemed to be thinking.

"So," I asked. "Were you anyone famous in some life? How do you know the Moirae?"

"Famous?" she asked.

"Yeah," I said. "Iris was Helen of Troy. Maybe you were like, Cleopatra?"

"You are a buffoon. You know some famous people were just human. Not Eternals. The Moirae and I shared the same mother, Nyx. Nyx groomed me to be an assassin. I love the night."

"Weren't you the master of deceit or something?"

"You read all that trash? How I associated with the goddess of lies and the god of trickery? Pseudologoi and Dolos?"

I nodded.

"You're more of an idiot than I thought. Back in those times, you made one mistake and they pinned the role on you forever. I got caught stealing a basket of apples, and I was suddenly the goddess of deceit. Pseudologoi tried to defend me, and she was the Goddess of lies."

"Okay," I said. "Can you table your little rant? Where to, from here?"

The trail seemed to end at a granite wall. However, looking around, we found the wall diminished in height to the left, so we followed that and the trail reappeared.

Apate did not pick up on her complaining again. Eventually, we came across the spot where the Marble Fork of the Kaweah River flowed over huge granite boulders. The water cascaded around them in sheets. We crossed back into forest growth that, framed by the canyon walls, was a beautiful sight. Entering this area through the forest, we came across numerous fallen logs.

A few more moments of quiet hiking brought us within sight of the huge granite formation known as the Watchtower. According to the guidebook that I had taken over, it towered sixteen hundred feet over the Marble Fork River.

"There's another trail, the Lakes Trail to Heather Lake," I informed her, reading from the trail guide. "It takes you to the top of the Watchtower."

"We should take it. Imagine the magnificent view from up there." The words tumbled out of her.

"It says you have to navigate this very narrow ledge along the formation."

She looked at me and wrinkled her cute little nose. "Oh. Never mind. You falling off some steep mountain ledge was not in my plans for the day. I think we're on the right trail for us. You fall, and suddenly, I'm the goddess of mishaps or something."

I ignored her caustic murmurings. We continued on through the forest, passing an area with many downed trees.

"The guide says Horse Creek flows from out of Tokopah Canyon, and just before it meets and merges into Marble Creek, it splits off into three branches. We're crossing them on these bridges, and will gradually enter an area where the forest thins out and there are more stone outcrops.'"

April ripped the guide out of my hands.

"Gimme that damn thing. You're turning into a walking travelogue. Just enjoy the view and the pretty day." She tossed the book into one of the creeks. "I already know the way to where we're going. We don't need that silly thing."

From here, we could hear Tokopah Falls crashing down on the rocks even before it came into view. The forest had rapidly come to an end and we had entered an area littered with granite boulders and sparse vegetation. As we closed in on the falls, we witnessed its thousand-foot plunge. It crashed down the boulder-strewn rocks, to the lower cascades. Once in sight of our objective, we sat in silence on a circle of boulders and observed the power of the water colliding with the base of the falls.

After watching for a short period of time, we got up and I followed her as she traced the path of the small creek leaving the falls.

"I remember the guide said its ultimate destination is Heather Lake," I said.

"Yeah, yeah, Mr. Know It All. I'm only interested in the fact that the cold water of the creek flows into that clear, sheltered pool up ahead."

April ran over to it, took off her shoes and waded into the frigid water. When she waved for me to join her, at first I gently refused. Finally, I complied with her incessant waving by walking over and sitting on a boulder while she pranced in water that was not very deep. I thought of the story Mark relayed of Circe the water nymph.

"Were you a water—?

"Nymph?" she interrupted. "You bet your ass. That's how I met Circe."

I completely understood why she enjoyed the cool fresh water.

"Oh," she said suddenly as she looked around. "We're alone." With that, April Sunshine turned into Apate. "Better?" she asked, a wave of her lilac hair draping over a like-colored eye.

"You are one beautiful creature," I replied.

Finished with her water sprite act, she walked over, jumped up on the boulder and sat next to me. Her feet were practically blue from the cold, but she didn't complain. Shivering involuntarily, she wrapped her arms around herself, then lay back on the boulder and stretched, trying to get some rays of the sun.

Suddenly, an inspiration came to me. *Why don't you try warming her feet?*

The instant my hand touched one of her feet, Apate shrieked and kicked out, striking me full in the chest and knocking me off the rock and into the frigid water of the pool. I hit with a big splash, and I swear I could hear laughter in my head.

"Oh, for the love of Zeus!" Apate yelled when I surfaced. "You idiot. I'm so sorry. What the hell were you doing? You need to be careful where you touch."

"I was trying to warm your toes," I replied as I sat in the cold water. "You know, be spontaneous?"

She bounced up off the rock and splashed over to me. With a half-hearted swing, she hit me on the side of the head and said, "Are you insane? I could have fallen off the rock into the river."

"Oh, like me?"

She started to snicker and bent low, facing me.

"By the way, it's a creek," I corrected her. "Actually, it's technically a pool."

"Well, I'm sorry I pushed you in the pool."

"Kicked. You kicked me into the pool."

"Serves you right for touching my foot."

I couldn't help it. Her face was no more than six inches from mine, and she was not showing me a shred of sympathy or remorse. Still sitting in the pool, I reached over and grabbed both of her ankles and pulled her toward me.

"What are you—?"

Those were the only words to escape her lips before I yanked her legs out from under her and she fell, butt-first, into the water with a splash. I was instantly up, out of the water and on top of her.

"Alex—"

That was all that escaped her lips before mine were on hers. What I didn't expect was her reaching around and grasping me behind the neck, pulling me down to her. Before I knew it, her head was fully submerged and she continued to drag me with her under the surface of the pool. When we were both underwater, her tongue pushed through my lips and she wrapped her legs around me. I finally managed to pull myself, and her, out from the depths and up to a sitting position.

"What are you trying to do?" I sputtered, gasping in air. "Drown us both?"

"The water is like two feet deep, you pansy." She hugged me close to her. "Now, that was impulsive," she whispered. "Nevertheless, you should never mess with a former mermaid in her environment. I can still breathe underwater."

Water ran in rivulets down her cheeks, but she was grinning broadly. Kneeling in the frigid waters, she slid her hands behind my head and pulled me close. I had thought Circe had given me the sweetest kiss possible, but I was wrong. Apate tenderly touched her lips to mine and then lightly rubbed hers across them. That put me in a place I did not know was possible. We kissed for a few moments, but it seemed like a very long time.

"Let me give you an FYI, Alex. Former mermaids had to give up their tails for legs and feet. Their feet are always very sensitive to touch. Be warned."

When she finished, it occurred to me the water was very cold. I stood and gently raised her to her feet. We quietly kissed again, longer this time, and I took advantage of the situation by slipping my hands down the back of her jeans and massaging her bare backside. I was surprised she momentarily let me.

"No," she whispered when our lips parted, slapping at my hand. "We can't." After we slowly made our way back to shore, Apate unbuttoned her shirt, slipped it off and, after squeezing the excess water out of it, laid it up on the sun-kissed rocks that sheltered the pool. She did not remove the lemon yellow tank top that was under her shirt, choosing instead to knead it against her skin to get the excess water out.

"I know better than to excite you by stripping down to bare skin," she smiled. "Put your shirt on that big boulder next to mine."

I shook out of my wet shirt and laid it up on the rock.

Together, we sat there quietly. And I must admit, I was in heaven sitting next to her. Suddenly, she turned to me and gripped my arm.

"You must remember this place. I have brought you here for a reason. In this lifetime, you and Clotho were born at the same instant in time. It was not an accident or a coincidence. We must go back now. But remember, it's important."

I was disappointed by her insistence we return, but stood up with her as she gently tugged my arm.

"In this life I was originally supposed to be single, and then I met you," she stated. "When you touched my bare skin, I realized you have the power to turn my strength of will to jelly. If you asked me to be with you, I might not say no. But I can't disobey what has been decreed. Please, don't tempt me again."

"But—"

"NO!" She said it emphatically. "You don't understand. Circe is my best friend and, after her sisters, I am hers. She felt terrible that first I was tasked to kill you, then she had me manipulate my way into getting the assignment to kidnap you for Eris. And, to prove my loyalty, I had to again beat you. She didn't want you to hate me, so she convinced Decima to let me do this one small part of your quest. Decima agreed because any Eternal friendly to your cause was being watched. It was not in Circe's, or my, plans to steal you from her. You're not like the other male eternals. I see her attraction. But, you and I are not to be."

She then squirmed out of my grasp and picked up her shirt. "Come, Alex," she pleaded. "Please. Ask me no more questions. If you really care for me, you'll just do as I ask. Hopefully, our time will come in a later life."

Confused by her conflicted emotions, I followed her. We traced our way back up to the return path that led to the Lodgepole Campground. As soon as we got on the trail, she grabbed and hugged my arm.

"We can be friends," she said. Her smiles told me I had obviously pleased her by not pushing her to do more when we were in that passionate mood.

As we walked, I put my arm around her and drew her close. Suddenly, she stopped and looked up at me with a serious expression. "I'm going to further disappoint you terribly."

"What do you mean?" I asked.

"I can't stay the night," she explained. "You have to be alone tomorrow. Plus, we're tempting fate the longer we stay together. I was to only show you the pond area and leave. Eternals can keep track of me mentally, but not you. If they knew I was with you, I would no longer be useful to Decima."

She looked down at the ground for a moment before continuing.

"Listen," she urged. "Decima, Merope, Circe and I came up with a clever plan, the start of which was executed while you and I were at the falls."

"Plan for what?"

She explained as she pulled me along. "All of us Eternals need to distance ourselves from you, while you proceed alone to some hidden location. That will leave your whereabouts in doubt. So, before we reach the point where you saw the Lakes Trail sign, you will see one for the Twin Lakes Trail. There you and I will separate; you will take that trail while I return to the Lodgepole Campground. Use the trail signs and take that route as far as Clover Creek. There you will find a brown and yellow tent already set up for you by Martin, a trusted human friend. It has dry clothes and a sleeping bag inside and is the only tent there. Stay in it tonight. Tomorrow you will return to the pool by the falls at the exact hour of your birth. Wear the clothes in the tent and take the backpack to aid in your disguise. Martin is an experienced hiker and will have left you a map of an alternate route to the pool. Use it and trust no one on the trails. That is important, as they have the ability to disguise themselves as friends to you. If all goes well, you should find the Moiraes' baby sister. If the two of you are together at the hour of your birth, she will regain her memories at the same time you get yours."

"But will you be alright?" I asked.

We had stopped in front of the Twin Lakes Trail sign. "They would only track me to find you; they dare not hurt an original daughter of Nyx. They don't know I'm with you, and search for you with some other Eternal. But it is already late in the day, and they will undoubtedly look for you at the falls or on the path we took. It is important you move quickly to the tent and stay inside until it is time to return to the pool. I will stay in the yellow tent you found me in so that I can help if needed. Go now. Quickly." With that she returned to April Sunshine.

I paused only to give her a half-hearted kiss, then followed the alternate trail. Did I want to leave her? No, I didn't, but I knew that finding Clotho was important.

This trail was a little more difficult than the trail to Tokopah Falls, as it rose in elevation constantly. It was four miles to Clover Creek, so I hurried for the first mile or so, then took it a little slower. Other than a black bear rustling in the underbrush, there didn't appear to be another soul on the trail.

Upon reaching the camping area, I saw only one tent, and it even had a note pinned on the flap that said, Do Not Disturb. It was signed with the name Martin. Upon entering, I found a sleeping bag still rolled up, a small camp stool, a knapsack that contained a replacement set of clothes, a canteen of water and a gas lantern, along with a box of matches.

After zippering the tent shut, I sat on the stool and checked the pockets of the knapsack. As Apate had mentioned, there was a map containing an alternate route written out for me. On it, Martin had noted it would take me about thirty minutes to reach the falls going at a slow speed. One side-pocket contained several candy bars, one of which became my dinner. Then I crawled inside my bag and did my best to sleep.

I struggled fitfully through the night. I did sleep some, but wondered about all that had happened. A week ago I was in high school, and now I was supposed to be some kind of Eternal? I thought about what Merope had told me about each one knowing small pieces of this puzzle. My mind went over the dream sequences I had experienced and wondered about that huge bridge. When Circe and I talked, she knew of no such bridge on Trivane, and I knew there was no such structure on Earth. When and where was it?

Finally it seemed to lighten outside and I was thankful that, despite my fitful sleep, I was wide-awake.

It was still dark, but my watch told me it was seven, so I ate another candy bar, drank from the canteen and went about changing my clothes. After stuffing the old set of clothes in the knapsack, I cautiously unzipped the tent and looked up and down the trail, then went into the woods to relieve myself. While I did so, the sound of someone coming down the trail came to my ears. Hurriedly, I moved behind a large tree and watched as two young women approached from up the trail. They walked up to the tent and called out, "Hello?"

Apate's admonishment to trust no one overcame my attempt to answer them back.

"I told you we should have checked it last night," one girl said to the other.

"I still say he's just some camper," girl number two replied. "Where would he get a tent and have the time to set it up?"

"Someone else could have set it up for him. And I say it might have been him, and now he's on the trail."

After opening the tent and looking inside, girl number one said, "Camping gear. Okay, you're probably right, but let's split up. You go back down the trail a mile and I'll go up about the same, and let's both find a hiding place to watch, just in case he went this way. However, I'm sure they'll find him on the trail to the falls."

After waiting until my watch showed eight, I used Martin's map to make my way through the forest. About forty-five minutes later I found myself at the end of the wooded area. In front of me stretched a meadow that led to the sheltered pool below the falls. There was just fifteen minutes to spare as I made my way cautiously over to the rocks that concealed the pool from anyone watching from the area of the falls.

* * *

When my watch registered it was ten, I braced myself for Clotho's appearance—but no one came. Nor, at that hour of my birth, did I regain any memory of who I supposedly was.

* * *

It was close to noon on my watch when I decided to return to Apate's campsite, hoping that she would be there. Apparently, I was nobody, and that was good news in a way.

As I rounded the huge rock, which sheltered the pool from the falls, I ran straight into a girl coming down the path.

"I'm sorry," I said. "I wasn't looking where I was going." I looked up at her face, and my heart stopped.

"Alex?" she said. "Alex Monroe?"

"Brenda?" It was impossible. "What are you doing here? I mean, in California?"

"I live here. We moved here at the end of my second year in high school. What are you doing here?"

"I'm planning to go to college here." I couldn't very well tell her I was looking for a Greek goddess.

"Me too," she smiled. "Wait, how come you never answered my letters? Was that your way of dumping me?"

"Dump you? I would never do that. I...uh...never considered us...together."

"You always were a little inexperienced, but I never thought you that naive. I practically committed social suicide by hanging around you. Didn't you know I was deeply attracted to you?"

"Me? You mean like boy, girl together?"

"Of course I mean boy, girl, silly. I never went out with anyone from Lindblom, even after you left. I kept hoping you'd return for me."

"But why are you here, today?"

"I don't know." She reached out and squeezed me in a big bear hug. "What does it matter? We found each other. It must be fate."

"So," I said as we parted, "you're a California girl now. Hang out at the beach?"

"Well, I love the water, but I don't do the beach and sun thing. I do a lot of hiking and climbing. I guess that's why I'm on this walk today." She kind of trailed off the last few words and stared at me.

Looking at her, she reminded me of April yesterday, with a radiant smile that seemed to invite you in. I took the plunge and kissed her softly. What I didn't expect was her reaction. She kissed me back with feeling.

"Wow, you've gotten a little more confidence," she smiled. "I like the new you."

After we kissed again, she asked, "I told my parents I would be back by lunch. Do you know what time it is?"

As I looked at my watch, the second hand passed the fifty-second mark after noon. I had forgotten the time difference and my promise to keep my watch at Central Standard Time. When I got to California I had absent-mindedly set it to California time while listening to the radio. It was now the exact hour of my birth, Chicago time.

"Alex?" she whispered. "I'm... I feel funny..." Her voice drifted off.

"Brenda? Are you okay?"

"Clotho," she whispered back. Her eyes had changed to a beautiful, deep emerald color. "My Eternal name is Clotho...and you are...Oceanus."

"I'm Oceanus?" I asked. "Then it worked! My god, and you ... But I'm not remembering anything! What unlocks that knowledge?"

"I can do some of that," Circe said, stepping from around the rock and embraced the two of us.

"Lachesis, I've so missed you," Brenda/Clotho said as she momentarily separated from me and embraced Circe.

"I like your new look," Circe cooed. "Especially the gold in that reddish brown hair."

"And now, the three of us celebrate," Brenda said, as she pulled me into them and kissed me. Her emerald eye color flashed with specks of amber, while strands of her hair took on more of a gold cast. At the same instant, Circe joined us in a three-way kiss I'd have thought impossible.

With the kiss, it all came rushing back to me. I was an Eternal, an explorer. My last mission, from the ruling council on Aldebaran thirty-five thousand years ago, was to come to Greece as part of Zeus's exploration team. However, there was much dissention that a former Pleiad—I was that Pleiad—was Zeus's chosen second in command. So I returned to Aotearoa ... But then it was hazy.

I looked at Brenda hopefully, the question in my eyes. Did she know I was a Pleiad?

"Yes, there was a reason for all of this," Brenda said. "You were selected for a future quest to locate and assist Zeus. He had left on a mission to civilize a planet right after the Greek experience on Earth so long ago and never returned. Your memories will return gradually. Over the next few years, Decima will assist you in getting a crew and will provide you with a cover mission to hide the secrecy behind your search for Zeus."

"Are we free to leave the park?" I asked. "What about those who pursue me?"

"Now the danger is past," Circe replied. "She doesn't realize it, but Hera has failed to prevent the three of us from putting the plan into motion."

Having not slept well the last night, and exhausted from the revelation, my eyes were heavy when we finally got to the large yellow tent and went inside. Apate, I noticed, was not there. I lay back on one of the cots, Clotho next to me, and fell asleep.

* * *

I was in a huge store. It bore a vague resemblance to a fancy, multi-storied department store in Chicago called Marshall Field's, but I honestly cannot describe this enormous edifice. I would go from one spot to another in the store, but I was unable to recall seeing anything or anyone specific, except for one girl. She seemed to be in many of the same locations I was in. However, I could never make out her features. It was like looking into a haze. I stood on a balcony that overlooked an enormous courtyard, and gazed down on an unending sea of sales counters with people crowding every inch of the store. What were they selling? I had no idea. How many floors? I had no idea.

Upon walking into an area that appeared to be outside the building, I found people waiting to catch an elevator to other floors. The location was dark, and the elevators were small and hard to catch. They didn't always stop, and when they did, they were frequently full. When there was room on one, the crowd around me would surge, and I would be pushed away. When I finally caught one, I found myself alone in the strange contraption. It shrank down to just big enough for me, and then shot straight up to a higher floor. I crawled out of the elevator and looked down from between two columns, down into what seemed like black nothingness.

One second I was staring down into the black night, the next I was back in the store. I stood in front of stairs that seemed to float in the air.

Trying to get to another floor, I walked up the set of stairs, and suddenly they ended with no way to proceed any further. When I looked back down, it seemed impossible to retrace my steps. It was at least twenty feet back to the floor. When I looked right or left, I saw stairs continuing on up and a set going down, but they were at least ten feet away. I seemed to be marooned on the isolated stair.

Again I was whisked away, and now stood by what looked like an escalator going up. Suddenly, I was being pushed by some unseen person onto it, moving steps with no handrails.

The ride ended with the same results as the floating stair, dropping me in a high place with the next escalators about ten feet away and no apparent way to get to them. Somehow, the shadowy girl managed to successfully navigate this strange place and now stood next to me.

"You have been brought here as it is the only place we feel safe to talk," she suddenly spoke to me. "My name is Nona. I'm the youngest sister of the Parcae."

"Where is here?" I asked.

"Our planet's name is unimportant. It's in the constellation Taurus."

"And the bridge? Is it from your planet too?" I asked.

"No, that was on your home world. You'll recall all of that when the timing is right. I need to explain something else now." She took a deep breath as the stairs and escalators moved around us, and then began.

"Zeus is a planetary explorer who leads teams to civilize new worlds. After his time on your Earth, he went on a mission to another planet to set up that planet for a future migration. Zeus had no intention of returning from that mission until the colonization was completed, and he knew Hera would probably hope he was forgotten during that time. She has always wanted to rule alone. So, thirty-five thousand Earth years ago, when he left, a plan was developed to locate Zeus after a suitable time had passed. Zeus left one of his most trusted explorers behind to command part of that mission. That person was instrumental in setting up the great civilization on Earth called Lemuria, but has since gone through many

anonymous lifetimes. It is now time for him to assemble his crew for the mission to discover the whereabouts of Zeus.

"Over the next few months, possibly years, you will come in contact with a number of Eternals. Some mean you harm and others will aid you. Eventually, four of them will be chosen to go with you in your quest."

"Me?" I thought. "Why me?"

"You are that explorer. The person Zeus has entrusted with this mission. You would be tempted to choose all three Moirae sisters to accompany you. And, although the three are eligible, they cannot all be on your team. The Parcae will save you the problem of you having to choose by making certain choices for you. The Moirae choice will be your final team member."

"Why would that be a problem for me?" I thought.

"Because you think yourself in love with all three, and would be very sad to choose only one of them. We will allow you to choose the other three participants. However, if it proves difficult, the Parcae can make the choices for you. All those involved, besides the Moirae, will come in contact with you at some time over the next few years. They will not know why they do so; however, it is for you to decide which you trust. I, or Decima, will come to you as I do now, to tell you when you must choose. In these matters you may count on our assistance.

"When you wake, this vision will not be recalled except when one of us appears to you, so that there will be no danger of another Eternal scanning your mind and learning of our meeting. Once you have your Eternal abilities, there will be no need for our aid in covering your memories. Do you understand?"

I nodded, then woke up.

CHAPTER 16
CLOTHO'S REVELATIONS

I awoke in the tent I shared with Clotho and Circe, numb with the knowledge that Brenda, the girl I had befriended at my first high school in Chicago, was Clotho, the missing Moirae sister. Now I could see why it had to be me that found her. As I pondered this realization, she came over and sat on the cot that held my sleeping bag.

"I'm so happy to have finally found you," she remarked.

"I thought you'd be happier to have discovered your Eternal heritage," I replied.

"You are naïve. Don't you remember the great times we had back around our Chicago neighborhood?"

"I didn't think you'd remember me, let alone those times," I said.

"Are you kidding? I used to ride downtown with you, remember? We walked from school to Garfield Boulevard. Sometimes we'd walk, and sometimes we took the streetcar, down to State Street and then downtown. You used to like to go visit that hobby shop with the train layout in the loop, and as my treat for going with, you always took me for coffee to Marshall Field's. The Walnut Room, remember?"

Unable to believe she remembered that, I nodded.

"I loved Garfield Boulevard with all those tropical plants in the summer." Her eyes were alight with recall. "What were those flowering trees called?"

"Oleanders," I said.

"Remember how we used to watch them dig them up before winter, then replant them in the spring?" She was excited with the memory.

"We used to go to that little store on the corner of your block," I said. "Wasn't it Angelina's?"

"Yep. I heard it's all gone now." She got sullen. "My friend, Anna Stapleton, said Angelina's closed down. It couldn't compete with the big supermarkets. She said the boulevard no longer has those trees and they don't even keep it that clean anymore. You remember Anna?"

I nodded. "Yeah, cheerleader. She used to call me, 'that wimp.'"

"Sorry, I forgot that." She then leaned over and planted a kiss on my cheek. "I thought I'd never see you again, and now this. We're both Eternals."

"Do you have any idea of what's going on?" I asked.

Clotho explained what she now realized had been implanted in her thousands of years ago.

"Apparently it was planned that you and I meet at this point in time," she clarified. "I don't know if it was intended that it be in Chicago at Lindblom High School, or that you move away and find me here."

"Who set this mission up?" I asked. "That's not yet in my recall."

"Zeus's brother, Poseidon, is responsible for our being thrown together and for your future search," Clotho replied. "Lachesis and Atropos were not privy to those details. This happened a very long time ago. My involvement was much by accident."

"How long have you been involved?"

"After being born to Zeus and Nyx, I was only fifteen and in my first life on Earth. One day—this was before the Eternals left Earth to return to Aldebaran—I was alone in the house with Zeus and his brother, Poseidon. Hera wasn't around and, since Poseidon used to always treat me like a grownup, I was allowed to be with them when Zeus brought it up."

"Brought what up?" I asked. "Wait a minute. You were fifteen? I thought—

"The age thing doesn't apply to the first year we're on a new world. The three of us had to approve our being born on Earth, and we realized our being Eternals at age five. At that time, we could have asked to be reborn somewhere else. On subsequent births, we would recover our memories at seventeen. Zeus brought up that they were planning the return to Aldebaran. The council there had contacted him about going to a new planet. He told Poseidon he was ready to leave, but he feared that they wouldn't return from the new expedition for eons, maybe never. He suspected that Hera would do whatever she could to see that the rest of his plan was forgotten."

"Rest of his plan?" I asked.

"Yes, there was more, but I don't remember what it was. Anyway, together they planned a secret future mission for someone to come after them."

"They wouldn't return?" I said. "They planned their own rescue?"

"They never called it a rescue. Since Poseidon was leaving too, they thought that the plans for the relief mission—that's what he called it, a relief mission—should remain with someone who was not returning to Aldebaran with the rest of the party. Poseidon knew that Nyx had planned to run away with her daughters, so he suggested me."

"You?" I said. "Why?"

"I was always his favorite of 'Nyx's girls,' as he called us. He also said he had an idea for who should be in charge of the actual mission. I guess that was you, an eternal from Mu. That's what he called Lemuria."

"I don't understand why it had to be someone secretly on Earth," I said.

"Aldebaran is very mentally challenging, they told me. It was relatively impossible to keep a secret there from lifetime to lifetime, as they are all Eternals. Here on Earth, humans go from life to life relatively unscanned. Putting the secret in an Eternal who would be lost in time was the only answer, Zeus had said. They just needed another Eternal to unlock those memories. And, of course, one of the Fates to unlock the secret in that Eternal." Clotho smiled.

"So they picked you as the Eternal to do the unlocking?"

"And you, a non-Greek Eternal, as the one lost in time. Remember, I was fifteen. I had no idea what this Eternal stuff was they talked about. Poseidon said it wasn't important; they were just putting instructions in my brain that would awaken at the right time—now. I had no idea that thousands of years and many lifetimes would pass. Even when my Eternal memories came back each time I was reborn, I was still ignorant of your quest. "

"And me." Circe joined us. "I was the Fate. Celaeno and her sister, Merope, were involved as backups, too. If someone discovered part of the plan, they would not suspect Pleiads to be involved."

"Why wouldn't they suspect a Pleiad?" I asked. I had not shared with them the knowledge that I was long ago a Pleiad. They obviously did not know that, so I assumed it was still blocked from anyone reading my mind. I recalled Pollux telling me that Clotho was a Pleiad who had done the full conversion to human. Did she recall that?

"The Pleiads were not a part of the Eternal scene back then, and they have always been shunned by other Eternals jealous of their beauty," Circe revealed. "However, among the Eternals, Clotho was always the exception. If not for her, the Seven Sisters would have returned to their home planets eons ago."

With those words, Circe pulled Clotho over and hugged her tight. "I've so missed you," she added when they parted. "Decima told me that it was actually Poseidon who had put those latent plans in various Eternals and set them to come to light at this time."

"Various Eternals?" I said.

"Yes, including you, Celaeno, Iris, Circe, Decima and me," Clotho said. "Decima was the first to become aware of the plan, as she had to make sure that Iris, Celaeno, you and I were all born together in the Chicago area. Then she had to arrange for Iris and Celaeno to become aware just before your incident in the railyard. Iris was the real watchdog, as she has been born near you in every life since this plan was conceived. Although no knowledge of this expedition was within her, Poseidon had ensured that if the plan were prematurely discovered somehow, she would be there to protect you. You knew her in Germany and here, but usually she was unknown to you, just close by in case she was needed.

"Finally, Circe and you had to awaken the memories in me in the park, and by our three-way kiss, we stirred the recollections in you. Everyone else was clueless and just along for the ride. Some had minor roles, but only five of us were tasked with the actual quest. It was up to the Parcae to add others if we needed them. Like Apate. She was Circe's choice. The attraction between the two of you was not planned, but Decima noticed it right away. That's why she let her lead you to the meeting spot."

"Wait," I replied. "How did Zeus even know me?"

"It's strange that your past life memories have not returned," Clotho replied. "I know he knew of you in Lemuria. I guess we'll have to wait until either your memories return or you find him to discover the reason."

"I was not involved at the beginning," Circe acknowledged. "I really showed up at your school clueless. When I realized that Iris was Heike, it tripped something in my brain, and before I left Irene's apartment, Decima told me I was deeply involved. Decima is in charge, but I was tasked with the direct responsibility for the successful conclusion of this initial part of the plan. I had to see that you arrived at the place where you might find Clotho, and by the three-way kiss, facilitate the recollection of our involvement. To cover my role, Decima let on that I had been dismissed for getting too close to you."

"I'm still in the dark," I said. "Wait. You knew that Iris was Heike?"

"Yep. When I called her on it she told me to keep my big fat mouth shut. Decima echoed that in nicer terms."

"What about Iris? Is she further involved in all this? I just spent several years in school with her. Was her only role to guard me during my lifetimes? And how is Celaeno involved in all this? Not much of a role to just ignore me in high school. You didn't mention either of them."

Circe and Clotho just stared at me, and I knew. Neither they, nor I, knew the complete plan.

* * *

An hour or so later came a sweet female voice in my head. "At last. It's Decima, Alex. Now that you are once again an Eternal, I can speak to you directly."

"I'm not an Eternal yet, I don't think." I thought the words in my head. "I don't have any memories of past lives or who I am."

"Part of your past lives will be restored when you consummate the relationship with the woman who is to share this life with you. That will happen soon."

"Why is that a mystery?" I asked.

"While those that would see this mission fail monitor known Eternals, they do not yet monitor you. Putting you with someone known to be connected with this expedition puts it at risk."

"What about Apate?" I asked. "They wouldn't suspect her."

"And just what do you think would happen if Apate was called by Eris to do a mission involving you? Apate is valuable in the position she is in. Trusted by Eris. We cannot put her at risk."

Disappointed, I grew quiet.

"As to more of who you are, that will be restored by you being kissed by the right person. That person will then recognize you. It has been my pleasure to serve Zeus in this way. It will be up to you to locate him in the future." Decima then exited my head.

That evening we drove to Circe's apartment, which was in the town of Big Bear, near San Bernardino and Riverside. She lived up in a mountainous area, where there were few houses.

When I commented on its remoteness, she said she liked privacy.

"Remember Irene's room?" Circe asked. "Her pictures?"

"I remember her bed," I replied.

"I want to show you my favorite picture," she said. "The bed can wait."

The walls of her little refuge were hung with different pictures and paintings, seemingly from different eras. They were primarily of her and her sisters, but there was a fourth girl who always seemed to look away from the camera.

"That oddball is Celeano," Circe said from behind me. "As you can see, she hates to have her picture taken, and back then she had just mastered the shimmer cloud to further hide her form. She hardly ever appears anywhere anymore except as some other identity. Like at your high school, where she was Patty Zerbean. I forgot her name in this shimmer."

I glanced over and was astonished to see a painting that I immediately recognized as done by Claude Monet. It was a variation of his painting, *Women in a Garden*, only the women were Circe, her sisters and one other. A short distance away was a very old photograph of Claude Monet standing on a bridge over his garden at Giverny. Standing next to him was a beautiful girl that was unmistakably Circe. I thought this was impossible, but it didn't look like it was faked.

Circe's voice broke into my thoughts. "I thought you might still not be taking me seriously in my explanation of my history," she said. "That's the main reason why I invited you up tonight."

"But this is impossible," I replied. "Monet died in 1926. This photograph..."

"Taken at Giverny in 1922," she said, and then nodded to the oil painting. "He did that painting especially for me. I had told him my favorite of his was *Women in a Garden* in which he used his wife, Camille, as the subject. He said if he'd have had such lovely subjects as the Moirae or Pleiad sisters, he would have included us. Three months later, that painting was delivered to me. He also had re-done the original using the Seven Sisters as the women. Merope has that one. Here in mine, he painted me sitting on the grass and looking at him. That's Clotho smelling flowers and Irene doing the dance in the background. The one in profile next to the tree who is sticking her tongue out is Celaeno, who happened to be with us that day. That girl is a real treat in her shimmers. She must have half a dozen now. I've always treasured the painting. Oscar was like a father to me. We met when I was briefly dating his son Michel in 1915. While that relationship didn't last; my friendship with his father did."

"But you were only..."

"I was around twenty. I was living with my sisters and Iris then at Giverny in France. In 1922, the Seven Sisters, each trying out a new shimmer, were on their way to visit Nyx in Germany. I asked them to detour to Giverny for a mini-vacation. That's when they met Oscar, and he did this painting and the one for Merope. Celaeno stuck around with us for a time. She ended up joining us in that trip to Germany the following year. The rest you should know."

I was stunned by all of this. How could she retain these mementos when...?

"Relax, Alex," she put her hand on my shoulder. "I have a semi-permanent home in Paris. Before I die, I send all of my things back there. In the following lifetime, when I age to the point where my memories return and I'm living on my own, some of my possessions, collected over various lifetimes, are returned to me. I pick and choose what I want and where I live. In this lifetime, I chose to be born in Giverny in 1900, moved to Paris in 1925, to the United States in 1945 and came to California in 1956. The rest of this existence is already planned, but it's not for you to know."

"But what if you die unexpectedly? You said that was possible." I asked.

"Other Eternals would take care of it. We're all pretty tight. They would know what to do."

Later that evening, I found myself alone. It appeared that everyone but Circe had left. Circe finally came over and led me upstairs.

"You can stay in my room tonight," she grinned. "Enjoy the bed."

We had stopped by the painting, which somehow seemed different.

"I don't understand," I said. "Is this the picture I saw before?"

"It's been changed," she replied. "You see, the figures in it can move about, if they like."

She chuckled at my cluelessness, then said, "I'll make us breakfast in the morning."

After she left, I turned back to the picture to find that all but one were still in the same pose as before. Clotho no longer smelled the flowers and seemed to be speaking with a Pleiad. I assumed the beautiful creature had turned off her shimmer and it was Celaeno. They stood by the tree, now staring out of the picture and smiling at me.

"Someone wants to see you, Alex." Clotho said the words from the picture.

"Who?" I asked. Why was I talking to a painting?

I was surprised when the Pleiad in the painting, Celaeno, suddenly appeared next to me. She squeezed her tiny blue self between me and the painting, stood on tiptoes, and kissed my cheek, then clutched me around my neck and pulled me down to her. "Welcome to our world," she said softly, and then kissed me passionately on the lips.

There was a rainbow of colors in my head and the memory of having a birth sister poured into me. Her face was obscured in my vision, but I realized she and I had come to this planet millions of years ago. While I continued to stare into Celaeno's eyes, her face registered a huge smile.

"Oceanus," she said. The picture in my head of my birth sister focused into...Celeano. "I knew someday I'd find you," she said. "I love you, my twin." With that she hugged me tightly.

"Surprised?" she said. "Disappointed?"

"Disappointed? No, just confused."

"Let's sit," she said, and pulled me to a stuffed chair in one corner. I did, and was instantly whisked away to that huge store.

* * *

This time I was standing in front of what looked like a jewelry counter. I was amazed because, in my previous experience within the store, I had never been able to remember seeing any merchandise. I knew right away this time would be different. I could hear voices, see things.

When I wondered if the elevators were still where I had found them before, I was shocked to see the girl behind the jewelry case turn and smile at me.

"Can I help you, sir?" She had a slight grin on her face, as if she knew something I didn't.

"No," I said, "I was just looking for—"

"Decima." She whispered it like I should have known. "I am Morta. You want to talk to my sister, Decima. Go out to the elevators and take the express up to the roof. She'll meet you there."

"Thanks," I nodded. I turned in the direction she pointed. As I walked, I had the sensation of floating. Coming to the elevator doors, I pushed what I thought represented the up button, a sun with the rays pointed upward as opposed to the other button where the rays pointed down. The doors instantly opened. I floated inside, almost striking the back wall before I managed to stop. I came back forward and hit the highest button, which I assumed would take me to the roof. The doors closed with a 'swoosh' and the elevator shot upwards. Then it came to a sudden stop and the doors opened.

I stepped out into darkness. There was a crunching sound as I walked on the roof material. In my previous encounter, there was no sound. I didn't see anyone at first, so I went toward the edge of the building. I had to be careful, as I seemed to glide instead of walk, and I didn't want to end up going over the edge. All I could see was blackness, except for some pinpoints of light below.

"It's two miles straight down." I turned at the sound of the voice.

"Decima?" I said.

"Things should now be a little clearer, but I will try to make them more so. You talked to my sister Nona previously, and were told that Zeus picked you to find him if he failed to return from his last mission many years ago."

"Shouldn't this 'rescue' have been launched thousands of years ago?" I pointed out. "Aren't we a little late?"

"This mission was many thousands of years in the making and execution. This is the time that he requested us to awaken you to your destiny. You may have heard others mention a 'plan,' but no one really knows what that is. Rumors have always persisted among the Eternals of a great event happening

around this time. This is that event, and you will lead it. However, note that you will join Zeus, not rescue him."

"Join him?"

"You are to assist him in completing what he started. You have been in contact with each person he considered capable of making this mission a success. You will pick three of them. I will add one of the Moirae to accompany you."

"I assume the ones I pick are needed for a purpose. What if I pick the wrong people?"

"Zeus is confident in your judgement. There is a separate mission concurrent with yours. A sort of cover mission, as no one must know of yours. While you are the overall leader, it will have its own Eternal in charge. At the appropriate time, you will meet with that assignment leader to coordinate your missions. Like you, she is an unknown Eternal and will have a crew of both Eternals and Earth humans. She has also been handpicked by Zeus and Poseidon.

"For your protection, I will temporarily keep all knowledge of this mission secret from you to avoid prying scans. Each time I appear to you, you will instantly remember all of our previous planning.'

* * *

I awoke to Celaeno perched on the arm of the chair. "You've probably wondered what the reason was for me being at your school. Decima originally chose me to be your companion in this life. She thought that as a Pleiad I'd not be considered a threat. However, neither of us knew you were my long-lost brother. So, while Decima reconsiders that, we can still spend the night together—platonically. You can ask me anything. But first I want to show you that wild Lachesis's crazy bed."

She then pulled me over to the bed in the middle of the room. "Go on the other side." She poked me in the ribs to get me moving.

I walked over to the far side of the bed. I had expected something like what I had experienced at Irene's apartment, but I was surprised to find that it looked like a normal Earth vintage, king-sized bed.

"Not quite." She smiled in response to my thoughts. "Pull back the spread and take a closer look."

When I pulled back the sheet, I was surprised to see it looked like a bed of sand. Across from me, Celaeno was gesturing at the sparkling grains. "It's not sand; it's queezium from a distant star system. While it looks like sand, it's actually sort of a quasi-liquid with amazing properties. While you sleep it'll massage your skin and, like crystals, has healing powers. Once we Eternals reach the age of memory restoration, we don't really need it, but it is nice to sleep in. And don't worry, it's very porous, even though it doesn't look so. You can breathe even if you're lying face down in it. Want to know the most amazing thing?"

"Yes," I said. "Impress me."

"Oh, you want to be impressed, huh?" She looked down at the bed, and then looked me up and down. "Turn the other way," she said.

I did as she asked, and then turned back to face her at her command. When I did, I saw only her head sticking out from the sand-like material. The gown she had been wearing was draped over the top of the bedpost.

"I don't understand," I said. "What am I supposed to be seeing?"

"Correction. Not seeing," she smiled. "I'm almost sans clothes under here, Alex. And yet you, standing there right next to me, can't see me. That is, unless I want you to see me."

"Or, I want you to see her." Circe had quietly come up behind me. "So I'm wild, am I, Blue Girl? Are you ready to be really impressed, Alex?"

"Yes," I said, a bit eagerly.

"Queezium can be thought controlled," she said. "It has two states. You now see the sand state, but don't forget she said it was a quasi-liquid; it has a state almost like water. Clear water."

Then, amazingly, the sand turned into what looked like a crystal clear liquid. And frowning in full view of me was an almost naked Celaeno. She only wore what looked like panties, a thin, midnight blue piece of material. The tiny garment left little to the imagination. Just as quickly as she had turned the bed to water, it was back to sand.

"Lachesis, are you insane?" Celaeno said loudly. "And you, Alex, you looked a little too eager." She broke into a smile. "I'm your sister, remember?"

"You were his sister. That was millions of years ago. Turn around, Alex, so she can get dressed and out of here."

* * *

"I hope you didn't mind my little demonstration," Lachesis laughed after Celaeno scampered out. I heard her bare feet pounding away.

"Decima didn't want to disturb you further, so I thought I'd come and tell you: for now, you're by yourself. Your life companion will have to be reconsidered. And, Decima soundly rejected my volunteering to show you the intricacies of my bed, so you sleep alone. Night, Oceanus."

She smiled and left, shutting the door behind her.

* * *

The next morning, when I woke up, I saw Celaeno in the doorway.

"Good, you're awake. Come down when you get dressed. We're waiting."

I didn't bother to ask who, just got dressed and hurried down. In the kitchen, I found Celaeno, Lachesis (Circe), Iris and Clotho sitting around the table.

"Iris was never fond of the name Susan, so she prefers you call her Iris," Clotho said. "Circe and I prefer our current names, so call me Brenda. Your sister wants you to call her—"

"Sis," Celaeno said. "Or what you called me when we were growing up. Peanut."

A little shocked at the gathering, I nodded.

"Are you disappointed in how things turned out?" Brenda suddenly asked.

"Disappointed? No, I'm with my favorite people in the universe. I'd like to know though, what's your story? What happened in Germany? You must recall that life now."

"When Decima came to me back in Germany, after you died in that crash, all I knew was that you, as Herman, were a suspected Eternal and there would be a need for me to terminate my life then and be reborn on the same day you were. She told me of us meeting in high school, and that seemingly being abandoned by you would be the key to my being ignored by those that would do harm to your important quest. My memory of being an Eternal would be lost until you found me later. Of course, I didn't remember any of that until we got our memories back in the park. I had no idea of the eventual level of my involvement or that the quest was this important."

"Are *you* disappointed, now?" I asked.

"Are you kidding? No," she said.

I felt a knot loosen in my stomach that I had not been aware of until then. "You told me you were there when this was planned. Tell me about it."

Brenda began, "After Zeus disappeared on that mission to civilize a planet that had previously been seeded, it was a thousand years before a follow-up operation was launched. That research party, I was a part of it, found no signs of Zeus's civilizing team, but they did an initial catalogue of the planet. After that the council on Aldebaran suspended expeditions to civilize distant worlds. They needed little encouragement in reaching that decision, as it is extremely expensive to launch physical beings into space. The alternative is spirit travel, but that is very time intensive."

"How do you mean?"

"Spirits can travel the great distances almost instantly, but must take residence within a life-form on that planet without delay. That's why there are always seeding missions and civilizing missions first."

"How long does it—" I started to ask.

"It takes years to fully learn the ways of the life-form you reside in on each world. After you have gained the knowledge of that species, you are reborn as that organism. Several life cycles are then needed to actually transition to being that creature."

"Did you know how I was involved in all this back then?" I recalled that Decima had warned me it would take considerable time before they would feel safe enough to enable my memories of the past.

"I'm getting there," she said. "When the council met again after having made that 'No More Expeditions' decision, Poseidon schooled you in what to say and urged you to attend."

"I went before the council on Aldebaran?"

Brenda turned to Iris. "He wants the whole story," Brenda told her. "You tell it. You were there."

"The Council on Aldebaran? Yes, I was there," Iris said. "Poseidon dared not go himself, so he sent me because I, as her sometimes messenger, would not be considered a danger to Hera. I sat unnoticed in the gallery and watched as this brash young Eternal entered. You," she poked my chest, "implored the council to allow you to continue explorations in the Orion sector."

She turned to me so that we were face to face and pretended to imitate my voice. "'There are still many unexplored areas. And always some unique species of life that needs a new planet to go to. That has been my chosen field of work. Exploration and resettlement will always be needed.' I had no idea back then that this outspoken Eternal would turn out to be Celaeno's twin brother."

"I said all that? Did it do any good?"

"Your efforts to have the council fund future explorations were rebuffed, but because of the publicity of those efforts, the ruling body from the planet of Flammeria came to you. They offered to pay to outfit a ship for you and a crew to tame a portion of a planet for a small, fairy-like race called Distans. The Distans' home planet had been heavily harvested of its natural resources, and the few that were left had come under the care of the Flammerians, who hid them somewhere here, on Earth. Decima told me it was on the east coast of the United States. The Distans possess some unique capabilities valued by certain humanoids, and fearing for their continued safety, Flammeria sought and found a relatively uninhabited planet in the constellation Serpentarius orbiting the star Wolf 1061 that would meet their needs. That was our name for the constellation. I think Earth astronomers now call it Ophiuchus. It just happens to be the planet that Zeus was sent to civilize."

I nodded in understanding, and she continued. "When Flammeria pledged to finance your mission, the council quickly approved it and agreed on a start date around the Earth year 2025. There will be a Flammerian woman in charge of their secret Earth station at that time, and you are to meet with her in the Earth year 2020."

"Wait," I interrupted. "How do they know that this woman will be in charge sixty-some years from now?"

"Just who do you think you're dealing with? I'm Iris, I know these things. She's an Eternal that has just been reborn to Flammerian parents with that mission implanted in her. She won't be conscious of being an Eternal until she gets to that planet near Wolf 1061. Now, your sister wants to tell you about what she went through herself, coming to Earth."

"Are you doing okay with all this, so far?" Celaeno asked as she walked over and took the seat that Iris vacated for her.

After I nodded, she started her tale.

"You know the ones that are now my Eternal sisters and I came to Earth over a million years ago. After looking for you everywhere, we finally moved to the area around Greece thirty-five thousand years ago as celestial nymphs, but of the Pleiad race. Unlike you, we refused to change our look, because it reflected our heritage."

"But you weren't really sisters, I mean, back where we came from?"

"No, except for Merope, who you know was our baby sister on Celaeno. You do remember that little rock was our home world?"

I didn't, but I nodded and she continued.

"The seven of us came as Pleiad sisters, and you were my actual twin brother who chose to migrate to Lemuria as human. As my Eternal brother, I trust those memories will one day return to you. The seven of us, as did you, came from small planets located in the Pleiad system. You went to Lemuria and assumed the human form, but our request to continue in the natural form of Pleiads after converting from the spirit world clashed with what was allowed by the then council, and we were eventually banned to the mountains of Greece.

"Poseidon discovered us there, and after he heard our tale, personally approved our request to remain as Pleiads, with the stipulation that we be very cautious in showing our true form to humans. He and Zeus suggested we only interact with Eternals. At least, that was our experience with the civilization of Greece. There were Pleiads in other places on Earth, including with you on Lemuria and in Atlantis, but we had no direct contact with them. Zeus guided us through the process of transforming to our particular version of the humanoid body. Spirit migrators who preferred to stay on land had a choice back then of assuming a human or cat body, while some who were nymphs of the sea or ocean, called Oceanids, could choose to migrate to a creature of that realm, mostly whales, dolphins or sharks. Some celestial nymphs could choose to be eagles. Zeus, however, convinced all seven of us to choose the female human form, albeit a special blue one. We were among his most loyal subjects for many years. Until he left."

"I don't understand the attraction of Zeus to all nymphs," I cut into her story.

"Zeus is everything a female wants in a human. He's kind of like you, in ways. I assumed that's why so many of the Eternal women felt attracted to you. They can sense certain qualities in you, ones I remembered from our childhood. We seven have remained very close after that first Greek experience, and have been reincarnated together through all of our lifetimes. We long ago made a choice to stay in our own strata of society. However, with the aid of shimmer clouds, Alcyone, Merope, and I have finally chosen to take Zeus's advice and meet other Eternals. Starting in our last life, the three of us also began to live in Earth's world."

"You said Merope is our baby sister? That remembrance has not surfaced."

"Yes, millions of years ago. Merope's first foray into the social order of the Eternals was with the seven of us in Giverny. She met you in Germany where you were Herman. She shimmered under the name of Nicolette Green. You two were quite cozy for a while."

"So Merope was Nicolette and she knew me in Germany?" I asked.

"Let me tell the story! You were first enthralled by a girl named Heike, whom you now know was..."

"Iris," I said as she waved to me from next to the refrigerator.

"Yes, the two of you met at a meeting regarding the secret flying boomerang war machine you were to be the test pilot of. All of those psychic German women fascinated you." Her hand came down and tugged playfully at my nose. "Even though you were twenty-two years old, because of the block that had already been implanted, you had not recovered your Eternal memories of who they, or you, really were."

"Did I meet you there?"

"No, I did not go to any meetings with humans. It was attended only by Eris along with Heike. You were immediately drawn to Heike's very long, reddish blonde hair and her beautiful face."

"Don't forget I had those sparkling green eyes," Iris called over.

"Like jade," Celaeno called back to Iris, and then returned her attention to me. "You had no idea then that she was Iris. At our Eternal meetings, back then in France, they all laughed about your complete surrender to Iris's beauty. I got jealous hearing about it, because Iris seemed to attract all the males, and I was always hidden in the background. Even though I had never been with a human male, I began to wonder if I could catch one with my shimmer cloud. So, one night, I asked Eris.

"She laughed and said, 'Truth be known, you're the prettiest female of us all, Celaeno. And our little Iris needs a lesson in humility. So yes, go for it.'"

As I listened to her words, I suddenly recalled how I had chased after Iris, and through that beautiful creature eventually met...

"You," I said aloud. "You and I had a secret affair..."

"Yes, I used the Luna Mist shimmer."

"You never revealed yourself as a Pleiad back then," I said.

"Of course not. I only slept with you, as Luna, because of Eris's encouragement. I had no idea you were my long-lost twin brother. However, sleeping with you awakened the beginnings of a plan in me that had been put in place thousands of years ago. Shortly afterwards, Clotho came to Germany with the Moirae, and in our very first contact, we looked at each other and both recalled we were part of some future plan instilled in us by Zeus. Everyone else was in the dark. Including, of course, you and any other little Eternal nymph you picked up along the way." Her hands came down and playfully slapped my cheeks.

"I think you exaggerate."

"I think not. You were a sly one back then, a veritable lady's man. Do you recall when you secretly—at least you thought it was clandestine—met Heike one day at her parents' apartment while they were at some Nazi rally?"

The memory of Heike slipping off her clothes that day and whisking her beautiful hair across my equally naked body filled my head.

"Her assignment from Eris, who was leery of you, was to find out which Eternal you were. However, Heike was Iris, and even back then, as part of the plan, she protected your identity."

"Iris knew who I was?"

"Back then?" Iris shouted as she came away from the refrigerator holding a plate of sandwiches she had made. "Of course not. I did it unknowingly. It was all preprogrammed into me by Poseidon. Sandwiches, anyone?"

As I waved to Iris, in response to her sandwich request, Celaeno gripped my chin and shook me.

"She told Eris that she could only read one lifetime in you," Celaeno smiled. "That usually signified you were not an Eternal, just a normal Earth human. Of course, we now know that was because of the block placed on you."

CHAPTER 17
PICKING MY CREW

I later found that Pleiads—most of us, anyway—were not the only ones who had decided not to adopt human characteristics. Decima and her Parcae sisters had also rejected the idea of human type bodies, or any other for that matter. They remained on their spirit home world, which was located somewhere in the constellation we call Taurus. From that point on, I continued mental contact with Decima, and she removed several additional mind blocks.

She reiterated that the mission we were on was conceived by Zeus and Poseidon years ago. It was to be put into actuality if Zeus hadn't returned from his voyage to a planet in the star Wolf 1061's system by this time.

Hera had been overjoyed with the disappearance of Zeus, and had circulated the tale that his ship was lost somewhere in space, which would prevent his rebirth in the known universe. However, Zeus had apparently not planned to return. Whatever his reasons, he placed his trust to carry out his goals in several of his most favored Fate children: Decima of the Parcae, Clotho of the Moirae, Celaeno of the Pleiads and his faithful messenger, Iris.

I was a fledgling explorer on Lemuria back then, and he had selected me to lead the quest because of my limited exposure to the political climate of Aldebaran. Decima reiterated what Clotho had told me: that there had been an exploratory trip to Wolf 1061, a thousand years later. They found little trace of his party, but based on conversations with the indigenous people of the planet, it was certain that Zeus did arrive there. But there was no recollection of his leaving. No one knew where he might have gone. My job would be to find and make contact with him.

So what had happened that night in the railyard? I mentally posed the question to Decima. She told me that despite Zeus's precautions, Hera had always known there might be what she thought a rescue attempt. While Hera didn't know the specifics of the Zeus plan, she had always assumed that either Pollux or I would be involved.

After I was considered lost to the Eternals, Hera couldn't track me as Oceanus. But she could track Pollux, and eventually, in this lifetime, through Eris she found me.

Although she did not know for certain who I was, my friendship with Mark, who Hera knew was Pollux, made me a target of her wrath. Suspicious of my relationship with Pollux, she had used Iris to relay a message to Ker, who was another of Nyx's offspring that had migrated to Hera's side. She was instructed to stage an accident in which I was run over, then to do the same to Pollux/Mark. Whatever our role, we would then be lost to any plan, and Hera assumed it would die with us.

To maintain her trusted position, Iris relayed the message. But she also stepped in and alerted Mark, and then planned to take control of my senses to save me. Celaeno, as Patty, was always part of Zeus's alternate backup plan, however, and it was she who ratcheted up my hearing and planted in me the suspicion of something amiss that night in the freight yard. Decima explained what I had partially figured out. It was Eris's voice projected through Moe, while the voice from my left was apparently Iris, pretending to be her consort to cover up the fact that she was actually on my side. The overhead voice, of course, was Decima. Upon hearing this, I recalled Moe's words, 'that little blue wench.' When Patty saw me in school the next day, her mind was blocked to the deed she had performed the night before.

* * *

Almost a year after, Brenda, Circe and I met by the pool in Sequoia National Park, I drove alone to Red Rock Canyon. The desert landscape, located about twenty-five miles from Mojave, where I had stopped with Merope, had become a place I went to for communications with Decima. She recalled me to the area whenever she wished to guarantee our conversation was private. Something about one of the rocks possessing strange properties. I think she called it a scatterer. I was in a foul mood that morning, as I had been rebuffed by Clotho who I had met with earlier.

"It is time you know that Clotho and I have started preparations for you to lead the expedition to locate Zeus," Decima imprinted the words in my mind. By this time, I had also recalled my earlier experiences as a member of Zeus's team in the exploration of suitable planets.

"We are also in agreement that Pollux will be involved, but in a different capacity. I may reveal that to you later, but you must tell no one who he is or his mission." After a slight pause she continued. "We have important things to plan, and yet I have heard you're unhappy?"

"Did Clotho talk to you? Irene had Pollux, Circe's gone and I felt lonely. Clotho was there, and I was led to believe I'd live this life with someone, but you ruled out the Moirae, and Celaeno turned out to be my sister. I'll cope."

"I have already told you that you have previously expressed to one Eternal your undying love. Through all time, remember? Besides, all the others you came in contact with would raise alarms if you were to live with them. Did we not discuss this?"

"As you said, we have important things to discuss. I told you I'd cope. I don't want to discuss my love life with you." I said. I had no idea who she was talking about. Had I known then that my refusal meant that I would go years without a girlfriend, I might not have been so hasty.

I needed to change the subject, so I mentally asked, "Tell me again. Why did Zeus pick us for this?"

"You and Pollux are the most respected of Eternals. Hera never actually determined it was you in the railyard. Apate has the ear of Eris, and she has convinced her that you are most likely Castor, which is why Pollux was involved. So, Hera has been led to believe you were someone of no consequence who was lost to the world of Eternals when they left thousands of years ago. And now, to her, you have once again been lost.

"Zeus was always impressed that of all his faithful leaders, your group was the most loyal. To you and him. You always knew how to pick people for any given task." she continued. "Clotho and I have sampled opinions of the other female Eternals who were involved in the unveiling of your mission. There are next to none who would not jump at the chance to accompany you on your quest or to be with you in a life experience."

"I find that hard to believe," I replied. "I've been lost to the Eternals for thirty thousand years."

"And missed for thirty thousand years. Yet, when you returned, you aligned with the Moirae and the Seven Sisters of the Pleiads. The Moirae sisters are the most selective of all Greek Eternals in their relationships with males. But, they accept you. The Seven Sisters hardly ever mate with a male Eternal. However, today you could live with Celaeno or Merope, who, among the sisters, despised male Greek Eternals most of all."

"That's not exactly fair," I pointed out. I was embarrassed by all of her praise. "Celaeno and Merope are my sisters. What would you expect them to say? Enough talk of female Eternals. Exactly what is it you want me to do?"

"Your quest is to locate and join Zeus on the planet IO27. I assume, if you are successful in locating him, he will instruct you further. You will take an exploration party of five, all of which are female Eternals. There are few males left on Earth, besides Pollux, who can be trusted. The five will know that it might be a one-way trip. To avoid suspicion of Hera, Pollux cannot go with you, and we must mix the five who will accompany you."

"What do you mean?"

"You can't take five of the Pleiads, nor more than one of the Moirae. Your crew must be scatter picked, and include some trusted by Hera. I will assist you with that, and over this lifetime we will make the selections."

"Am I to die for this to happen?"

"No. No one knows I have granted you, Clotho, Iris, Circe, Merope, and Celaeno an extension of this lifetime. To avoid the suspicion of Hera, the new civilizing attempt had to be added to the long list of future events, and by my calculations it will not come up for approval for close to sixty-five Earth years. You, Celaeno, Iris and Clotho were all born in the Earth year 1939, and are now nineteen years old. Lachesis is much older, but that may be to your advantage. I will speak with her and see if she would prefer to be younger. You will continue to live here in California for at least five or six more years. Because as Eternals you do not age after twenty-five, you will need to move around every ten years. You are living your own life now, so the choice is yours.

"Over those years, you'll be picked to serve as crew on several other expeditions, which will result in you being selected to lead the one to Wolf 1061, contracted by the Flammerians. You may take one of the Sisters, and that will, I assume, be Celaeno. Merope will join Pollux on the mission that parallels yours, of which we will talk another time. To avoid you having to make a choice, Clotho has insisted on Lachesis being the Moirae on your crew. Clotho will be accompanying Pollux on his part of the mission. I search to find a way to include her that will not raise suspicion. The remaining three for your quest will be selected by you, Clotho and me over the next fifty or so years. They will make themselves known to you during that time."

* * *

In 1975, the first of our additional crew became apparent when a radiant Susan Stage reentered our lives while Patty (she had adapted to that name) and I lived in Glasgow, Montana. Clotho, as Brenda, lived nearby with Circe, and I visited them often. Patty and Susan had been invited to attend a reunion of the cheerleaders of our high school that had been planned to occur that year. However, neither Patty nor Susan could attend, as they still maintained their teenaged high school looks, while the others were now around forty-five years old. Of course, they could have gone with shimmer clouds, but instead, Susan and Patty, together with my ex-cheerleader, Brenda, had their own reunion at our home.

Before she left, Susan casually mentioned she'd see us in about fifty years. Later, Decima confirmed the choice of Iris as one of the crew, someone who would please Hera. It was something I had always suspected. What I did not realize at the time was that I had not seen the last of Susan.

* * *

1980 was a hard year. Irene told us that Pollux had died, but we were not to be sad as it was positioning him for the backup mission. Decima had never explained to me the mission of the backup crew. All she would tell me was that 'backup crew' was really a misnomer, and I'd find out at the right time.

* * *

In 1995, Circe, Patty and I lived in Singapore. Merope, as she often did, had left us for France, her favorite country. Brenda had moved to New York. While Patty and I still looked twenty-five, we were now actually fifty-seven years old. We had taken to privately calling Circe, who lived nearby, The Old Lady.

One day, while the three of us were at the Singapore Zoo, we boarded a tram that was being driven by a familiar face. The shimmer of one, anyway. April Sunshine, who I recalled was Apate, the girl who had twice beaten me to a pulp. She turned her gorgeous lilac eyes from Circe, to Patty and finally me, and winked.

"We're together in twenty-five years," she whispered to me.

Two days later, Decima confirmed that Apate was indeed the fourth member of my team. Another choice meant to please Hera, who was unaware of Apate's closeness to Circe. Hera kept close track on any expeditions, except those that had her minions as crew. Little did she know Apate was now my minion. Shortly after, Circe informed me she had made her decision. She had no desire to be the 'Old Lady.' She had herself scheduled to die in the year 2000 so she could be reborn and would be twenty-five for our mission. In that year, Clotho left New York for a week to be with Circe when it happened. I was heartbroken for days, until Irene called me and told me that I should realize I was an Eternal and sacrifices came with the territory.

* * *

In the year 2009, the two of us moved to London. A year later, Decima contacted me to meet her in a remote place. "I couldn't stop her," she revealed.

"Who are we talking about?" I asked.

"My little sister, Nona. She entered the human world in 2000 and is now nine years old on Earth."

"Why?" I asked. "I thought you three vowed to stay spirits."

"Nona had previously entered the conversion program, and even though she completed it, at the last minute she chose to remain with us. However, while assisting me in the selection of your crew, she became enthralled with your quest. When I labored over your fifth crewmember, she suggested that the unlikeliest choice would be someone new to the exploration world. Like herself. So, she is your fifth crew member."

"Are you opposed to her being—?"

"Sorry, that wasn't clear. I was opposed to her conversion, not to her being with you. Actually, that solves an important issue. I needed someone with Fate training on the mission, but I feared making it one of the Moirae to avoid suspicion. Nona is a natural fit, and an additional Fate to go along with Lachesis, who, you may be interested to know, is now a nine-year-old tomboy in New Haven, Connecticut. In addition, you now have Apate and Iris, both trusted by Hera, along with you and Celaeno. Which is further reason for Hera to discount your expedition, as she abhors Pleiads. Pollux's backup and recovery team will consist of six; besides Clotho, he has two other Eternals and two nymphs in the process of conversion to humans."

"Who are his other Eternals?" I asked.

"You know one is Merope, the other you'll learn in time. Meanwhile, I have one more request. I want you two to move early. By 2020, I need you to be back in the states, preferably somewhere in the southwest. Nona is working on a surprise for you."

* * *

By 2017 we had moved to New Mexico, and I was hardly surprised when a slightly beat-up silver Valiant appeared at our ranch one day. A black-haired beauty, wearing a jeweled top, jumped out from behind the wheel and said, "Guess what I found out four days ago?"

Circe said she had been in high school on her birthday when her memories returned. She had lost no time getting on the road after mentally conversing with Decima.

"What's your name now?" I asked.

"To my Eternal sisters I'm still Lachesis," she said. "I figured you weren't smart enough to have to deal with a new name, so I kept the old one, Circe. Same look, too. Are you happy?"

"Kind of," I answered.

"Well, I'm here to make you a whole lot happier."

"What do you mean?" I asked.

"Nona picked you a partner."

"You?" I asked.

"No, not me. I'm way too young for you." She looked back to the car. "Hey, you blond wench. Get your skinny little ass out here." The passenger side door opened and Susan got out.

Circe explained. "Nona got the idea to have Susan pass on. At least to Hera's knowledge. As far as Hera's concerned, Iris won't be reborn again until 2027. By then the quest will have started. So Susan—by the way, she now goes by Heike—needs a place to hide out for ten years. You interested?"

"Wait," I said. "Hera thinks she's part of my crew –"

"Your quest is off Hera's radar. Having Apate on it was all we actually needed." With that, Circe silently slipped away and went into the house.

Susan... Iris... Heike... walked over. "I don't have a fancy bed," she said. "But I still have the 100-6 in storage. I can get it shipped here. But in case you didn't want me," she waved a key in my face, "I have a room at a hotel."

"I don't think you'll need that," I smiled.

"Remember the time, in Berlin, when my parents were out of town?" she asked.

I nodded, as I really did now recall it.

"Want to relive it?" she asked. She shook her now long, blonde tresses in my direction. "Did you notice I grew my hair out? For you. You always loved it long."

"And it's back to that reddish tinge," I marveled.

My long, self-imposed drought of 'close' female companionship ended that night as Heike swept that hair over my naked body. I found myself remembering the last words I said to her in Berlin before I perished in that plane crash. "You are the jewel in my life. I will love you forever. Through all time."

Sixty years after high school, I finally had a real girlfriend. Heike was all I remembered. And…all I ever wanted.

Epilogue

Prelude to IO27

Despite my pleas to stay with us, Celaeno moved into a home close by with Circe. They remained our constant companions.

Three years later, Heike—as Heike Earhardt—and I drove the 100-6 to Maryland. Amazingly, like us, it never appeared to age. It was probably due to the expertise of the Eternal friend of Iris's that took care of it. We never took vows of marriage, as Heike said it was pointless. Eternals never married, but sometimes two would live with each other through countless lives. Such was our case.

When my memories returned, I found the vision I'd had when I was Admiral Idomeneus sent to rescue Helen was meant to recall our first meeting. While being close to Iris instigated the dream remembrance that evening in her little sports car, at the time she was totally unaware of what I was recalling. On that voyage back to Kaptara, Helen, who was considered an unearthly beauty even in those times, and Oceanus, who was unaware of his Eternal self, fell in love forever and ever. Little did anyone know then that Helen, that unearthly beauty, was the Greek Goddess, Iris.

In Maryland, we met with Laura Foley, a woman from Flammeria, who bore overall responsibility for the Distans that we'd transport to the Wolf 1061 star system. Flammeria had unknowingly provided us with a cover story for the secret mission to locate and join Zeus, and in turn, Decima told me to placate the Flammerian in any way necessary.

As I still had not recovered all of my abilities, I had asked Heike to scan her for any information she could provide. Heike reiterated, as I had been told, that the Flammerian woman, born on Earth, was a Lemuria Eternal like me.

Lemuria had been wiped out in a catastrophe on Earth many thousands of years ago. Her heritage shouldn't have surprised me, as by now I could readily tell women who were Eternals by their signature beauty. Laura was no exception. But there was something about her that my memories would not reveal to me. Neither was Heike able to discover that something in her scan.

To further complicate things, Heike said Laura was completely unaware of her birthright. She had no remembrance of former lives, and there apparently had been no effort made when the mission was planned eons ago to cover her long ago past. Laura actually thought she was a Flammerian born on Earth.

Laura would not be on the initial voyage, but she would come later, once we were established on the planet. Decima told me that being with another Eternal and Fate on her birthday at the hour of her birth would reawaken those long lost memories. Circe and I planned to be the ones to do that. Yeah, it was shades of Clotho discovery all over. However, I felt that would unlock her real identity to me. What I didn't know then was that we wouldn't discover the answer until she came to 1027. We did learn that Laura had a brother in this life, named Jake, who would be accompanying us on the mission along with Sheila, his half-twin sister.

Heike was to function as the contact between the Flammerians and us. Celaeno and Circe were to be going as my two second-in-commands. Celaeno was tasked to keep an eye on Laura's Flammerian brother, Jake, while Circe took it upon herself to be responsible for the twin sister, Sheila. How they had come to that arrangement, I never asked.

Later that year, Decima confirmed that the exploration start had been cleared for 2025. Late in 2024, Heike and I met Circe, Celaeno and Apate at an assigned desert location in the American Southwest. There, we were picked up by a planet hopper for the short trip to the underworld base on Phobos, one of the moons of Trivane.

The big surprise was the pilot of the saucer-shaped craft. Irene welcomed me as I climbed through the circular hatch in the bottom.

"Remember that paper you wrote?" she asked.

I nodded. "We get that ride together. But what are you doing flying this thing?"

"What?" she smiled. "Like it's hard? They practically fly themselves. I had to do something when Pollux left me, so…"

Behind me, Circe let out a huge shriek at seeing her Eternal sister. This trip would be fun.

When we settled in our seats, I noticed that across from us, a girl with thick, reddish-orange hair was looking me up and down with her black eyes.

"I studied you," she said as she came over.

"Are you talking to me?" I asked.

She nodded.

"You studied what?"

"You. On my first mission as a humanoid, I wanted to make a good impression on you, so I studied the various missions you were part of."

"You what?" I was confused.

"Sorry, Alex," Decima's voice came into my head. "I meant to warn you about Nona. Later, I'll explain some things to you, and you'll understand her reasoning."

So – this was Nona. Like Irene, Nona was of medium height, taller than all the other girls going on the mission. However, when she had appeared to me in that store dream previously, I remembered her as a small girl. She sat next to me and immediately started a mental conversation.

"In the dream, I was using a shimmer. Now you see the real me. And, yes, Spirit beings can use shimmers. In this current life, Circe and I were born on Earth at the same time. She and I wanted to be the same age on this quest. That's all of my personal history you need to know for now. Decima will tell you that I try to reduce everything down to traits. She told me you have some intangible traits that make you different. She said that was what Zeus saw in you, as he possessed similar attributes.

"One more thing," she continued. "The Flammerians see this mission as theirs. They do not know our ultimate goal is to locate Zeus under the guise of exploring the planet. They think they are to leave once their mission is done. You, as well as they, will soon discover they are not who they think they are. My part of this mission will be to convince them to stay and assist us. Jake, their leader until Laura arrives, knows that you are in charge. However, you should tell him that I, not Iris, will handle most communication between the groups. This is not to cast doubt on your abilities, however. Both missions are important, and it is too much to expect you to deal with alone. You see, Zeus had a backup for you, too. And that is me. I'll share this small part of your command. Once we are on IO27, I am available to you to do whatever mission details you see fit. Of course, my part is just between you and me. Is this all agreeable? Do you accept my role?"

"Just a minute you little pipsqueak, first of all you were in the spirit world just a few years ago, so I'm sure Zeus didn't appoint you as my backup. You've never even been on an exploratory mission. So you will do what I tell you to do when we get to IO27. Is that clear?"

I responded, and she sheepishly nodded. "As previously planned, Iris will be my contact between groups. Is that understood?"

"Whatever you say, Oceanus." With that she got up and sat alone across from me. While I had gradually accepted the fact that I was not who I thought I was growing up, and at times I still doubted the trust that Zeus had placed in me, nevertheless if he thought I could, I would certainly try my best. Still, I had worried that if the follow-up expedition years ago had not located him, how would I?

Knowing I was not alone in formulating a plan to find him and, having the utmost confidence in my team, I relaxed. . And while I knew nothing of the attributes that I shared with Zeus, I put trust in the opinion of Decima and others.

Nona had turned away from facing me and was now in animated conversation with Celaeno and Circe. It was obvious they respected her greatly, and she would be an excellent addition to our crew. As we entered Mars's vicinity, I recalled that Decima had said something about a backup mission that involved Pollux and Clotho, but that was never explained. Something to ask Nona about, I reasoned. As if reading my mind, Nona came back over to me.

"Alex?" Irene called down to me from her pilot's position above us. "We're approaching Phobos. Can you come up here? Nona, dear, is it okay if I pull him away from you?"

"Yes, Mother, I'm uh…finished explaining things to him."

"Mother?" I'm sure my face mirrored my confusion.

"You heard correctly," said Irene. "I couldn't go on your mission, but Decima asked Pollux and me to be Nona's birth parents. The first-time birth is special, and she wanted her parents to be Eternals. Didn't you notice the resemblance?"

A quick glance took in those long legs. I nodded, as now I did. Nona looked a lot like Irene.

"So, in a way I am going with you." Irene added.

"I saw that look," Nona interrupted. It was my choice to copy Irene's look, but don't get any romantic ideas. "I'm Irene's daughter, not Irene. Besides, you have Iris. Understood?" Nona's eyes flashed as if to emphasize her statement.

"Nona," Irene said, "I told you not to come off strong, didn't I? Wait, he put you in your place didn't he?" Irene then turned to me. "So our little car ride did teach you something. I still have that Speedster. Maybe we can go for a ride like old times if you ever get back."

"All I am today I owe to you." I acknowledged. It was true. Irene was the one who showed confidence in me and I had responded in turn. Just as I had years ago on my first mission with Zeus.

From her assigned seat, Heike yelled out, "Hey, Nona, you skinny little wench, Oceanus is taken. You want a job on this expedition? Always go to the woman in charge. That would be me. Come and talk to me."

Now I knew the quest would be interesting.

* * *

"Join us up here, Alex," Irene called down.

After ascending the ladder to the upper part of the craft, I was surprised to see a girl with long, blond hair sitting in the co-pilot's seat.

"This is April, Alex. She is the Flammerian pilot of the ship you're taking to IO27. She wanted to get some flying time in a hopper, so I invited her along. By the way, she is no relation to Apate so put April Sunshine out of your head."

"Hey, Alex," said April in way of a greeting. "It's April Elliot." She then looked to Irene. "Isn't Apate the girl with the aqua hair? Why would he confuse us? We look nothing alike. She's gorgeous. Who's this April Sunshine?"

"I'll explain it sometime," Irene smiled.

"Okay." April looked confused. "Time to switch?"

I nodded in acknowledgement to April as she and Irene switched seats.

"April will take us the rest of the way so we can talk," said Irene. "Come sit in the middle seat."

After settling in between the two women, Irene smiled over as Phobos loomed in front of us. She pointed out a huge crater that covered a large section of the moon. "That's Stickney Crater. See that smaller crater inside of it?"

I nodded. In my travels, I had not been to the base on Phobos, and in my eagerness to see it, I forgot about Heike and Nora for the moment.

"That's Limtos Crater," Irene said. "That's the entry point to the underground base. I'll be sorry to see this place go. It's been in use since the great upheaval."

"Go?" I replied. "And what upheaval?"

"Earth has a number of projected space explorations aimed at Phobos, so we have to close it down next year and completely remove all signs of the base so it's not discovered. After you all leave, they will start moving the equipment to the new base on the dwarf planet, Eris. The upheaval is what we call the collision that caused most life to flee Trivane."

"Most? You mean some people still live—"

"Of course. Many live underground. It's always been the way to dodge planetary cataclysms."

"I wish you were going with us," I told her, deciding to change the subject from planetary disasters.

"I think you have more than enough females to handle," she replied with a chuckle. "You met my daughter, Nona, and I'm sure you and her clashed. Expect a lot more from my little angel. She's tough to control. Plus, I brought the other group up here yesterday." Irene turned her attention to April. "Alex once had a crush on me."

"Well, if you like someone like Irene, wait until you meet Jake's little sister, Sheila," said April. "She's a handful. Although she's smaller, she looks a lot like Irene here."

"Actually," Irene interrupted. "I think Alex will find Sheila looks more like my younger sister.

"Hey," I said in hopes of stopping this litany of eligible women. "I have the love of my life now. Iris is all I can handle."

"Still, I'd like to see Jake's face when he meets Ceellia, your co-pilot." Irene's chuckle quickly turned into both girls giggling.

"Where's our ship?" I asked, to break up this unwanted discussion while wondering who Ceellia could be to elicit that reaction.

"It's in orbit on the other side of Mars," April answered. "It's out of Earth's prying eyes. Ceellia and some of her Distan friends are going through the pre-takeoff checklist like I taught her. You'll meet all the Distans when you get aboard."

I recalled Laura's talking of taking the Distans to IO27. But she talked of small creatures. I assumed this Ceellia must be the one who interfaced with them.

"I'll take both of the groups up to the ship early tomorrow morning," Irene said.

"How early is early?" I asked.

"We leave at the crack of dawn," April laughed. "Trivane's dawn."

* * *

About twenty minutes later, we entered the base location. As we waited to exit the craft, Nona and Iris moved in front of me.

"Iris, Alex," Nona said, as we followed her out of the saucer-shaped craft, "This is Jake and Sheila, the Flammerians we'll be working with."

"And this is Rachel," Jake added.

I studied the three as we greeted each other.

I thought all three were familiar. It was the same feeling I had about Laura, when we met her in Maryland. But I just could not place them. Sheila did indeed look a lot like Clotho. However, a bigger surprise was that Jake bore a startling resemblance to – Pollux (?).

But, that couldn't be, could it?

Continued in IO27.

Acknowledgments

Thanks to Zora Knauf for doing a fantastic job of formatting both the printed book and E-Book. Thanks to Fiona Jayde of Fiona Jayde Media for her cover ideas and design.

A huge thank you goes to my beta readers. Erin Ruth Carter, Evi Mourellou, Malika Kahn, Michelle Browne, Samantha Reid, Thomas Tomaszewski and Zola Copeland-Monehen gave fantastic feedback, pointing out so many things that I messed up or missed. An even bigger thanks to my editor, Calee Allen, without who this would have remained a mess.

This novel has undergone many changes from the original that was started back in the very early 2000's. Thanks to all in the Schaumburg Scribes who read that and offered their suggestions. What they read eventually got split into two novels, this one and the upcoming (hopefully) Shadow Lake.

Coming is the second novel in this series, Moonglimmer.
Watch for it!

MOONGLIMMER

Jake Foley and April Elliot, whose parents trace their lineage to the planet Flammeria, were born on Earth and have embraced Earth as their home. Flammeria's mission on Earth, headed by Jake's sister, Laura, is to monitor Earth's volatile climate which has devastated past civilizations. Jake and April attended the US Naval Academy in Annapolis, Maryland, and after rejecting a Flammerian mission ten years ago, they made a pact to separately pursue their own Earthly interests. Jake resigned his Navy commission and left the east coast, abandoning Laura, along with Rachel, his Earth girlfriend, and his life in the Annapolis area, while April went on to become a Navy Fighter pilot. But Jake's search for an alternate life for himself went nowhere, and he ended up living in the Midwest with his father.

Now, ten years later, Jake has been strangely driven to return to Maryland and the life he abandoned those years ago. While he reconnects with Rachel, Flammerian things are not the way he left them. He finds he has a twin sister, Sheila, who tells him that she and the Distans she cares for, both of whom he never knew existed, are threatened by the Zantites, an alien race.

The Distans, a species of eight-inch-tall, fairy-like creature, live in the huge gardens by the Flammerian house situated along the James River, in St Michaels, Maryland. The tiny Distans, with their human-like bodies, have wings and can fly. In addition, they can read human thoughts and telepathically send them hundreds of miles. To aid in his communication with Sheila, Jake is assigned two Distans, Moonglimmer and Ceellia, who go with him everywhere. Jake and Laura gradually become aware of a deep-seated hidden mission they have been tasked with, the particulars of which, unknown to them, were set in their minds thousands of years ago and are now being brought to light. Put off by the reality of the Distans and the fear of once again being deserted by him, Rachel leaves Jake.

Together with April and the two Distans, Moonglimmer and Ceellia, Jake must aggressively oppose the Zantites, who seek to establish a base on Earth. They steal a Navy jet and engage a Zantite ship, which causes their aircraft to ditch in the ocean.

After rescue by the Flammerian underwater ship, Jake is reunited with Rachel and becomes more aware that this was not the mission he came back for. Eventually, Laura informs him that along with Sheila and her, he is actually an advanced human species, an Eternal, and their memories had been shielded until now from their true mission: a mission that will take them a long way from Earth.

www.ingramcontent.com/pod-product-compliance
Lightning Source LLC
Chambersburg PA
CBHW030241200626
46816CB00002BA/462